THIS MUST BE THE METAMATRIX!

He began to rise like a bubble drifting to the surface of a sea. Something deep inside his skull clicked, a metaphysical switch, and the metamatrix came alive around him. The silence was riven by an avalanche of sound. It was a terrible, rasping rhythm, the breathing of a wounded god, ancient and appalling. He was very close to the Demon Star.

He wanted to scream, but had no tongue. The sound pounded at his ears, but he had no hands to cover himself.

The Demon Star began to change. The great circle went white around the edge, but in the center grew a crimson pupil, a hunger of an eye. Slowly the eye scanned the universe. Alive with lust, it twinkled. It beckoned. It summoned him. . . .

DREAMS
OF
GODS
AND
MEN

W. T. Quick

A SIGNET BOOK

NEW AMERICAN LIBRARY

SIGNET TRADEMARK REG. U.S. PAT. OFF. AND FOREIGN COUNTRIES
REGISTERED TRADEMARK—MARCA REGISTRADA
HECHO EN CHICAGO, U.S.A.

SIGNET, SIGNET CLASSIC, MENTOR, ONYX, PLUME, MERIDIAN
and NAL BOOKS are published by NAL PENGUIN INC.,
1633 Broadway, New York, New York 10019

First Printing, February, 1989

1 2 3 4 5 6 7 8 9

PRINTED IN THE UNITED STATES OF AMERICA

This book is dedicated to:
Sarah Mitchell, Aunt Sally
and
Ernest E. Quick, Uncle Ernie
You are missed . . .

And
Tracy Cogswell
Teacher and Friend

SPREAD OUT IN the narrow valley below, the cabin was a smoking ruin. The sharp miasma of spent high explosive filtered up to the niche where Toshiro Nakasone clamped his hands to the sides of his head. His fingers knotted against the insidious trap he'd unwittingly triggered in what should have been a straightforward assassination. But who could have predicted this awful, pervasive mental attack? Particularly from a victim whose body was now bloody shreds? Finally, by sheer, teeth-grinding will, he forced his throat to work.

"Ahhh!"

"Hang on, Tosh," Levin said. "I'm working on it."

Toshi stared at a tiny figure picking its dainty way through the rubble of the God's retreat, moving slowly toward the fifty-meter wall of rock which sheltered Toshi's hideaway. He knew that form. Blades of God, they called themselves. He squinted at the little yellow killer, trying to estimate how much time he had left. Not much, probably. Those fragile-looking samurai were unbelievably effective at search and destroy.

"Levin?" Toshi mumbled. It was hard to subvocalize. His mouth was filled with peanut butter, his tongue a swollen sausage of rigid flesh.

"Try to relax," Levin said. "When you fight, you make things harder for me."

"I killed that God. I know it. Nothing could have survived inside the lodge, and that's where it was when the bombs went off."

"Well, you got its body, I think," Levin replied slowly. "But *something* is still with us. There's got to be a source for that control process. I'm trying to analyze now—it's either autonomic or psychomatic, but I can't tell yet. That God was one of the newer entities. I haven't been able to find out as much as I'd like about the Church's latest engineering techniques."

"That's nice, Levin. Very encouraging." Toshi took a deep breath. Levin was partially controlling his respiratory system, exerting a psychonomic calming effect. The air smelled clean and cool. There was a taste of pine to it, and damp earth and still water: a fine mishmash of odors, heavily spiced with the charring tang of Hyundai number four industrial-grade explosive.

"I think I understand," Levin said suddenly. "Arius didn't retreat to the metamatrix when his avatar was destroyed." His clear tenor voice turned puzzled. "But that's impossible, too. At least we thought it was."

The Blade moved alertly across the base of the cliff, head swiveling like a good hunting dog on a scent. Short lemon man with death in his chromosomes.

"Listen, old friend," Toshi said. "It may be impossible, but it's happening. And we don't have a hell of a lot of time. That Blade down there is gonna find me pretty quick—and if I'm still in my present condition, he's gonna rip me into small bloody chunks with his delicate little fingers. You do understand that, right?"

The soft breeze shifted slightly, carrying with it the sudden stench of burned God and scorched rock. Toshi decided he'd done a good job on the building. It was just bad breaks that his intended victim seemed unexpectedly immortal and that one Blade had remained outside on guard duty when the shatterbombs went off.

"We've never tried a full feedback loop, Toshi. But the theory's okay, and you're wired for it."

"No!" The harsh suddenness of his reply startled him. It betrayed levels of fear he had never investigated, some dangerous lapse in the web of controls by which he governed the disciplines of his life. He was replying to logic with emotion, and that might be the worst thing of all.

Down below, the Blade froze, his face toward the cliff. Then he smiled and slid forward into the underbrush like a sword drawn suddenly from a sheath.

Nervously, Toshi tried to raise his right hand to wipe sweat from his burning eyes, forgot about the mandrakes and, but for the slow freezing of incipient paralysis, almost blinded himself. "Damn it!" He paused, then swallowed heavily. "Uh, Levin, I take it back. Whatever you're gonna do, you better get started. I don't think there's much time—"

He didn't finish the sentence. Levin took control of his vocal cords. And everything else.

It was an eerie sensation. Toshi felt as if he were watching himself from a distance, slow and dreamy, but without connection. Yet he was still in his body. Levin was pushing buttons, pulling all the nervous wires.

The implants which connected him to Levin were modeled on some very nasty wrinkles in mind control the NASA-INTEL people dreamed up in the late nineties and later discarded as too dangerous for even their arcane purposes. Levin actually used him as a remote input-output unit. He watched from Toshi's eyes, heard from his ears, shared his enthusiasm for the taste of dark beer and the smell of fresh bread. In their strange relationship, Toshi functioned at times as an ultimate Waldo. Berg said it was safe. Toshi trusted Berg. And Berg had designed Levin. But, he thought uncomfortably, we've never truly put it to the test—and when the Blade flowed into his rocky nest like a striking bushmaster, all his emotions clamored blindly against the prison of his skull. Toshi's hands, covered with electrified, razor-studded mandrakes, moved suddenly, a blur faster than he could follow. The unbidden movement shocked him.

Amazing, Toshi thought. Nice set of reflexes.

The Blade sported his own set of jumped-up nerves and muscles, backed with genetic memory grafts. The Church augmented Blades as bodyguards and assassins, and the resulting samurai were the best ever known at those poignant trades. A single Blade was perfectly capable of chopping a battalion of ordinary troopers into prebreakfast snacks. This one grinned flatly as he flicked a pair of steel-spiked nerve balls at Toshi's eyes. As part of the same fluid motion he raised his left foot, toes inward, for an immediate killing strike.

Toshi watched this with an intense concentration. Two score answering moves jittered through his shrieking brain, but the synapses weren't passing on any messages. Time slowed down. A deep hum began to pulse at the base of his spine. The Blade's foot came up and up. Toshi's left hand rose slowly, batting the nerve balls away as he turned. His right knee blocked the foot strike, moved forward to drive at the Blade's groin. The little man backed away, beginning a roll, but Toshi's right hand, 'drake buzzing and spitting power, brushed his face.

The Blade convulsed. His spine arched like a broken bow.

Toshi's left hand came down. The Blade screamed once, but it was too late. He was already dead.

That fast? He felt himself go numb at the ease of it.

Levin broke the loop. Toshi found his voice.

"Jesus, Levin, what was *that*?"

"I told you it would work."

"Yeah." Toshi stared at the body crumpled at his feet. He had always wondered if he could take one of them even up. He still didn't know. Had he done it? Or Levin—or both of them?

The God was still at work somewhere. Free of the feedback loop, Toshi felt ghostly tendrils of control begin to surge again at the walls of his mind. Certain problems were now painfully evident. The efforts of the dead God were almost immobilizing him. Sooner or later the situation would turn fatal. He had to get out, and only Levin could do that for him. He carefully considered the logic of it, but the deep levels still recoiled at turning over control once again.

Yet the word had to get out. The interminable war with Arius and New Church, Inc., had probably been futile from the start, but he still fought. And so did Berg, and Calley, and all the others. They had to know about this new mind control weapon—it was deadly in itself. But perhaps only Berg could truly gauge the threat embodied in the system itself—that Arius could somehow function in the real world without a body, or at least a brain, for physical support. He recalled Berg's often muttered question: What *is* real? He shook his head. It was Berg's question. Let him answer it.

At the moment it was all beside the point. The contract was definitely busted. He had to get the hell away. And do it now, he reminded himself. Nevertheless, he asked the question again. Maybe there was a different answer.

"Okay, Levin. Now what?"

"I can put you out while I take over." Levin's voice was soothing. As always, he answered the unspoken words first.

"That would be better." Toshi exhaled slowly. "I don't like it much the other way."

He could almost see Levin nod agreement. Then came the sudden dark, and Levin marched him out of there like a big, blind baby.

When he opened his eyes he saw night. He shook his head and watched faint starbursts flicker at the back of his eyeballs. The medicinal odor of fir trees and pine cones enveloped him as he inhaled sharply. A sharp, chill breeze ruffled his dark hair and tugged at his earlobes. In the distance he heard the thin whine of tires on concrete. A road, then, not far away, and big enough to handle freighters.

"Levin?"

"What?"

"Where the fuck are we?"

"Flip down your shades."

"Huh? Oh, yeah. Here." He groped for the mirrored silver lenses which were attached to his headband, and almost ruined himself with the mandrake again. "Mother*fucker*!"

"Be glad you're not powered up," Levin observed.

"Asshole," Toshi muttered. He carefully removed the monomole mesh gloves and folded them into a pouch at his waist, working slowly so he didn't slice his fingers to rags on the razors. Then he lowered the lenses, making sure the opti-fiber cable from the socket beneath his left ear was securely plugged into the edge of the frames around his eyes.

"Well?"

"One second," Levin said.

Suddenly the lenses glowed with sharp green lines. A map. A tiny red star pushed near one heavy green line, marking their location.

"Expand, please," Toshi said. Obligingly, the map

suddenly widened. The effect was as if he'd suddenly risen to a much greater height. A faint wave of nausea thumped his heavy stomach.

"Not so fast!"

"Sorry. I told you not to eat that second pizza."

"I'll worry about my own diet, thanks," Toshi replied. "Looks about forty klicks north of San Francisco. That right?"

"Forty one point two."

"And . . . let's see. The car's almost twenty more back up the road."

"Yes."

"So, you want to tell me why you walked us here and not there?"

"Certainly. About a dozen Blades are between what's left of that lodge and our car. Of course, if you'd rather—"

"No, thanks," Toshi said hastily. "This is just fine. I'd rather walk. Really."

"Thought you would," Levin said.

Toshi sighed and stared up at the night sky. The map faded away from his lenses as Levin kicked in the light-gatherers. A canopy of dark leaves moved slowly, far overhead. Redwoods.

"Picturesque," Toshi said. He checked his bearings one more time, then moved slowly off toward the road. After a time his lips moved silently.

"Hey, Levin," he said.

"Yes?"

"Thanks."

"Oh. Sure."

A fucking *awful* day.

The sun, rising over Montclair in the Oakland hills, cast Toshi's shadow across the hard black rocks overlooking the Golden Gate Bridge from the north side of the Bay. Far across the water, the towers of the city glittered in needles of steel and ice. He stared at bubblecondos strung like neon pearls from the lower level of the bridge as a freshening breeze whipped at his long black hair. The upper levels of the bridge still carried some traffic, mostly huge, low-slung freighters hauling food into the city. Their giant tires made a thick, throaty hum on the morning air. Brilliant needles of blue-green light danced above their cabs as they sucked laser power from the grids orbiting far overhead.

"It's gonna be a bitch," he muttered slowly.

"We have to get back into the city," Levin replied.

"I know. You got any ideas?"

"They'll be watching the toll areas. I can fool a portable retinal analyzer. Maybe you can bluff it."

"My face is different than last month. But my profile is pretty much unmistakable. There's enough assorted carbon and metal inside me—and my hand can't be missed by anybody with a scanner. Like I said, a bitch."

"Perhaps they won't be as vigilant as they might be."

"Are you kidding? I tried to kill a God. And I missed. The New Church knows I ran into that mind control thing, and they also gotta figure I'll be trying for the city. I would guess there's a platoon of Blades spread over all the obvious places, and probably half the Wolves in the country down there waiting for me."

"They can't be sure it's you, Toshi."

"Yeah? I hate to sound pompous, but they've had me tagged as Berg's number one hit man for at least the last two years. Before your time, even. Somebody takes a potshot at one of their bubble gum saints, their computers spit up my profile before anybody else."

"You do," Levin said.

"I do what?"

"Sound pompous."

Toshi licked his lips and glanced at the deserted parking lot behind the overlook point. Soon enough the first tourists would appear, laughing and waving cameras. No doubt some of the cameras wouldn't be cameras. And some of the tourists wouldn't be tourists. He exhaled slowly.

"Nobody likes a smart ass," he said. He turned around and walked slowly away from the rocks, his eyes squinted against the sun. He made a strange figure, a short, pudgy Oriental man with long black hair and a peculiarly graceful, rolling gait. There was a harmlessness about him, a roly-poly joviality only accentuated by the robelike Hawaiian-print shirt which descended to his knees. He carried a tattered green backpack slung over his right shoulder, and moved as if the pack was filled with feathers—but he'd loaded the pack himself and knew there was at least thirty kilos of gear inside.

He had the kind of face strangers smile at without thinking.

It took him a minute or so to trudge through the parking lot and climb back to the road leading down to the bridge. He paused at the edge of the road for a few seconds, until another gigantic freighter whined past. Then he shrugged and started walking.

"I'll think of something," he said.

The trucker was named Joe. He had a wife in Kansas City, an ex-wife in Baltimore, and a girlfriend in San Francisco. He was winding down the final few miles of a cross-country run, and his eyes, hidden behind mirrored sunglasses, were bulging from two hundred milligrams of tailored methamphetamine he'd chewed for breakfast. Six speakers placed strategically

about the cab of his freighter blared sym-rock—PetKillers
—at a decibel level guaranteed to cause hearing loss.
He didn't give a shit. He hadn't heard well for years.

He barely noticed the small figure in a godawful red
shirt walking along the edge of the road, but as he
blew past, the sudden heavy thump down low behind
his cab was impossible to miss.

"Oh, fuck," he said. "Oh, Mother of God, jeezus."
Something bright bounced once in his rearview mirror
and disappeared beneath his wheels. "Oh, fuck," he
moaned again, and slammed on his brakes.

As he raced to the back of the freighter a wave of
dizziness slammed into him; his heart tried to climb up
and kick his teeth out. He skidded to a stop and
peered into the darkness beneath the big wheels, almost puking with the certainty of what he would find
crushed there.

Yes. He saw the silent lump and turned away for a
moment, retching. Finally he turned back. Have to
pull the guy out. Shit. No time for San Francisco
Sheila now. Maybe no job. They'd test him for sure—
and DUI meant hard jail time.

His chest burned until he wanted to scream, but he
stooped over and began to tug at the crumpled body.
He was too buzzed to notice the man seemed very
heavy for his size. Finally he pulled the body out into
the light.

Strange. No blood. Maybe—

He reached down to touch the man's neck, trying
for a pulse.

Toshi's eyes popped open. "Hi, there," he said.

Joe felt a stinging sensation in his right calf. Then
his eyes rolled back into his skull and drank darkness.

"Now what?" Toshi had finished pulling the huge
freighter off to the side of the road. He stared at Joe's

comatose form slumped on the seat next to him. The bony trucker's eyelids flickered rapidly, then subsided. His breathing was harsh and irregular. "You think I gave the sucker a heart attack or something?"

"Get me a sample," Levin said briskly.

"Huh? Oh, right. Good idea." Toshi gestured once and a small, sharp blade magically appeared in his right hand. After making a small cut in the ball of Joe's left thumb, he put the thumb in his mouth and sucked.

"Enough?"

"Yes. That will do."

Toshi nodded and replaced the trucker's hand on his lap. He gazed stolidly at the tiny red ball of upwelling blood while he waited for Levin to finish his analysis. He knew that Levin monitored his physical indexes constantly, but it still seemed like witchcraft when the AI program inside his skull was able to dissect changes as minute as a few drops of blood on his tongue.

"Got it," Levin said. "He's pumped full of speed."

"Is he okay?"

"Yes. Use a mild hypnotic. He'll last long enough."

Toshi nodded and withdrew a small kit from his backpack. He loaded a silvery hypospray with the required drug, then leaned over and pressed it against Joe's neck. A sharp, low-pitched hissing sound filled the cab. After a moment the trucker's eyelids flickered again, twice, then slowly fluttered open. Toshi raised one hand, said, "Wait," and while Joe stared at him in amazement, placed a bright purple derm on the man's neck, below his collar where it wasn't readily visible.

"What—"

"Just relax."

And as the derm began to release its measured dose of powerful mood-altering serum, the thin freight-hauler's leathery face collapsed into an expression of blank repose.

"Okay," Toshi said. "Here's what you're gonna do."

Joe listened carefully. When Toshi finished speaking, he nodded once. "Yeah. I'm gonna do that."

Toshi grinned. "I know," he said. "I know you are."

The big freighter eased slowly into the wide concrete apron fronting on the tollbooths before the bridge. Joe brought the behemoth machine to a halt, rolled down his window and leaned out.

Next to him, Toshi scanned the booth, wondering who was monitoring the small glass lens eyeing the truck. He saw no one nearby, but the blocklike building just behind them would have people inside.

Joe leaned out and pressed his credit chip into the waiting slot. A moment of silence. Then a buzzer sounded, and a red light on top of the toll machine began to flash.

"What the fuck—?"

Toshi forced a grin and spread his hands. "Beats me, pal," he said. "You got any cash behind the chip?"

"Sure I do. This machine's busted, that's what."

"Do not pass," a speaker grill blurted suddenly. "A supervisor will be with you shortly."

"What the hell's the matter?" Joe asked.

"A supervisor will be with you shortly," the machine repeated.

Toshi settled himself back in the seat and pasted a calm look on his face. Below window level, however, his right hand crept slowly into his backpack. He rolled down the window on his side. After a moment, he heard footsteps.

"Three of them," Levin told him silently.

Toshi stiffened. Nobody needed three fucking supervisors to handle a routine credit refusal.

One man appeared on Joe's side. A man and a

woman walked up to Toshi's window and peered into the cab. The woman's face was badly scarred, and all the knuckles on her right hand were knobby and broken. Since cosmetic surgery would fix any of that, Toshi decided she just liked the way she looked. Tough broad.

He smiled out the window at her. "What's up?"

"You got ID?" the woman said. Her voice was deep and rasping. Toshi grinned again.

"Sure," he said. "What's up?"

"None of your business, pally. Let's see the ID."

"You a cop?"

Now the man with her stirred slightly. Toshi had been carefully ignoring him. He knew exactly what the long, canine face, the fangs, the big bunches of muscle where the human body was not supposed to have muscle meant. The tough broad's companion was a Wolf, and Wolves were New Church. Once Wolves had been Toshi's friends. No more, he thought sadly. The times do change. For an instant a fleeting memory of the Lady stuttered through his mind, bringing with it a faint hint of the adoration she'd once inspired in him. Things changed *that*, too.

"I'm a cop," the woman grated, and flipped an embossed silver chip. "You wanna check it out, loudmouth? You can, but it'll probably piss me off. Is that what you want? Think before you answer. Take ten seconds, even."

Toshi raised both his hands. "Hey, cool off. I don't want no trouble." He lowered his hands, then passed his chip across. "Just want to get this load into the city. Been a fucking long run, you know."

The Wolf and the tough broad both stared at him for one long second. Then the woman put his chip into a portable reader and watched a series of green letters and numbers scroll across the tiny screen. Toshi tried to keep his mind full of innocent, stupid, harmless thoughts. He didn't want to fight his way across the Golden Gate Bridge. He wasn't even sure he could.

She stared up at him, her flat face expressionless. "The eyes, pally. Give me a nice, big look."

"What?"

She raised the analyzer. "It does retinas, too. Open wide for momma, now." She smiled, revealing a mouth full of yellow teeth.

I hope you really can beat an analyzer, Toshi prayed silently to Levin. He lowered his face to the portable gadget. After a moment the machine made a tiny clicking sound, then whirred softly. No alarms. Toshi began to breathe again.

Finally the tough broad handed his phony chip back. "Tan Seng Kenner, huh? You Chinese?"

"Naw. My parents were born in Singapore."

Her face had gone blank and uninterested. "Yeah, cool, pally," she said. She turned partially away and raised her voice.

"Pass 'em through," she yelled suddenly.

Toshi was very glad Levin was controlling his sweat glands. He winked at the Wolf suddenly, and the Wolf raised one side of his thick, black lips, revealing a flash of sharp, white bone.

Yeah, you, too, mother, Toshi thought. The cab jerked as Joe engaged the laser feed. A moment later they pulled onto the bridge.

As always, Toshi felt his spirits lift as they entered the great green garden of the city. He thought San Francisco was the most beautiful place on the face of the earth. Once, before all this started, he'd made his home here. Now, with Berg in deep cover here, he could no longer afford the luxury of residency. This time he contented himself with the sight of the fairy-like waves of steel and glass which rose among the ancient, towering pines of the Presidio, now a playground for the city's richest citizens.

"Hey. Pull this rig over."

Joe obediently muscled the big freighter to the side of the road. Toshi took a scrap of paper and a pen from his backpack and scribbled a few words. He handed the paper to the trucker.

"After you get unloaded, take this to a doctor. He'll know what to do."

Joe nodded. "Okay."

Toshi grinned in relief. He hoped the hypnotic would hold long enough for Joe to follow his instructions. He didn't like to think about what the witch's brew of drugs was probably doing to the skinny trucker's brain cells.

He slid his door open and hoisted his backpack to his shoulder, then reached over and patted Joe's arm once. "Good driving, man," he said. "You take care."

Joe nodded, already half-forgetting his passenger. "Yeah," he said. "You, too."

Toshi waited until the freighter turned a corner and disappeared in the distance. Then, savoring the moist, clean smell of a San Francisco morning, he began to walk. After a moment, he was surprised to find himself whistling.

Too good to last, he thought bitterly, as he stopped in mid-whistle. Half a block up the street a crowd swarmed around the blasted shell of a small house. That house looked like any other on the carefully preserved Victorian block, but it wasn't. It was very hard to get into, and among other things, it was very fireproof. To Toshi's trained eyes, the damage meant bombing, heavy-duty stuff. He wondered if Berg had managed to get out in time.

Old reflexes took over then. Time for thought and investigation later. First thing was to get away.

He was able to retreat almost a full block before the thin, relaxed voice said, "Going somewhere, chubby?"

Only one kind of being could sneak up on Toshi like that. He felt something hot and bitter begin to burn in his stomach as he turned to face the short, insectile yellow man behind him.

"You want something?" he said, shifting his backpack.

"I don't think you're really that good," the Blade said. "Maybe my partner made a mistake, back at the lodge."

"I don't know what the fuck you're talking about, man. You crazy or something?"

The Blade's jade-green eyes were calm as antique marbles. "I think I can probably tear off one of your arms and beat you to death with it."

Toshi sighed, and waited for Levin to initiate the feedback loop, speed up his reflexes, and let him reduce this deadly little killer to fishbait. The Blade raised his left hand slightly and Toshi stepped back. Suddenly he realized what was wrong. Levin hadn't said a word since they'd hijacked the truck. "Fuck it, Levin, come *on*."

Not a thing. Nothing.

No Levin. For the first time in almost two years, Toshi was alone.

The Blade of God stepped forward.

2

"**I**T'S NOT GONNA work, darling," Ozzie said. His beanpole frame curled like a stork stuffed with barbed wire bones across an ancient, corroded basket chair whose cushions, pounded flat by decades of use, spilled the last of their gray polyfoam beads onto the floor.

Calley stared at him. Even after nearly three years, it was still sometimes hard to get used to his angelic face. At times her memory played tricks, fuzzy, two-bottles-of-wine tricks, and she saw him as he'd been before: cheeks a mass of thick, maroon folds, the residue of an ancient encounter with an algae designed to eat oil spills. She shook her head and the vision passed on. That was then—he was an angel now, a seven-foot, anorexic angel.

"Why won't it work?"

His left foot began to twitch. He was wearing a skintight pair of faded black Levis and one of his collection of two thousand equally worn tee shirts. This one proclaimed "White Dopes on Punk," a rally cry she knew was at least thirty years old.

" 'Cause Arius is blocking access again. I can't get into the metamatrix."

"What about a sneak job?"

"You remember what happened the last time?"

Calley nodded slowly. Her brain still ached from the

23

near-terminal brush with Arius's lethal feedback programs. "Berg can get in," she said.

Ozzie shrugged. "Sure. Anytime. It's that fucking program inside his skull. That and whatever he got mixed up with in there. But only him, and he's not here."

She turned away and caught a split glimpse of her reflection in a shard of broken mirror, slow and tarnished and shadowy. Have I changed, she wondered? She touched her frazzled mop of hair, still black but now worked with a faint weave of silver. Nose a blade, eyes the color of crushed emeralds. She'd once thought of her body as a knife. Now she just felt old. Rusted, maybe.

She blinked. "There's gotta be a way. I know there's a way. We did it once. If I can just—"

He spread his big, red, knobby hands apart and began to examine the tips of his chewed fingernails. "Course there's a way. We just wait until that sonofabitch Arius is back in his rotten little body."

"I don't want to wait. I want to get in there and do some ass-kicking."

"Anybody ever tell you you're not much of a lady?"

"Yeah. You. Pretty regularly." She scratched the side of her face, hard. "Goddamit, Ozzie, Arius isn't really a God, no matter how many conglomerate stuffed suits he cons."

"Maybe not, but inside the metamatrix he does a real good imitation."

She made a sharp, hissing sound and turned away. "I'll think of something."

"Just breaks your heart, doesn't it, darling? Not being able to stick in the knife?"

She turned back. Her face stretched slowly into a translucent mask. "Not funny, Oz. It's not a fucking game."

"I know," he said. "I do know that."

"Let's take a walk."

"I don't want to take a walk," she said.

"Sure you do. Look at you—prowling around this dump like some kind of panther or something. You may not want to, but your body does. Trust me." Ozzie unfolded himself from the chair and stretched. It made him look like an old-fashioned TV antenna.

"Fucking mysticism."

"Gimme that old time mysticism . . ." His voice cracked on the high note, and she giggled suddenly.

"A singer you're not," she said.

"I'm great. You just don't listen on the right notes." He snagged a battered black leather jacket from a pile of dirty clothes. "You better wear something heavy," he told her. "It's cold outside."

She grunted. "Chicago in January? Cold? And here I thought it was fucking Miami."

"Berg's okay. He's in San Francisco. I checked the weather. Sunny and fifty."

"Yeah? How much is that in Celsius?"

"Got me, babe. I don't think metric about the weather."

The gray dome of the sky was glazed with winter. A few snowflakes, already dusted with soot, drifted down to the cracked pavement running along the New Drive. They paused for a moment and stared across the dikes at the lake.

"Looks nasty."

A stiff breeze chopped off the tops of the stubby wavelets as they rolled into the face of the dike. The water was greasy and thick. Even in the aqueous afternoon light it shone with an unhealthy magenta phosphorescence. Odd, spiky bits of debris tossed uneasily between the rippled, flattened waves.

"It is," Calley said. She hugged herself, wishing she'd worn gloves. Her fingers felt thin and numb. She turned away from the water and stared at the Burger King behind them. She knew that from somewhere inside it a camera watched her as well. Burger joints bit back these days. If you went to stick one up, a guy hidden in a little room behind a steel wall killed you. It saved the real cops a lot of trouble.

"You get anything recent on Toshi?" she asked, her words a choppy tom-tom of steam.

Ozzie grinned suddenly, waved his arms, and did a strange little softshoe two-step. "Nope. Berg's running him on this. We'll find out when we find out. Why? You worried about supernip?"

"I dunno. He scares me a little bit. Didn't used to, but now with that weird Levin hookup . . . he's changed, you know. Different."

"He doesn't scare me," Ozzie said. "But the setup does. You and Berg did the programming, but I grew the fucking thing, and I did the wiring. Levin's all hung out in the metamatrix. He's meat—and the metamatrix is Arius's playground."

"Berg did the defenses. Even Arius can't crack them."

"You sure about that? You understand what you're betting, right?"

She shrugged. "We could lose Toshi, sure."

"Not at all, little lady. Arius could *get* Toshi, and there's a difference. You know what he is. You want Arius doing soft for Levin, and Levin doing likewise for Toshi? He's a fucking army all by himself."

She squinted against the glare of the Burger King subliminal bank. "He's our army."

"For how long?"

"You pays your money, you takes your chance. We've got this far. We're still alive."

Ozzie's perfect features turned glum. "We're gonna lose this thing, you know. In the end, there's no other way. Not unless something changes."

She reached out and touched his cheek. "Then something will just have to change. Won't it?"

He smiled sadly and took her arm and walked her back across the street. The Burger King sign flashed its message of modern apotheosis.

"*Eat me*," it invited. "*Eat me*."

"What time is it?"

Ozzie rolled over on his belly and propped his chin in his hands. His bony elbows rested just over the edge of the futon.

"Little after midnight," he said.

"I can't sleep." Calley slowly ran her fingers through her hair, squeezing her scalp as she did so.

"You got a headache?"

"Huh-uh. Just can't sleep." She stopped for a moment. "What you said this afternoon."

"About what?"

"That we can't win. You really believe that?" Her husky voice was flat, as if she had consciously tried to drain all emotion from the words.

"Uh, yeah. I'm sorry, darling, but I think I do."

"Why?"

He crossed one foot over the other ankle, suddenly tense. "I don't know if I want to talk about it. Maybe I've just been depressed lately."

"And maybe you haven't. So talk to me. I can handle it. You know me."

He sighed. It was a slow, unhappy sound. "You're like a blade, Calley. Nobody's ever broken you. But I don't know if you can bend—"

"I think that's probably bullshit, son. But I'll grant

you your worries. What I don't give you is the right to hold out on me. So spit it out. Okay?"

"Look around you," he said.

"Mmm." She was silent a moment. "Okay. So?"

"What do you see?"

"A dump. I don't know where you keep turning up these warehouses, but this doesn't look much different from your old place. It had half the junk in Chicago. This must have the other half. Is there a point?"

"Junk is the point. It didn't used to matter. But it does now. All our equipment. We're supposed to be the opposition, a strong point in the great war against the almighty New Church of the Spirit Corporate, and Arius, the latest version of God. Well, it just ain't far off—the New Church is fucking rich and fucking powerful, and Arius will do until a better divinity comes along. Big time people, kid. Very, very big time, and all we've got is what we can steal from the edges, what you and me and Berg can cobble together. And all the time, every minute of the day, this vast goddam *thing* has shooting our asses off as its numero uno priority. And I don't think it's gonna get any better. You got to see where a situation like that ends."

She puffed her cheeks in and out quietly. "Yeah, I see. We lose. So what does it mean?"

"I don't understand."

"Let me put it simple. Do we quit? Pick up the nearest phone and report ourselves to the local Corporate Chapel?"

He tapped one elbow nervously on the scarred wooden floor. "No. We don't do that."

"So then what?"

"We keep on keeping on, I guess. One foot in front of the other, and all that shit."

"That all?"

"I don't have to like it," he said slowly.

"You got any other options? If you don't, then you might as well feel good about it. It sure as hell won't make any difference, one way or the other."

"You're starting to mix logic and emotion again. Telling me reasons why I should feel good don't make it happen."

"How about showing you?" Her hands moved.

"What? Um—no, not there, lower . . ."

Later, they watched the wind scour eddies of snow from the skylight overhead. Calley lit two cigarettes, handed one over.

"Thanks."

"Yeah," she said. She inhaled once. "Besides . . ."

"Besides what?"

"We fucking will win. Bet your *ass* on it, buddy."

He blew a thick, roiling cloud of silver smoke straight up at the snow. "I already have."

"What do you think?" said Ozzie.

She raised one hand, motioning for silence, her face gone shadowed and chalky in the green backlight from encircling monitors. From the socket beneath her ear stretched a glittering length of optical fiber which, a few inches from the socket, split into five separate lines, each eventually ending at one of Ozzie's usual unfinished-seeming black boxes.

"I think I'm getting a handle on it."

"Any vision overlap? Breakage? Splitting?"

She shook her head. The cables moved softly, like jewelry made of spiderwebs. They sat like travelers from a forgotten time, pioneers camped in the round of their lit campfires, surrounded by ominous dark. Overhead, on the skylight, mounds of snow shut out the sound and sight of the city. Reefs and shoals of spangled refuse, rusted and glowing, slowly collapsed around their center.

Each one of their inhalations and exhalations was a specific interval in the silence.

"It's weird," she said at last. "Three-sixty vision, but not looking out. It's like I'm a huge bubble, focused inside, on a point. It . . . makes me feel funny. Maybe a human brain's not supposed to deal with this kind of perspective. I can't see anything, but I *know* I'm in the metamatrix."

He noted a thin, shiny film of sweat on her forehead, pulled a white handkerchief from the back pocket of his jeans, and gently mopped her damp flesh.

Her eyes remained closed. "I'm in. I'm definitely in."

"Good." He nodded once, gaze thoughtful. "Can you focus out?"

More silence. Her chest rose once, sharply, then relaxed. "I . . . uh . . . maybe. I think—"

"Maybe from just one quadrant?"

She shook her head again. "No. It's gotta be all or nothing." Pause. "I can see the programs."

"Whose programs? What programs?"

"No, I can see the meat defense. Around our stuff. I'm still looking . . . in. I think."

"What about Arius?"

"I dunno."

"Well, *look*, dammit."

"I *can't*!"

Ozzie leaned past her and tapped a quick command on one of the touchpads fronting the monitors. Quickly he scanned the scrolling series of symbols which suddenly appeared. Satisfied, he straightened up, and with one sure movement, plucked the tiny silver probe from Calley's skull. Sudden movement shook the optifibers, and they responded with a quick flash of color, red, blue, magenta.

Her head snapped up. "What the fuck—"

"Needs more work, darling," he said flatly. His voice was absolute with certainty. "Look for yourself." He gestured at the frozen monitor screen.

She turned. "Oh." She reached out and touched the screen softly. "Right there, huh?"

"Yeah. Autistic precursors."

"Autistic?" She shivered. "Nasty." She rocked forward on the edge of her chair, and shoved the heels of her palms against her eyes. After a moment she sat up. "You can fix it?"

His hollow shoulders rose and fell. "I dunno. Maybe. Probably. God, I'm tired."

"Get out the speed, Ozzie. This is important." She moved her face close to his, stared into his eyes. "I was in, Ozzie. That's a step. A big step."

He carefully turned away from her. "It's a first step," he said.

"Step's a step. Let me worry about that. You just get the goddam thing working right, okay?"

He faced her again, eyes startlingly wide. "Hey, it's me, Ozzie. Your *friend*. Remember?"

"Oh, God, I'm sorry." She reached over and cupped his perfect chin in one trembling hand. "I'm tired, too. So awful tired. I'm sorry."

He put his long arms around her but didn't squeeze, as if he held something thin, Oriental, and without price. "It's okay," he whispered. "We're okay. Really."

"It's another twist on the wetware," Ozzie said. "You really interested in the theory behind it?"

His big fingers, clumsy to look at, unbelievably precise in motion, moved like hurried insects in a clutter of chips and tiny boards. Calley sprawled on one of the dilapidated basket chairs, a glass of red wine in her right hand, a drawn expression on her face. The fingers of her left hand drummed intermittently on her knee. "I write programs, Ozzie. That's what I'm good at. But I write them for the boxes you build, and then I ride them afterward. So, yeah, I guess you could say I'm interested." She raised the wineglass and stared at the crimson fluid. "It's my fucking life, after all, if one of those things craps out on me."

He nodded slowly, his gaze fixed on what he was doing. "Once I told you the wetware perceives what it can perceive. And I built a box that changed the input, altered it into perceptions the human brain could handle. Which got us into the metamatrix in the first place. So now—" He paused, looked up. "Now I'm changing the parameters of perception. It should change the configuration a human presence shows in the metamatrix. Instead of a dot, a discrete point, it's a diffuse bubble. And the bubble should be invisible. There's nothing for another perception to focus on."

She sipped her wine. "Uh-huh," she said carefully. "But what about us? If there's no way for Arius to grab us, does it work the other way? Can we manipulate? Can we do anything ourselves?"

He shook his head. " 'Fraid not. It's possible we're not really in the matrix at all. Just a point of view. But it's better than nothing, right? At least we have access again."

"If I know what to look for, I can design in-and-out attack programs strong enough and fast enough to do some real work. Hey—" A sudden thought flickered across her features. "What about using it as a guide? Keying it to programs operating out of a meatmatrix? We've got several. Maybe even use Levin?"

Ozzie frowned. "Mmm . . . should work. Coordination might be a problem. But—" He brightened. "I bet I could work out something with hardware, a talk-to, talk-to kind of thing. Close a feedback loop. It'd be kinda roundabout, but it ought to work."

"That's my Ozzie," she said, and drained off the last of her wine. "Dream it up. We'll give 'em hell yet."

They went for breakfast at three in the morning. Streetlamps hissed and sizzled their endless litany of static overhead. Sometimes, Calley felt, in Chicago it was always three A.M., that the city was somehow bound in endless night. Ozzie's cloud of curly blond hair turned a garish yellow-green under the harsh lights. She grinned suddenly at the effect.

"Where do you want to go?"

His eyes were colorless. "Someplace that serves grease. All-night grease. Gyros, polish sausage, pizza, burgers. Hot dogs. I got the urge."

She stared at him. "Why don't you weigh six hundred pounds?"

"My metabolism's fucked up. How about up there?" He pointed at a pool of light spilling onto the next corner. The subliminals just managed to catch her eye, and for a crazy instant the vision of a giant dancing hot dog, wearing a short white skirt, tap-tapped behind her forehead. "Jesus."

He laughed. "You don't like dancing hot dogs?"

She sighed. "If it'll lay down while I eat it, I don't care."

A bell rang over the door when they pushed it open. On the left were several tables, their brown formica tops scarred with initials and gang graffiti. A narrow shelf ran beneath windows on the right, leading back to a high serving counter. Behind the counter a fat man in a dirty tee shirt, his massive arms a mosaic of glowing neon tattoos, regarded them impassively over a half-chewed cigar.

"I'll sit," she said. "You order."

"What do you want?"

"Whatever. No, one thing. No hot dogs."

She listened to the spattering hiss of French fries hitting hot grease, and marveled for a moment at how much, and how little, the world did change. Gods moved through the technological empires and miracles spilled from the labs like Christmas goodies, but people still ate hot dogs cooked in corner joints, even if what they paid with their parents wouldn't have recognized as money.

"Ten minutes," Ozzie said, sliding into a chair across from her. As usual, she was reminded of some lost, birdlike creature. Ozzie trying to cope with a normal-sized world made her think like that.

"What'd you get me?"

"Surprise." His eyes raised to the blank windows for a moment, then returned. "You okay?"

"What?" The question startled her.

"Are you all right? You doing all right, darling?"

She blinked. "Hey, what are you, the fucking Red Cross?"

He fluttered his fingers, and again she thought of birds. "You're awful fierce lately," he said. "Something's bugging you bad. And you're too important to me for me to ignore it. Is that okay?"

"You don't have any right—"

"Course I do. We went through all this before. Listen, Calley, I told you. I *already* bet my ass. I may get down every once in a while, but I tossed all I had on the table a long time ago. In a warehouse, remember?"

She wouldn't meet his steady gaze. "Ozzie, I'm still with Berg. We're joined. Always will be. I thought that was settled then, too."

"That shit in the metamatrix, right. I know. But, darling, can't you see? Don't you ever wonder sometimes?"

She knew what was coming, but made him say it. "Wonder what?"

"Berg. Whether he's even human anymore." He paused. Then he said, "Uh-oh. So that's the problem. He's got you fucked up bad again. Right?" He reached over and ran his fingers lightly across the back of her hand.

She pulled her hand away. Her brows came together, and for one instant she thought she might break down. Ozzie was too close. In his own scattered way, he wielded an acuteness about human nature that could sometimes pierce the hard walls of her own guarded personality. "He's so sad, Ozzie. All the time, ever since we got him back. And it's getting worse. You know, I think he really wants to die. Or maybe he's just forgotten what it's like to really live. He seems so knowing all the time, like he's got some terrible secret. And he knows everybody else's. Sometimes— honest to God—I think he reads minds now."

"I suppose my blubbering about how doomed we all are didn't help much, did it?"

"Oh, shit, Ozzie, you didn't tell me anything I didn't already know. Goddam, you think I like living this way? Being this way? Hell, I never lived like Berg. I never needed it the way he did, all those antiques, pictures, that hot-shit condo, but I lived good. And I didn't hide all the time, didn't have to watch my back, didn't have to worry that half the frigging giant companies in the world had their knives out for me. Yeah, it's bad. But for him it's even worse. I think he left a part of himself in the metamatrix. And I don't know how to get it back for him."

The counterman coughed, a thick, wet, rasping sound, and said, "You people wanna eat? I'm not gonna carry this shit over to you."

Ozzie stared at her one long instant. "Food," he said positively. "You need food. Hang on."

He slid a brown plastic tray in front of her. Her eyes widened happily. "Oh, Ozzie. Souvlaki. French fries. And baklava. How'd you know I wanted Greek?"

He grinned, and for one instant looked about fifteen years old. "Maybe Berg reads minds," he said. "I read stomachs. That's gotta be worth something."

By noon the wind shifted, the temperature rose, and it began to rain. She sat up on the futon, knuckling her eyes. Ozzie still snored next to her. She looked down at his face, at the tangle of blond hair framing his features like a cloud of golden wire, and grinned, remembering. Younger men did have their advantages.

After a moment she climbed to her feet and padded off to the bathroom. When she came out, she smelled bacon frying and coffee brewing.

"Hey, gimme some of that."

He was crouched in front of his workbench, and waved one hand without looking up. "On the table," he said. "I already put in the cream."

She sipped the hot liquid, savoring the taste. It was the last of the Jamaican Blue Mountain—Berg had taught her about coffee, and taught her well—and she decided to buy another couple of pounds.

"What's up?" she said.

"Not me. Not after last night."

"Piglet. None of that chauvinistic male posturing. Not before breakfast, at least."

"Calley." His voice was excited. "I think I got it this time."

"Yeah? Got what?"

"The new interface. It looks okay. It'll handle a feedback loop, so I can slave it to meat programming.

And—" He stopped a second. "I don't *think* it'll make you go crazy."

For some reason the night had purged her of darkness, and she felt almost light-headed. "That's a great recommendation, kid. Makes me feel real confident."

"No, really, I think it's okay."

"Good. Bring your coffee over here. Is the bacon about ready?"

"Bacon? Ohmygawd!" He broke for the tiny kitchenette, arms and legs a tangle of motion. "Aw, shit. No, wait a minute, here's a couple of pieces not burned. You wanna share?"

This time she laughed out loud. "I got a better idea. You sit down and I'll make breakfast."

"Deal," he said happily. "Keep 'em in the kitchen, my dad always said."

"Your dad was probably an asshole, too."

"Funny. Mom used to say that."

"Your mother," Calley said positively, "was a wise woman."

Cyberneural technology had turned out to be astonishingly simple in practice, she reflected. The meat-matrices developed by Bill Norton had not demanded vast support systems nor, once the tech was assimilated, great expertise. Berg had grown their first meat less than a year after his rescue from the metamatrix, bringing back the necessary knowledge as a by-product of the great Joining which had created Arius. As a consequence, they had a meat with them, the whole setup resembling not much more than a small refrigerator.

Ozzie checked the opti-fiber hookup one last time. "You ready, darling?"

She nodded. For a moment she listened to the steady beat of rain on the skylight and smelled the fresh, woody smell of Ozzie's hair. "Yeah, I'm ready." She tried to relax into the curve of her chair, but she knew it wouldn't help. She hadn't been free in the metamatrix since the day she and Ozzie had scooped Berg from the wreckage of the Double En matrix like a broken butterfly. "Let's get it done."

"Counting," Ozzie said. "And three, and two, and one—"

She was there.

"God," she breathed to herself.

Her brain fought against the globular vision effect, and she forced herself to concentrate on a single quadrant of the overall sphere. After a moment the riot of perception slowed, and she began to make out shapes.

The metamatrix had grown in her absence. Now the great, pulsing clouds of the meatmatrices were almost without number. Shag Nakamura must be selling hundreds of the damn things. Their shifting, plasmatic shapes, like so many neon amoebas, slid and throbbed slowly in the green-tinged dark of the data universe. From their sides and embedded in their guts hung gemlike hard edges of chip arrays, hardware extensions, ROM cores; she was reminded of monsters in costume jewelry.

The view awed her, as always, but after a moment she began looking for something else. It was odd; what she sought should have dominated the entire metamatrix, but she couldn't find it.

Slowly she began to rise. Of course—the data universe arranged itself in ranks of power. Her goal would be at the very top. As she floated up, she passed things of unbelievable beauty—vast, shining dreams of information. Quick shafts of light, chrome-yellow, halide-green, a blue so pure it made her eyes ache—I don't have eyes, she thought suddenly—flashed past her, databursts bound for the unimaginable ends of that strange universe.

And still she ascended, retracing once again the slow beautiful steps from hell to heaven. The meat-matrices grew ever larger, more complicated, more encrusted with glittering hardware, until finally they filled the entire endless dome of the metamatrix with hues so overpowering she wished she did have human vision so her brain could shut off the flow.

Now the light began to brighten. At first a fire, then a storm. The curtains of flesh and sand finally parted as the full glory of what she sought revealed its awful majesty.

Star. Sun.

White Light.

Arius. God and Godhome.

She looked on the face of the Enemy, and then she turned away, sightless. For she learned a secret in that instant—there were things in the world and out of it stronger than she was.

Beneath the pitiless light of the Demon Star she screamed and screamed, until finally Ozzie brought her home.

She felt him pull the cable jack from her socket, and opened her eyes.

It was very quiet.

"I'm blind," she said.

3

SHIGEINARI "SHAG" NAKAMURA turned slowly away from his desk and stared at the tall figure who sat calmly on a long sofa at the other side of his office. "Why is he coming here? You know I don't like to deal with him . . . face to face."

The other man raised his right hand in a slow, precise movement, barely disturbing the impeccable tailoring of his gray silk suit. He stared at his manicured nails as if something vaguely important might be written on their glossy surfaces. "I don't think—" his voice was a mid-tenor encyclopedia of upper-class nasal resonance—"that your likes and dislikes are of paramount importance to him." Pause. "Old chap."

Nakamura's black eyes flashed once, like sunlight striking broken onyx, but that was the only visible sign of his anger he allowed to penetrate the calm yellow mask of his face. Fifty generations of samurai breeding would not allow him to parade his rage before his filthy British assassin, even if the Gods had seen fit to elevate Collinsworth to a position well above what Nakamura's vision of nature could ever have allowed.

"Too damned well I know it. I knew him when he was human, and he was a beast then. Now he's worse. Listen to me, Collinsworth—I painfully understand my position. That I am anything more than a beggar on the streets is his doing. I know that. I even, to some extent, understand it. But Arius was once a fat, despicable, sloppy man named William Norton, and no matter what he might be now, I trust him no farther than I could spit. He saved me for a reason. Therefore, he has a use for me, even as he does you, which gives me a certain value. Do try to keep that in mind while you pollute my air conditioning, would you?"

The lanky man sighed. His eyes moved slightly, a candlelike flicker in the late afternoon gloom, in faint acknowledgment of an aristocratic dance older than either man; finally they dropped before ghosts of family more ancient than his by half a dozen centuries. "Shag, why don't we get on better?"

The little Japanese man shrugged. "If you were in my position, you wouldn't ask such questions. Since your aren't, it's well that affection isn't necessary to our relationship. I repeat—why does Arius feel it necessary to come calling in his divine person itself? After all, I'm plagued at this very moment with the presence of his number one mouthpiece."

Collinsworth grinned suddenly. "Don't let the Lady hear you say that."

Nakamura lowered his head slightly, his own grin flickering like a razor in the dark. "Ah, yes. Our Bitch of the Wolves. She is well? Happy? Gainfully employed torturing heretics, I presume."

Plainly uncomfortable with the conversation, Collinsworth shook his head suddenly. "I really wouldn't talk like that, Shag. I have a sense of humor, you know. But she has none. Absolutely none at all. Only Arius himself is a shield against her brand of faith. I certainly couldn't protect you. Even if I would."

"Which you wouldn't. Thank you, Collinsworth, but I prefer to take my risks in my own way. There was a time not long ago when the Bitch Mother lived in a sewer. The wheel turns. Such a time may come again.

Meanwhile, we unenlightened businessmen keep putting one foot in front of the other, no matter whose hand is on the wheel. You understand me?"

"What I understand is that you'd rather spit yourself on one of her penance sticks than bow a single inch in her direction. I understand pride, too, Nakamura."

"Then why don't you ever show any?"

The moment crackled and discharged suddenly, leaving the afternoon oddly limp. Collinsworth said, "I don't know why he's coming, Shag. I suspect the usual."

"Berg?"

"Of course, Berg. Is *he* ever concerned about anything else these days?"

"Evidently not. Of course it makes no sense, but when have Gods ever made sense?"

Collinsworth chuckled. "Now you're getting it."

"I always have," Nakamura replied.

A soft, chiming note hung on the air like a fruit. Nakamura faced his desk. "Yes?"

"Wolves," a machine voice said.

"Of course." He turned back and faced Collinsworth, his features golden and enigmatic. "Let them in."

"They are in."

Nakamura grimaced. "Doesn't anybody ever knock these days?"

He paced away from Collinsworth's quizzical gaze, his steps seeking the peace of his garden. After his fall, and after the incredible events following, when he had struck a deal with a devil he could barely imagine, he had reclaimed his old office and had it rebuilt so it was identical to what had gone before. The only change was in the Oriental rock garden, which dominated one side of the vast room. Where once the rocks had been few and smooth, rising like the backs of sea creatures from the carefully raked gravel, now thrust jagged points of stone, reminding him of hungry, blackened teeth. Although he could never explain it to someone like Collinsworth, he felt with the certainty of bone that the art of a man must reflect his reality. His own days were certainly filled with teeth.

Another tone, this one higher and more shrill, announced the arrival of the Wolves at his door, which meant the Lady, and Arius himself, could not be far behind. He clasped his short, thick fingers behind his back and squeezed, composing himself for the ordeal. No sweat would touch his forehead, but perhaps the Bitch could read his soul.

"Ah, Lady," enunciated Collinsworth's slow, cultured drawl behind him. He counted to three before turning, to let her understand his bow was one of form, not substance.

She regarded him silently, framed in the wide door-jamb like the central figure in one of those hideous Italian religious masterpieces, while her bodyguards—*his* bodyguards—drifted past like vampire dreams, full of snarls and silence.

"Shigeinari," she said formally, but did not return his bow. He understood. By her vision of things she could not bow to him nor to any other human; not as long as she cradled in her arms the monster whose bloody eyes now scanned his face with ancient longing. She carried God; how could she bow?

Worse, by her faith; how could he not? Such was the universe of assumptions in which he now found himself trapped.

"Lady," he replied.

"Hello, Shag," said the monstrously deformed infant she cradled in her arms, its delicate voice a breathy symphony of horror. "How the fuck are you?"

He had to turn away. It was always like that. Shaken by memories bred into his very cells through centuries

of Japanese myth, mother-whispered tales of tiny things
that crept and robbed, of animals that changed shapes
and man-things that didn't, he turned away from the
voice of the demon.

It didn't help that he knew what the being that
called itself Arius truly was. If anything, it made it
worse—that this wretched scrap of inhuman flesh had
once been his partner, Bill Norton. He couldn't really
grasp the joining of Norton to the Lunie Artificial
Intelligence nor the strange, near-mystical role that
Berg had played in that titanic event. Not grasping, he
ignored . . . and thus made Arius a more horrible
transformation of his one-time business associate.

"Hello, Bill," he said mildly, from the safety of the
other side of his desk.

The Lady trembled at this token disrespect for God,
but God laughed. "Calm down, Mother," he said.
"I'm never going to be God for old Shag. Never in this
world. Somehow, maybe I like it that way. A sop to
old days and old ways, eh, Shag?"

"Whatever you say, Bill."

The Lady carried her charge to the sofa and sat
beside Collinsworth, who moved inconspicuously away
from her. Arius laughed again. "My favorite Limey,"
he whispered. "Nobody likes to get close to me anymore, Shag. Can you under*stand* it?"

Nakamura forced himself to stare at Arius's face. It
was a broad, vacant visage, its features yet unformed
by growth, striking only by the great red saucers of its
eyes. Arius had been birthed by the Lady, whose own
eyes, once blind and then repaired with infrared inserts, glowed with her child's crimson light. Hers were
artificial, however. Arius had been born that way.

The tiny body seemed an afterthought beneath the
great, soft baby skull. Perfectly formed, its stunted
limbs twitched and moved without direction, vaguely,

like the contortions of a crushed insect. Nakamura wondered how that tiny chest could provide air for the obscenely adult voice, but after a moment pushed the thought away. If even remotely possible, he preferred not to think about Arius at all.

"Shag, I don't think anybody loves me anymore."

Now Nakamura felt something gelid and awful begin to creep slowly up his spine. It took him a moment before he realized what the feeling was; a terror so general, so unfocused, so all-encompassing that for a moment his iron will broke, and he closed his eyes. Even the barest taste of Arius's metal amusement had that power to affect a human mind, to bring home the essential difference between the Demon Star and anything even barely human. For one instant, then, Nakamura mourned his partner and what he had become.

"Bill . . ." He shook his head. Bill was dead. Finally, in the chill infant breath of Arius's unspoken laughter, he bowed before that undeniable truth and the unspeakable doors which opened behind it.

"Go on, say it," said Arius.

"Your aren't God."

"I never said I was. Only others."

The Lady shifted uneasily, disturbed by heresy, but unable to cope with its source. Shag regarded her pityingly; she had carried the infant body in her own womb, and at the point of delivery suffered the monstrous invasion that was the arrival of the soul—no, he drew away from *that* term—the *essence* of the Demon Star in the flesh she bore.

He shuddered at the thought of that birthing.

"Why are we here?" Nakamura said at last.

Again dreadful fingers played with the nervous strings inside his backbone. He gritted his teeth and watched the flat, doughy travesty of a face that was Arius in his physical incarnation.

"He is killing me," Arius said.

It seemed to Nakamura that the entire room shifted slowly, that time ground to a crawl, and that the features of the others in the room changed and stretched, becoming masks. He felt cold dampness on his palms, and listened to the sound of his own breathing, slow and terrified.

He brought himself back by sheer force of will. Pressed beyond his own boundaries, he was saved by the strength of others, by a concept of shame so foreign to these devils that it was as alien as the child monster himself.

I will not yield! Even as he chanted the thought, it chanted itself, fueled by generations of disgrace avoided. He would not yield because he could not. It was not allowed.

"Who is killing you?"

Collinsworth had shrunk into himself, his suit around him like a rag, his face drawn with an emotion that was almost fear, almost something beyond it. He wore his tan like a bandage, or a scab concealing wounds pale and puffy. His eyes ran between Nakamura and Arius like small hunted things, and finally rested on empty space between. Nakamura noted this, and realized that he had won a battle. Not the war, but this man would never trouble him again.

"Berg," said Arius. "The Key That Breaks and Joins has done both." The red eyes screamed in unknowable languages. Nakamura felt the backs of his hands begin to itch. "The sonofabitch poisoned me, Shag. He fucking *ruined* me!"

Nakamura stared at him and knew that death was very close. It was all he could do to keep the triumph from his face. He nodded. "What do you want me to do?"

It has to be an hallucination, he told himself. Arius's eyes began to bubble. Something thick and red grew there, expanding, filling the air of the room. Nakamura could feel the blood warmth of it, and fought the urge to choke on Arius's demon vision.

"Why, I want you to find him, Shag," said Arius. His voice seemed to drift from someplace far away, full of broken metal and tortured nerve. A choir of buzz saws sang hideous accompaniment. "Find him and bring him to me."

Nakamura glanced down, surprised by sudden pain darting in his hands, and realized that his fingernails had gouged deep furrows in the soft flesh of his palms.

He looked up at the hellish infant, and at the transformed face of its mother. Suddenly the dream which Arius had imposed on them all cleared, and the great office was gray and cool. The demon became a deformed baby, the mother only another witch. The Gods had decided to remove themselves from mortal ken.

"You think you can do that, Shag, old buddy?"

Collinsworth's face looked like an unwrapped mummy, desiccated with terror and age.

The Japanese executive nodded slowly. "Yes," he said. "I can do that."

He sat alone in his office, dusk settling gray on his garden of stone and running water, and wondered if he could make good on his promise. Outside the tall glass walls of his aerie, the towers of Chicago began to come alight in the autumn evening. A low bank of mist moved in across the lake, obscuring the firefly paths of high-speed commuter hovercraft, heading for

the safe, rich havens to the north. A few stars flickered above the flatwater horizon, far to the east.

A pensive smile played on his lips. He remembered
the small exodus, the Bitch and her Wolves, Arius and
his Blades, with Collinsworth, the high executioner,
moving like an old man in the crowd. Arius would
return, Nakamura knew, his appearance refreshed, his
confidence seemingly restored, but something had broken inside him; and Shag had witnessed that. Things
had changed between the two of them now, and for
the first time since the near-destruction of Nakamura-
Norton, the little Oriental began to see an acceptable
future for himself.

The Demon will respect strength, he told himself,
and I have that. As much as any of them, I have
strength.

"Light," he said softly, and there was.

"Yes, Mr. Nakamura?"

"Come in, Fred." Shag turned from the glittering
view of the night skyline, arranging his face in a wel-
coming smile. Frederic Oranson made him nervous,
but it was nothing he couldn't handle. Oranson was
human. Or at least he thought so. The nerves came
from—he even dared admit it to himself—feelings of
guilt. It was not an emotion he was used to entertain-
ing, but in Fred's case the power of it was renewed by
each day of the security man's continued usefulness.

When he discovered that Oranson had betrayed him
to Arthur Kraus, he'd taken the only road open to him
in those hectic times and broken down Fred's conditioning with the quickest and most brutal methods
available. That such methods had involved infecting
the security chief with lethal bacteria to counter those
already present in his body, setting up a tightrope
from which any slip meant death, had been of small

concern. He'd been in too much of a hurry to worry about details. The information he'd obtained had turned out to be of little worth—the time was late and the data had become obsolete. It did, however, reveal that Oranson had not consciously betrayed his chief, but rather had done so under the overwhelming influence of the combined talents of Bill Norton and Arius, before both had joined to create the final Arius entity. Shag knew from bitter experience that no human mind could have successfully resisted that fusion, and so, after Arius had restored him to his seat of power, he searched for Oranson. *Perhaps I owe this one*, he'd told himself at the time.

Frederic Oranson had not been hard to find. The various bacterial strains had done their awful work and, inevitably, begun to slip out of balance. Oranson was discovered in a cell in one of the Double En labs, barely alive, his mind only questionably functioning.

Nakamura spent a fortune. Money had done what it could. The security man emerged from the ordeal bound inextricably to his old boss, for the solution had been continued dosing with an esoteric virus which destroyed all the Bacterial Countermeasure Drugs in his system. Nakamura caused the virus to be created in the weightless environment of one of Double En's orbiting labs, and dispensed to Oranson. In Terra's gravity well the bug could only survive for a few days; without it, Oranson could not survive at all. It made for as loyal a relationship as either could expect. Thus, he was finally made as whole as medical technology could make him, and returned healthy by any clinical measure. The loss of affect which the original assault on his mind had entailed, however, remained with him; in essence, Frederic Oranson had no emotions left. He could feel no anger, no happiness, no rage or joy. Sometimes Nakamura envied him.

Oranson padded slowly across the slate-gray carpet of the office and sat in one of a small grouping of chairs around a low table next to the garden. He turned his vacant brown gaze on Nakamura. Shag, without realizing what he did, swiveled from the emptiness of those eyes, preferring the neon life of the city below.

"Would you like a drink, Fred?"

"Sure, Shag."

Nakamura prepared Oranson's Chivas and soda with his own hands. In private, he did things like that, fully realizing that as penance it was insufficient, but doing it anyway. The two of them were bound by something feudal out of Nakamura's own past, a richly figured tapestry of blood and debt. Despite the ever-present nervousness—*I can never know this man*—Shag felt surprisingly comfortable with him. *Nor can he ever know me . . .*

He leaned over and placed a thick crystal goblet next to Oranson's left hand. To the unpracticed eye, the security man looked normal enough. He'd regained weight and now carried his full hundred plus kilos spread across a frame that held no hint of his previous softness; the experience that had taken his emotions had also stretched the strings which held him together, so that he seemed dry and hard. His blond hair had turned a brilliant white, an albino color so showy as to appear artificial. That hair, atop a face smoothed of any emotional nuance, was incongruous. Oranson's face was that of a child's—until you looked into the amber emptiness of his eyes.

"Thank you, Shag."

Nakamura seated himself across from Oranson. Formerly he had dominated him with the conscious use of obscenity, enjoying the suppressed disgust this had engendered in Oranson's middle-class mind-set. Now

he spoke as to an equal. What did it matter? He had
decided to trust him long ago.

"Did you monitor our guest's visit?"

"Of course."

"What do you think?"

"I think we should find Berg."

"Yes. So do I." Nakamura leaned back in his chair,
feeling the automatics begin to knead the tension from
his muscles, and wrinkled his forehead. "Where do we
stand on that? I haven't been paying attention. It
hasn't been a high priority until now."

Oranson nodded. "We have searched for Berg almost two years now, ever since Arius expressed an
interest. I believe the idea at first was to keep tabs on
him, but he must have known something. It turned out
that he'd disappeared almost immediately after Calley
and the Japanese, Toshi, brought him back to earth.
All of them went underground, including their tame
genius, Oswald Karman. It didn't seem to mean much
at the time. As you recall, we were busy. There was
the Church to establish and treaties to negotiate with
the other Conglomerates. And Arius, of course, had
his own plans. Later, the sabotage began, and Berg
moved up the list a bit. Not much—what could a
handful of people do against us? Especially with the
new technologies Arius created from whole cloth. Remember, we spent almost eight months on the fast-
growth systems and the perfection of the Blades."

Nakamura sipped his drink pensively. It was true.
The time after the Joining, when Arius had finally
made good on his word and smashed Arthur Kraus
and the Consortium, had indeed been hectic. Later,
while Arius created his own tank-altered legion of
killers and began development of the subsidiary Gods,
the whereabouts of Berg and his small cadre had seemed
of little importance. Nakamura, in fact, conscious that

Berg had been manipulated from the first, was in-
clined to write the little man off, leave him in peace to
enjoy whatever fruits Calley and Ozzie had been able
to steal from the titanic event of Arius's creation.

Then somebody had assassinated one of the new
Gods, and the game got hotter. Arius took a personal
interest, and his analysis showed that Berg had been
responsible, in some shadowy way, for the killing.
Later, other events occurred. Data banks broken. Great
information nets poisoned. All these acts had one
thing in common—they were aimed at the New Church,
and carefully calculated to do as much damage as
possible. Shag thought about this.

"Why would he attack the Church?" he asked
Oranson.

"Our analysts say the attacks have no pattern. Perhaps it has something to do with vengeance. My understanding of it—limited now, I admit—would seem
to indicate he has reason."

Again, considering the role vengeance played in his
own life, Nakamura was comforted by the knowledge
that the man across from him could feel no such emotion, no similar burning need. He is truly mine, he
told himself, and one more time marked the ever-
present nervous itch to unrequited guilt.

"Berg isn't stupid. He has a reason, whatever it is.
But why the Church? He must know it's self-renewing,
as long as Arius exists to fuel the technology behind it.
Church-baiting was always feasible when the Gods
stayed safely in their heavens, but Arius is a bit more
lively than that. No one knows that better than Berg.
So why the Church? Why not Arius himself?"

"Perhaps he is unable to face Arius on his own
ground. Perhaps the Church is the only thing he can
reach."

"What kind of resources can Berg call on?"

Oranson shrugged. "Before he got involved in all
this, he was called 'The Iceberg.' He was known inter-
nationally for his skills in computer programming, particularly in the so-called 'black areas,' involving both
the protection of data banks and their invasion. He
had all the right contacts for that sort of thing as well,
particularly in the underworld. He knew the Lady
before we did, for example. Afterward, he came out
of the metamatrix changed. Nobody quite understands
how. Maybe Arius does. But the group that was created by our efforts to destroy Norton—Berg, his ex-
wife Calley, the Oriental assassin Toshi Nakasone,
and the rogue genius Oswald Karman—has many talents he can draw on. Moreover, Berg managed to turn
the information he gained from the experience into a
great deal of money. It is even possible that he has
reestablished ties with Luna, Incorporated. We have
been as unsuccessful in tracking his money trail as we
have in locating Berg himself, however, so we can't be
certain."

Nakamura sighed. "I didn't realize he had become
such a factor. Perhaps I underestimated him. I even
felt sorry for him, to tell the truth."

Oranson's eyes were, as usual, unreadable. He said,
"Logically speaking, he was one of the wronged par-
ties in this whole affair."

Nakamura glanced up sharply, stung by what sounded
like a judgment, but his security chief's face was utterly bland.

"Well, wrong or right, Arius wants him. What you
or I think has nothing to do with *that*. What are our
chances of finding him?"

Oranson spread his big hands. "The Church is looking. Double En is looking. Arius himself is looking.
How long can any human hide from that?"

"I don't know. You tell me. He's avoided us for two years."

"As you say, he was never a top priority before. I can run it through the machines, but offhand I can't conceive of him keeping away from us for more than a couple of weeks. It's only a matter of time, with as much as we can bring to bear."

Nakamura's eyes found the stony peace of his garden. The restored brook made soft, bubbling noises in the background. He could almost feel the delicate balance between earth and water. "Who finds him first, do you think? Us? The Church? Arius?"

"Does it matter?"

"Possibly. Just answer the question."

Oranson was silent for a few seconds, but his gaze never wavered from Nakamura's face. The Oriental wondered what those thought processes were like now. He had once speculated on the mysterious wars which must have been fought in Oranson's skull, as exotic bacteria battled one another for dominance. He shook the thought away.

"We have the best chance," Oranson said. "We have the teams in the field. We have the experience. We have the mercenaries. The Blades of God are bodyguards and killers, as are the Wolves. They aren't trackers, not truly. Arius rules the metamatrix, but he must work his will through humans and their machines. We have more of the necessary resources. I think it will be us. And I ask again, why does it matter? I'm not simply being curious. What you want may make a difference in the way I pursue the matter."

Nakamura wasn't sure what he did want. To oppose Arius, now that he controlled absolutely not only Double En's data processing heart, but every other meatmatrix within the metamatrix, was absolute insanity. Yet it was obvious Arius feared Berg. Nakamura couldn't imagine why, but that didn't matter. And though strange twists of the Way might have brought him beneath Arius's iron dominance, Shag knew he could never truly submit; it wasn't in him. Berg might be a weapon. He was obviously trying to attack Arius. Perhaps he only needed another to point the way.

"I want us to find him. Is there any reason we are less efficient than the Church? No, we find him, and we find him first. Then we turn him over to Arius."

Oranson stared at him blankly. Nakamura wondered if there was any possible way the man could read minds. He suspected that Arius might be able to accomplish it, and decided at that moment he would have to avoid any further face-to-face confrontations with the Demon Star; for what was slowly growing in his thoughts was a plan. If Arius were to know it, it would mean his death.

Phrasing his words to avoid anything incriminating for the omnipresent spying devices, which he supposed Arius monitored constantly, was already second nature.

"Very well, then," Nakamura said. "Get on with it."

"Yes," Oranson replied, rising.

Nakamura watched him walk to the great double doors of the office. "One thing."

The security man paused, but didn't turn.

"I want him alive," Nakamura said.

His eyes glared up at her, answering crimson. She held him carefully, as befits a God. Their armored car rode smoothly, a monomole egg filled with luxury. For a moment she compared her present estate with that of her previous life in the Labyrinth, before the Demon Star had selected her to mother a new religion.

The life-style was more opulent, but the snares had

grown more deadly. Life makes trades, she thought, not for the first time.

"I don't trust that man," she said.

Arius's breath voice moaned at her breast. "Of course not. But you don't understand him. Your weakness, Mother. You don't understand men at all."

She bridled. "No man can equal—"

"I don't mean that," he told her. "No man can ever be as tough as you, make the kind of choices you do from instinct. That is your strength, and you are right not to trust him. But I do."

"Are you sure?"

"Yes. I trust Shag Nakamura to do what he will do."

"You risk much in the riddle of your trust," she reminded him.

"I risk this body, yes. Perhaps I risk more."

"And still you trust?"

"I understand treachery," he breathed softly, his eyes molten pits. "I trust that."

4

STRANGE ORPHANED BITS of memory filled split seconds in Toshi's brain as the Blade of God twisted into his first-strike movements. He had a sudden vision of himself as a skinny child playing on the crowded streets of the teeming Sunset neighborhood where he'd been born. When he was seven years old there'd been skateboard gangs— his board had sported the challenge "Thrasher Death!" And one kid, Katao, ruled them all with the usual childhood tools of fear and terror. Katao was bigger than most of the kids, but his true power derived from his attitude; all he wanted to do was win, and at the age of eight, used anything from his rudimentary karate training to rocks, clubs, and knives to enforce his dominant position.

One dusky fall evening Toshi turned a corner and realized he'd strayed from his own turf, caught in the gliding rush of the board beneath his feet. His friend Mikyo was with him, but around the corner, leaning against the graffitied wall of a crumbling Victorian, lounging on its steps, were five kids, all members of the Striking Dragons. Katao's gang. And Katao himself, his smooth face creased with two slits for eyes and a third for a grin, rising from their midst and raising his hand.

"Look," he said. "Babies. We've caught babies."

Toshi crashed his board and pulled a one-eighty, but not fast enough. He tangled with Mikyo's legs, and they fell in a pile before the other laughing boys.

"Babies," Katao said again. Now he skipped lightly forward, his weight on the balls of his feet like a dancer, and tapped Toshi sharply, once, on the top of his skull.

"Ow!"

"The babies are afraid," Katao announced. "I tap this one—" he repeated his quick motion—"and he cries out. Frightened babies." Now his expression turned ominous. "Frightened babies must be spanked. Is it not so?"

Seriously, his friends nodded assent.

Toshi slowly disentangled himself from Mikyo's legs and stood up, ignoring the raw strawberry on his bare knee, feeling a sick helpless feeling deep in his gut.

"We're leaving, Katao," he said. "We didn't mean to intrude. We apologize." For he did acknowledge that the rules had been broken.

But other rules had now come into play. "Oh, no, that's not enough," Katao laughed. "You must pay a penalty, frightened babies. You must learn never to trespass on my territory."

"We're leaving now."

Katao's voice went as hard and flat as his black button eyes. "No." His right hand darted out, and Toshi's head jerked back, a red stinging imprint of four fingers splayed across his cheek. "Frightened babies must fight," Katao announced.

Behind him, Toshi heard Mikyo make a small sound. He didn't turn around. A moment later the harsh sound of skateboard bearings and feet slapping concrete told him all he needed to know. Mikyo had deserted him.

Katao smiled. "One baby runs away. But what about the other? Will you fight me, baby?"

Toshi felt the tears hiding behind his eyes, but he nodded. If he didn't fight now, he would only add the humiliation of cowardice to his mistake, and everybody would know and avoid his eyes.

"Then fight!" Katao screamed as he leaped forward.

Katao was perhaps fifteen pounds heavier and a couple of inches taller, but Toshi discovered he was the faster of the two. One heavy punch caught him a glancing blow on the cheekbone, and he saw stars, but he turned enough so that Katao went rushing past. Without thinking, he kicked up; his sneaker caught Katao square on the butt and sent him sprawling across Toshi's skateboard.

Somebody laughed. Toshi wished very hard they hadn't. Now Katao would have to prove something. His guess was confirmed when the bigger boy lunged to his feet, breathing hard, his eyes nuggets of black fire.

Katao moved forward slowly, taking his time, measuring his punches. For a while Toshi was able to dodge, using his greater speed, but finally one clumsy fist connected with his forehead and left him standing, shaking his head back and forth, unsure of where he was.

Then Katao was on him, flailing with arms and elbows. Toshi felt his nose splash, tasted wet salt on his lips. He realized he was crying. His arms still moved but his legs wouldn't answer, and then he was on the ground, belly down, with Katao's full weight on his back. Rough hands grabbed his hair; they rubbed his face across the dirty concrete. Dimly he saw a red smear there.

Finally the weight lightened. From far away he heard

a satisfied voice. "Babies must be punished," the voice said.

After a while he was able to stand up. *If only I'd been bigger*, he thought. That was a rule to remember. He wiped his hand across his face, felt oily blood, and winced. Bigger and faster was better. Winning was better. Very well . . .

Never again.

"I think you got the wrong guy," Toshi said, "but . . ." He wondered what had happened to Levin. Overhead the sun began to burn off the morning fog. The Blade's face was flat as an ax, and as full of expression. He moved like something made of metal and silicon. Which, in fact, he was, to some extent. The Blades were tanked constructs, warriors whose genes were selected at birth for intelligence and ferocity of reflex. At fifteen, the New Church put them under, turned them off, and submerged them in special growth containers in which carefully tailored proteins invaded their bodies and laid down tiny channels of carbon fiber and silicon wire. Even their skin was strengthened.

The result, though small, was fearsome. Strong men, hardened brawlers, ruthless killers, turned away when a Blade of God strolled past.

At least I'm bigger than this little shit, Toshi thought.

He blocked the first hand strike by turning slightly and raising his right hand, palm inward. The strength of the blow surprised him. When he'd fought this one's mate earlier, he'd felt nothing. Levin had insulated him from his own nerve endings. Now Levin was gone, and he was on his own.

As the block spun the smaller man's arm, he followed the motion with his entire body, launching a circle kick at Toshi's knee. Toshi backed suddenly, squatted, and took the force of the blow on his thigh. The power, the speed of it, staggered him.

"Nice," he said between slitted teeth.

The Blade stepped back and nodded. "A taste," he said. "I'm going to chop you into little bits. Slowly . . ."

"Your momma's ass," Toshi said, and began his own attack.

He began his formal karate training at the age of eight. By his twelfth birthday he'd won several state-wide California competitions and was beginning to fill out. He branched into other, more esoteric forms of the martial arts, worked with the steel balls, the odd-shaped weapons, the straightforward knife, and sword and ax. Later, in his adolescence, he became addicted to firearms, and celebrated his eighteenth birthday by competing and winning a gold medal in the Olympics.

And all through medical school he learned about the body, about its hidden physical secrets, and kept himself on the cutting edge of the technology for improving those strengths. He had his first implant, a highly experimental technique involving synthetic additions to his adrenal glands, before he graduated from Johns Hopkins. As it turned out, he never practiced medicine. And he was never beaten again in a fight. Any kind of fight. Winning *was* better.

He felt the gravely, rotten concrete beneath the sensitive pads of his feet as he arched into a flying kick. The Blade of God crossed his hands in a perfect block, but Toshi's foot, clubbed into a ram of muscle and callus, crashed through the interleaved fingers like a spear and thrust the smaller man back into the wall of the building which had shielded them somewhat from the scene of the explosion in Berg's safehouse.

The Blade made no sound, but his eyes sparked and a certain wariness crept into his movements.

"Bigger is better," Toshi grunted.

When he was nine years old he sought out the same Victorian stoop where Katao still ruled his little empire. Katao was advanced for his age, had discovered drugs, and was no longer the fearsome physical specimen of his heyday, but he was still formidable. The fight lasted less than a minute, and when it was over Katao ruled nothing.

Toshi didn't hurt him as much as he could have, and at the end felt a strange, empty hollowness in the victory.

That was how he taught himself about oppression and the weak, and how his feet were set upon the path his life would follow from that day on.

The blur of their movements was like a hysteric dance, the sheer art of it visible only to those whose training was long and detailed. The two of them accomplished small miracles of attack and defense; hands, feet, and bodies moving to patterns so arcane they appeared beyond violence.

A moment came when motion stilled and they strained for half a second against their own stasis. Toshi looked into the eyes of the Blade and smiled. Something answered him from deep within the body of the Blade, something that he almost responded to. He remembered that Blades tended toward homosexuality for a simple reason: Their awesome strength, sometimes uncontrolled within the sexual moments, was prone to accidentally destroying less endowed partners. And it was said many of the Blades enjoyed the interplay of great forces checked and balanced more than sexual release itself. Of course, Toshi reminded

himself, some of them preferred more human partners, seeking the darker sexual release of murder.

Combat as sex. It was an interesting thought. He
wondered why it came to him.

The Blades of God were older than the New Church.
Their history of mercenary service went back a thousand years. The techniques of genetic intervention were
impressed not as novelty but as improvement. Only
the Church's most recent technologies, such as tank
augmentation, were truly new. Now some brothers of
that ancient order of killers flocked to the Church not
from loyalty, but rather seeking yet more weaponry,
more power. It was a lust bred into their very souls.

I understand that, Toshi thought.

Silicon and carbon and muscle fiber strained against
the momentary stillness as the Blade exerted all his
strength. Toshi smiled, then straightened his arm. Two
of his fingers thrust into those empty eyes. His thumb
slipped between the grinding teeth. And feeling a bal-
loonlike expansion, a sudden freedom, he closed his
hand into a fist.

He heard a sound like the flat of a cleaver crushing
cloves of garlic. He stepped back and let the smaller
man fall. He wiped his fingers on the Blade's shirt
front, a predator marking the spot of his kill.

Then he moved away, falling into the traceries of his
retreat. He was surprised. The entire encounter had
taken no more than twenty seconds.

A lifetime.

At four o'clock in the afternoon the steady breeze
rising from the Pacific dragged long, shaggy wisps of
fog across the observation lookout atop Twin Peaks.
At his back the fog already covered the Sunset and the

Richmond, out in the Avenues where he'd been born, raised, and shaped. Toshi blinked, then turned and faced across the city spread below him like a giant's candy table. Stands of pine and palm dotted the glittering hillsides like earthbound green clouds. Lines of light snaked between jewelbox houses, which themselves shimmered in the long afternoon.

The city, as always, lay in a dream.

He could almost taste the salt of the ocean, borne on the creeping fog. Around him tourists did their camera dance, uttering short plosive sounds and long exhalations at the view. He wanted to laugh. Many of them, garbed in the shorts and light tee shirts of their native Omaha and Indianapolis summers, were shivering at the twenty degree drop in temperature—a usual San Francisco occurrence but one they simply couldn't comprehend. Some took it personally; "Goddam it, why didn't the guide *warn* us?" Toshi decided he could get rich up here with a coat rental concession.

Then the visitor gabble faded away as he regarded the city. He'd killed a man today. Which was all right. That was his business. But—

But what?

Something stirred inside him. Feelings repressed by an endless sense of discipline. Always he'd served, as much a mercenary as any Blade of God. That his causes had been his own, his choices equally so, had always excused the means employed to his various ends.

Was it enough?

Berg was missing, possibly dead. Levin had disappeared from the safe confines of his skull. Had Arius triumphed at last? Was a similar smoking ruin rising somewhere in Chicago, over the graves of Calley and Oswald Karman?

He didn't know. Only one thing was certain. He was still free. Still alive. Arius hadn't gotten them all.

If he would serve Berg, then he must serve himself. Duty demanded it.

Besides, if the others were gone, he really wanted to plant his fingers in the mad God's brain, wherever and whatever it was, and squeeze. He would enjoy that a lot. After all, he'd beaten the Blade of God today. Did that not make him a kind of god himself?

Where was Levin? It was a frightening thought. He'd managed not to think about it for almost a day as he covered his tracks from Berg's safehouse. Now he rested in a small apartment looking out from Potrero Hill, the dark liquid waves of the Bay an oily tapestry beneath him. Alcatraz Island glowed like a Christmas ornament, its rocky surface covered with the domes of the Funhouse. Farther out, the shadowy, knifelike sail of a tanker sub cut the surface of the water.

He had the windows open. Occasionally the scream of a shuttle or a big lasercab cut the night air, which was thick with odors of pine and nameless flowers. The night was fogless. Stars glittered over the Golden Gate.

He missed the voice in his head. But it was more than that. Levin was *important*. Berg had designed the computer, had done the programming, and had supervised the surgical installation of the remotes inside his skull. Levin was designed to be a weapon. In their war with Arius, Berg told them from the beginning that the Demon Star had great advantages. They would have to make up for their lack of money and numbers with speed, tactics, intelligence. Levin provided all three, as well as access of a kind to the metamatrix. For security reasons, Levin's location was known only to Berg. Like all the bioelectronic brains, Levin had a presence, a reality inside the metamatrix. He was capable of self-defense, Berg assured them. But was this true? They depended so much on Berg. Now he was missing. And so was Levin.

Dead? Captured? Hiding? Was this the end they had feared so long?

Toshi shook his head. He felt the wings of his dark hair brush the base of his neck. Somewhere a single bird called, a mournful sound. I can't do this, Toshi thought suddenly. Can't let myself get this way.

He leaned back in his chair and felt his chest rise and fall. He felt clean dark air flow in, flow out. Fill his belly.

After a while he closed his eyes.

In the dream he felt detached. He became a discrete point floating in vast space. Off in the distance things shimmered faintly, promising light. He felt himself drawn toward that distance, felt speed begin to build, sensed that great silent vistas were flowing past him in nameless waves.

The light grew. Then over the invisible horizon thundered glittering white sands. Above the sands hung suspended incredible constructions, amorphous, shifting shapes that bellowed silently. Lances of color darted like elongated fish. Higher still hung clouds of luminescence in a hundred shades of green. They were gray with spectral jewelry, hard, metallic forms embedded, dangling, barely connected.

Burning down on all, bonfire of white and red, blazed the Demon Star.

This must be the metamatrix, he thought. He felt detached, warm, and safe. Somehow he knew that none of this could hurt him. And somehow he felt the presence of friends.

Now he began to rise like a bubble drifting to the

surface of a sea. He slowed as he approached the Star. Something deep inside his skull clicked, a metaphysical switch, and the metamatrix came alive around him. The silence was riven by an avalanche of sound.

Juh uh duh. Juh uh duh! Juh uh *duh!*

It was a terrible, rasping rhythm, the breathing of a wounded God, ancient and appalling. The whole metamatrix echoed until it seemed even the endless stretches of light moved to a ghastly dancing beat. He was very close to the Star. He began to see things on its surface and beneath its surface. Strange, truncated shapes, twisted in agony, pounded knobbled fists against invisible barriers. They rose close to the edge of fire, screamed, sank back again. Rivers of molten red swam there, carrying freights of claws and lips and teeth.

He wanted to scream, but had no tongue. The sound pounded at his ears, but he had no hands to cover himself.

The Demon Sun began to change. Scarlet flowed, melded, congealed. The great circle went white around the edge, but in the center grew a crimson pupil, a hunger of an eye. An invisible ripple crossed it, and Toshi thought of translucent membranes, an eyelid opening.

Slowly the eye scanned the universe. Alive with lust, it twinkled. It beckoned. It summoned.

It knows I'm here . . .

But the fearful gaze passed on. Where it touched pieces of the metamatrix, darkness warped and sizzled. The metamatrix was filled with screams. And it passed.

Toshi tried to awaken. The nightmare went on. Finally, just as the eye was swinging its focus in his direction again, he found himself sinking. His face burned. He knew the skin there was ruined. Yet as he sank a coolness overcame him. Soothing, restful.

He was lowered to a diamond floor. Infinitely far above, the beat went on. JUH uh *DUH!*

The light winked out.

His eyes slid blankly open. Fog mantled the hills outside, muffled Alcatraz, dampened his cheeks.

"Levin?" he said.

There was no answer.

When he woke dawn was silvering patches of low fog on the Bay. The cold had seeped into his bones like groundwater. Every muscle screeched when he moved. At moments like these he was conscious of all the technological flotsam and jetsam which lived in his body, aware of its alienness, the inhuman strangeness of it. He felt full of metal, of carbon, of tiny things that moved of their own volition.

And full of something else.

He groaned when he stood up. He shook his head and turned the chair away from the window. Falling asleep in a chair. Good way to get killed. He scratched his head and limped toward the front door and checked the lock. It was fine.

He kept this apartment under a web of false names, one of many such in many parts of the world. Even the hunter needs a place to hide at times.

It was an anonymous place. The kitchen cupboard was full of canned goods. He'd taken a couple of six-packs of Amstel beer from beneath the sink and put them in the fridge the night before.

Rubbing tiredly at his eyes he found a skillet and opened a package of powdered eggs. He found some dehydrated onions and poured them into the skillet with a little olive oil. As the eggs cooked he heated a can of Campbell's Cream of Mushroom Soup.

He poured it over the eggs and ate them from the

skillet, flapping his lips against the heat. Then he opened a beer and fired up the little Braun coffee maker.

He didn't have Berg's taste for the finer things in life, but he was glad he didn't have to live this way all the time. He glanced around the room. The kitchen was an alcove off the main room. There was a sofa bed unopened against the inner wall, a small table, and one easy chair half-turned away from the window. The wallpaper had faded till its former flowered pattern was only a sketch against the mustard background.

The place smelled empty. An involuntary shiver ran up his spine. To spend the rest of his life in places like this, waiting for the door to crash inward . . .

He shivered again, drained the beer, and poured coffee. After awhile he padded across the industrial carpet toward the bathroom. A shower would help. Something was crowding at the corners of his awareness. He wanted to let it in.

Levin?

By noon the fog had burned off. Toshi finished shaving his skull, then carefully opened his small makeup kit and found a bottle of pills. He took four and washed them down with water from the sink, bending over to place his lips beneath the rusted faucet. By two o'clock his skin had turned an even, weathered chocolate color.

He spent another hour filling his backpack with items he thought he would need. He finally glanced at the small chrono set into the fingernail on his left hand pinky. He decided to give it another hour. Dusk had always seemed to him a good time of day for leavetakings. He glanced at the chair by the window and sighed. A few moments later he leaned back and placed his feet on the windowsill. Clouds scudded across the blue sky, bound slowly across the Bay toward the gray breakers of the Pacific.

Pursing his heavy lips, he tried to put it together. There was no use in returning to Berg's safehouse. It would no doubt be watched. His disguise wouldn't be easy to penetrate, but if any Blades remained, the very way he moved would be a giveaway.

He thought about the Blade he'd killed. There had been a single instant when the little man had known he was outmatched. One breath before Toshi had straightened his arm and closed the Blade's eyes forever.

"Winning is better," he mouthed softly to the blue sky, and nodded to himself. But that seemed cheap as well, and the thought of his triumph brought a queasy, rolling sensation to his gut. He shook his head. That wouldn't do either. Somewhere in the future was more killing. As certain as bones, he knew it.

One cloud seemed to shape itself slowly into the likeness of Berg—big nose, narrow, foxlike chin—and Toshi smiled. Dimly he remembered dreaming, but about what? Something scary. When he tried to recall it, a part of his mind recoiled. Perhaps Levin could have dug it out, but Levin was gone, too. And what had happened to Levin was beyond any of his strength. His fingers were good for squeezing, not finding missing flesh computers. Yet he knew he would do something now. It was a vague, formless idea, but he thought the feeling would grow stronger, more concise. Even to himself he couldn't explain it, but he was packed and ready. Soon it would be time to go.

The Berg cloud drifted past, slowly dissolving. He waited until nothing remained but tattered wisps. Then he stood up, hoisted his backpack, and walked to the door. He checked the lock once again. Easy and sleazy; anybody who wanted to could get in. It wouldn't matter. He would be gone.

He stepped outside, locked the door, and walked down the hall. Within a few steps he began to whistle. He felt light and simple. Outside the building he tossed the key into a patch of low, thick-leafed shrubs. He wondered where he was going.

As he walked down Potrero Hill, the weight of the pack bounced nicely below his shoulder blades. He smelled the sea wind. Somebody had just turned a small flowerbed. The earth there was clean and black and redolent of the changing season. Any season.

Where the hill leveled off there was an intersection. Army and Potrero came together at a tiny park. Across from the park he saw a relatively new single-storied building. Redwood covered the walls and made a low fence around the flagstone plaza in front of the building. Tall windows faced out on the plaza. He stared at the building and read the sign which swung softly in the breeze. Somebody had carved the words into the thick slab of wood, then filled in the carving with red paint.

"New Church of the Spirit Corporate"

Something moved him and he walked across the street. He stood in the plaza and watched the empty windows. He saw reflections of clouds and sky in the glass. A dim figure moved within the darkness. The door opened and an elderly man stepped out. Toshi smiled at him.

"Hello, my son," the man said.

"Not hardly," Toshi replied. "You're the wrong color."

The man was short, thin, and stooped. His left hand was missing two fingers; the rest curled into a half-fist that looked permanent. Toshi wondered why the New Church didn't fix it for him. They had the money. Perhaps a man like this found converts more easily.

He seemed harmless enough, perhaps even wise. Toshi thought people would trust this man.

The man laughed softly. When he did this his face lit up and became beautiful. "Figure of speech," the man said. "Although the New Church is father to us all."

Save it for the peasants, Toshi thought. Suddenly he wanted to get away. Nothing was as it seemed anymore. Things changed too quickly. He'd thought himself on the forefront of that kind of change, and suddenly realized he was as unmoored as anybody else.

Berg gone. Levin gone. There was nobody to sell his services to. He raised his hand and wiped his forehead. Suddenly he felt dizzy.

"Are you all right? Would you like a glass of water?"

Stupid, Toshi thought, so stupid. Stand in front of the enemy in your new disguise and be as noticeable as possible. Why not throw a fit, fall down and foam at the mouth, and twitch a lot? Bet this churchly cripple would remember *that*.

He blinked and shook his head. "I'm fine. Just stopped to rest a moment. Coming down the hill took all the breath out of me."

The Churchman stared at him dubiously. "You should get more exercise."

"I'm too fat, I know." He shrugged. "But exercise? Who has time?"

"They have to give you a new heart, son, you'll wish you'd made time."

Toshi turned away and stared back up the hill. "I guess you're right." He paused. "You have services tonight?"

"Every night of the week. Six o'clock sharp. And dinner after, if you're hungry."

Feed the poor, Toshi thought. It's what churches

are supposed to do. New Church didn't miss a trick. But why should it? It could *prove* the existence of its God.

He grinned and nodded. "Got to go. Maybe another time."

The man grinned in reply. "Sure," he said. "When you start exercising."

"Right, uh, father."

Now the bent little man's smile went wide. "Nope. Not the right color."

They both laughed. Toshi walked on.

Just at that moment a picture came to him, so clear he could almost reach out and touch it. Tiny machines. Millions, billions of them. Infinitesimally small, little moving parts going *racheta-racheta*. It reminded him of something, a message perhaps. That was it.

A message God would never forget.

"Good day to you, my man," he said. He moved back to the sidewalk. His stride swung into an easy rhythm. Juh uh duh. Juh uh duh!

Now where had that come from?

5

"**T**HAT'S IT, THEN,**" Ozzie said. His voice was shaken and dispirited. He sat in a chair next to the futon in his apartment. Calley sat cross-legged on the futon, her face upturned, her green eyes focused on his face; but she was staring at some invisible point just slightly to the left of the sound of his voice. Some trick of the acoustics, he supposed, and wanted suddenly to cry.

"Ozzie, I'm not a doctor," she said. "But can they be right? It sounds so stupid. I mean there's nothing physically wrong with my eyes. And I've been in the metamatrix before. There's no reason for—what did they call it?—psychosomatic trauma."

"There's no reason, because it's bullshit."

"Huh?"

"Oh, Calley darling, psychosomatic only means *they don't know*. It's a code word they use to cover up their ignorance. And you know it, too, if you stop to think."

She lowered her head. A stray lance of golden light broke across the ragged black mop of her hair, and for a moment it seemed to him that her entire skull blazed. He shook his head. She'd turned away from the light, but she hadn't blinked. Not a twitch.

Even amoeba showed more reaction to stimulus.

She inhaled heavily and placed her hands on her thighs and rubbed hard. "So, then, what?"

"I don't know," he said. "Let me think about it."
"Don't take too long," she replied.

Calley woke to a gray Chicago morning, though she didn't know it. She opened her eyes and for a moment wondered why it was still dark. Then a wave of panic seized her. She clenched her fist as a hammer of blood pounded in her ears.

I will not scream!

This was the third day. The second had brought a dreary procession of doctors, with Ozzie jittering nervously somewhere close, his long, nail-bitten fingers occasionally resting on her forearm until she wanted to shake away his presence.

Her body told her it was morning. She had to go to the bathroom. Even the thought of that simple task filled her with panic. Then it all came down, the weight of the things she could no longer take for granted.

I'm blind!

The two words didn't fit. She couldn't make them fit. Blindness happened to other people. Poor, helpless creatures. Or worse, those who proclaimed a virtue of their ability to cope yet were forever dependent on the goodwill of the world around them.

She tried to picture it. "Hey, Ozzie, walk me to the john, would you please? Where's the door? Do my clothes match? What does my hair look like? *What does the fucking world look like?*"

This last thought echoed in the windy space of her skull like a judgment. Then she felt hopeless, absolutely dark. Better to be dead. They were so limited. If it had been her eyes, for chrissakes, if her goddam *eyes* had been burned out, that could be fixed. The small cameras, or the infrared inserts, the microneural wiring—they could do that. But it was her brain! Nobody there, nobody home, in the good old neocortex to take those signals from the right visual field and the left visual field and make sense out of them. It was as if a cameraman was shooting with no film in the camera. The machinery was fine. It just wasn't loaded.

She could see, all right. But she was blind.

Did the world still exist, that part of it she could no longer see?

She ground her teeth together in anger and frustration. Reality was so *subjective!*

Not like having to ask if your ass was getting close to the toilet seat . . .

Ozzie mumbled something fragmentary in his sleep next to her. She felt his long warmth stretched out beside her icy frame and was grateful. She'd never tried to examine her feelings about the young genius who snorted softly next to her, lost in an Ozzie dream. Now she forced herself not to think about him.

Worst of all was the uncertainty. The medics could find nothing physically wrong. "Maybe it will pass. Things like this often do," one had told her reassuringly.

She hadn't felt reassured. Often didn't mean always, and Ozzie had been right. They told her what they didn't know, which was everything, and what they did know.

Nothing.

Of course—and she grasped at the flimsy straw with sudden passion—they hadn't been entirely honest with the medics themselves. But how could they?

She imagined trying to explain the reality of the metamatrix, the burning existence of Arius within it, the uncertain genesis of the Demon Star itself, its terrible power.

How could they believe that? They would laugh, shake their heads, and take even less interest in her case. Obviously some kind of delusional system. Drugs perhaps. Maybe that had caused the psychosomatic blindness. Just quit taking those nasty drugs, lady, and you'll be okay pretty soon.

She could hear it. She could also imagine one of the doctors laughing with the rest, shaking his head, then later punching a code into his comm unit and making a call.

Seven-foot kid and nasty broad. That might stir interest in certain circles.

So they were on their own. She'd never gut-felt it was any different, but it was depressing to arrive at the same conclusion through the slow cold steps of logic. Which brought her back to the original question.

What about Ozzie? More important, what about the combination of Ozzie and Calley? Her lips moved in a short sigh. There it was, and now she had to think about it. A part, perhaps the largest, most important part of her had always belonged to Berg. Even after the divorce, even after all that ugliness, there still remained a connection. And when she'd ridden a spear of ravening numbers into Berg's flowered heart, deep inside the metamatrix, his key had unlocked her door forever.

What had he said? Forever joined?

Yes, forever. And though the exigencies of his enigmatic, ceaseless war with the new God forced them to be apart, the connection still remained. But Ozzie had been here, with her, all that time.

And the thought of going to Berg with a simple plea—help me, love me, I'm blind—was beyond even her own strength.

I'll fight it, she thought wildly. I'll fight it and win. Like I always do!

She sank back against the congealed lumps of the futon and stretched her eyes wide until the muscles in her forehead ached.

Come on, dammit, *see!*

But it wasn't her eyes.

She thrust one elbow into Ozzie's ribs. "Come on, bozo, wake up. Mama's got to go to the john."

It was better than having him wake up and see her stumbling into walls, she decided bleakly.

"I'm going to let Berg know what happened," Ozzie said.

Abrupt terror made her lips numb. She stared out into the darkness, listening to the sound of his voice. She heard indecision, and fear. Ozzie wanted somebody else to share the responsibility. And who else would he think of but Berg?

"No!" She was surprised by the force of the word. She'd meant to calmly object, but instead one passionate syllable had exploded. Where had it come from?

"You always attack," Berg once said.

"Calley, I don't know what to do." The sentence was flat and miserable. "I'm not any kind of medical expert."

"You said it wasn't medical. They couldn't help." Again, she was amazed at the passion in her own words. Of course Berg had to know. There were only a few of them, herself, Ozzie, Toshi . . . Berg himself who knew the name of the real enemy. The rest of their allies worked second hand, taking instructions from one of the four. And none of the lower levels had any real idea who they worked for or what they worked at.

All Berg's idea, of course. Everything set in cells, so that no one could betray too much. She and Ozzie didn't even know his location beyond that he was somewhere in San Francisco. Levin handled communications for them. Maybe Levin knew everything, could put it all together. The thought made her uneasy.

Levin existed, as did all the meatmatrices, within the metamatrix itself. Berg told them it was safe and they trusted him. Levin was, after all, his creation.

Yes, certainly Ozzie had to tell Berg. She didn't denigrate her own value to their cabal. Nobody constructed attack programs the way she did, strange, sharp-edged webs with points and teeth, boring things, burrowing things. It was mainly through her skill at breaking and entering that they still kept things financed. The pot of gold she and Ozzie had brought back from the end of the sinister rainbow had carried them for a while, but later she'd returned to her usual occupation. "Icebreaker," they called her. And she did that. She could break the ice shrouding any data bank, any at all.

Except for one.

Berg had to know. She blinked, felt the strange sensation of flesh sliding across the surface of her eyes in utter darkness.

"You're right, Oz. Give papa bear a call. Mama isn't doing so hot anymore." No one would ever know what it cost to keep the panic out of her voice. Or the fear.

Ozzie had fired up his own machines. Now he wrinkled his pug nose. Overhead the gray above the skyline was slowly giving way to streaks of watery blue. He glanced over at Calley, who sat silent, her eyes aimed at the shoals of junk which filled the big room. Unconsciously he followed her gaze, took in the boxes, the shattered furniture, piles of corroded, shapeless metal.

Why do I live this way? he wondered. The thought made him squirm. Calley had always made fun of his wreckage-strewn homes, but left to himself, things just seemed to accumulate. He didn't know why. Things interested him. Things were full of possibilities.

The place smelled of moldy upholstery and rust and dust. Funny, he'd never really noticed it before. Calley staring at it, transfixed . . .

Then he remembered and closed his own eyes. She wasn't staring at it. It was just where her face was pointed. He turned back to the box which controlled the small meatmatrix and tried again with the entry codes.

Nothing.

"Calley?"

"What?"

"Something's wrong here. Levin's not coming on-line."

"Huh? Run it again."

He snorted in disgust. "Already did. Twice. Same result."

She put both palms down flat on the futon and pushed herself up. "Here, let me—" Then she stopped. Her lips moved in a small twitch of disgust.

He stared at her. "Maybe that's not a bad idea."

Her thin features seemed dry, pinched, hard as old wood. "What are you babbling about?"

"No. Really. We haven't tried jacking you in. The implants are all over your brain. Maybe you can function in . . ." His voice trailed off.

But her voice began to vibrate. "Yeah. The metamatrix. Maybe I can see there."

"Calley." His voice was gentle. "That was what blinded you— "

"—In the first place. Right. But I wasn't blind until I came *out*."

"I don't think this is a good idea, darling."

"Don't take this wrong, Ozzie, but right now I don't give a fuck what you think. Now get your skinny ass out of that chair and get mine into it."

"Skinny?"

"Move it, pal."

She guided the long optical fiber cable into the jack beneath her ear with her own hands. It took a moment; her fingers trembled. She was aware—astonished at how quickly her other senses had sharpened—of Ozzie hovering just off her right shoulder, his breathing jumping on a ragged catch of nerves.

"I've got every cutout rigged I can think of," he said. "If any of your vital signs start to go whacko, the box will cut out and bring you back. Any mechanical signs—software breakdown, wetware jam-up on the little meat—same thing. And I'm gonna stand right here, you understand? Right fucking here!"

She pictured his new angelic face screwed up in little boy determination, and repressed a smile.

"That's right, Ozzie, you stand by me." Her fingers sought the touchpad. She'd always said she could operate blind. Now she'd have a chance to find out.

"Ready?" she asked.

"No. But go ahead anyway."

"Right." She began to punch in the opening cascade of instructions, the piped series which brought the meat on-line to its shadowy doorway into the metamatrix. She knew that what she really did was use the neural tissue of the artificial brain as a filter for her own impressions, a sort of secondary neocortex.

Though she was braced for it, the sudden wrenching shift from darkness into the shifting, luminescent green light of the metamatrix was a shock.

She could see! And though she was completely cut off from the sensations of her real body, she imagined it slumping into a slow slide of relief. Ozzie would be worried. "Don't pull the plug," she commanded, even though he wouldn't be able to hear.

For a moment she simply hung there, hovering over the diamond-dusted floor of the data universe which was the incalculable net of billions of PC-users. She hung in the long green silence like an ornament, glorying in the darting tapestry of color: the reds, blues, greens of burst transmissions, the sudden, bubbly explosions of net interaction, the hard glitter which represented silicon interacting with flesh. So *much* flesh.

Again, she was struck by the vast increase in the numbers of the meat machines. Where once had only shimmered seven of the spectral constructions, majestic in their singularity, now the metamatrix throbbed with thousands of swollen, ghostlike shapes.

She knew that far above this shifting cloud of analog flesh blazed a sun—the Demon Star—but she had no intention of journeying in that direction. It was fine to just sit a moment and glory in the avalanche of vision.

I may never come out of here, she thought slowly. A choice between darkness and this, that's no choice at all. Somehow it was a good thought. Somehow it comforted her, as if out of all possibilities she'd made the correct choice, and somebody, somewhere, was applauding.

A brilliant pink shaft of light darted past and startled her out of her reverie. Levin. That's what she was here for. Now where was the mouthy little meatmatrix?

The problem was less simple than it seemed. She was capable of inserting various codes from her console which were then replicated within the metamatrix. And she did have codes for Levin: identification and come-talk-to-me series. But she had no search-and-locate codes. Berg had set it up that way. Always before when they wished to comm with Levin, they did the equivalent of firing off a flare. Levin would investigate, and if the ID codes were okay, he would initiate communication. The entire process took only nanoseconds, but now Levin wasn't answering. Because he couldn't, or wouldn't?

The thought of Arius in control of Berg's nerve center scared her shitless. Although a part of her denied the possibility—surely Levin would self-destruct before being captured—she knew that nobody, even herself, was fully cognizant of the Demon Star's capabilities. Probably not even Arius himself.

And now she began to feel a strange pressure. She extended her focus outward in a full globe. Nothing had changed, but now the full weight of the uncounted meatmatrices began to press her down. So *many*. And why did she feel as if they were all watching her? It was like being in the center of some kind of accident, with the silent crowd, neither pushing forward nor retreating, but simply standing there.

Waiting.

Something with many cold, hard claws skittered up the path of her spine.

But of course it was ridiculous. Or was it? Except for the few meats Berg had created—and how had he done that?—each meatmatrix was a cyberneural extension of the original. And that had come from the brain of Bill Norton himself. In effect, each of those great flesh machines was another lobe of the Demon Star's brain.

Could they *all* be connected?

It was a sickening vision, and for one ghostly moment she felt that soft lash of agreement which had touched her so lightly before. Was this right, too? If so, the danger was far closer, far greater, than she'd ever supposed.

It was one thing for Arius to raid other data banks. It was quite another for the Demon Star to *become* a universal data bank. If that were to happen, the real world would be simply a slaved extension to the dominance Arius already held in the data world, the metamatrix.

She shivered again and thrust the sickening concept away. Levin. Levin was the problem. There was no way to find him in this great mass of electro-fleshly brothers. She would have to discover a way of making the missing computer find her. And then *talk*, dammit!

Calley keyed in the shutdown sequence, then reached up and pulled the opti-fiber plug from the socket. Her eyes were closed.

She opened them slowly, mentally crossing her fingers.

Darkness.

She let out her breath in a long ragged sigh. "Well, I guess you can hope for miracles. Doesn't mean they're gonna happen."

"Calley?"

"Yeah, babe?"

"You see anything?"

"Here or inside? Nope, I'm still blind in the real world, kiddo, but, yeah, it's still the same in the meatmatrix. Big and green and probably nasty. Jeezus, Nakamura or somebody's been building meats."

"You can see inside?"

She wiped her forehead with the back of her hand. Wet. Why was she sweating? "I can see fine, Ozzie. You were right. Thank you."

She was astonished to feel his long, skinny arms wind around her shoulders. Then his lips felt warm and dry on her cheek.

"Hey, buddy, you forget how to kiss?" she asked, and turned her face up. Ozzie made a sniffling sound as he bent over.

"Ozzie, I'm gonna have to trust you on this."

He looked up from his touchpad. "I know you're a tired old experienced lady, babe, but I've done a fair bit of programming in my time, okay? It's not like you're asking for anything complicated."

The huge room seemed completely disassociated from the city around it. Only a faint pink glare from the skylight betrayed the outer world. Ozzie was curled like a question mark at his work, his clear, childlike features wrinkled in concentration. The green glow from three video data terminals caught the amber flecks in his gray eyes and turned them into brass. Calley sat beyond the futon at the edge of a beach of junk, feet curled under, leaning back in a tattered wire chair, protected from the rusted metal by something that might have once been a horse blanket. The only sounds were the faint scrabble of Ozzie's fingertips on the pad and their shared breathing.

Absently she wiped a fringe of hair from her forehead. From my eyes, she thought, and then didn't think the thought anymore.

"I'm sorry."

He paused. "You're what? What did you say?"

Her rough voice began to develop an edge. "What's the matter? You forgot how to understand English or something?"

"You never said you were sorry to me before."

She thought about it. He might be right. The only person she could remember ever having sincerely apologized to was Berg, and the circumstances then had been extraordinary.

"Maybe I should try it more often," she said. "Circumstances change, you know. Even I change, somebody pushes me hard enough."

"Calley, I'm not trying to push you." His voice trembled slightly. She could imagine his face.

"Not you." Abruptly she slapped the side of the chair. "Not you, dammit!"

Silence. Then, "Calley?"

"What?"

"Don't change too much."

This time, she thought as she gazed at the diamond floor of the metamatrix, *we'll see what I can stir up.* Dimly she knew she was marshaling the phalanx of programs Ozzie had created for her. In the metamatrix, when an operator was riding the jack-initiated programming, he was able to see an analog of it. Since she was operating through a meatmatrix, that meat would generate the analogs. Now she began to see a dim web, a circular ring of shadows, take up a dancing station around her. At first it resembled a horde of tiny bats. As the web sharpened, it devolved into a trillion jittering motes. It hardened further, becoming an elongated spear shape, metallic in its growing solidity.

Finally it began to flash colors, strange unearthly colors that she had no name for. And at the end, when the colors quieted, the whole thing became translucent, barely visible.

It was huge.

She laughed then, sucker-punched at her own powers. Ozzie wrote it, she thought, but I told him how. She'd niggled at the hunch she had, that Berg had built his meats without using anything from Arius or Double En. Which meant most likely he used his own brain tissue as the original culture.

That she could access. It took her awhile, with Ozzie guiding her verbally, but she'd cracked every medical data base in Chicago until she found Berg's records.

It took longer still to design hunter-seeker programs keyed on certain cellular characteristics she discovered there, bits and oddities and genetic quirks that had to be reflected in the structure of anything Berg created. It would have been simpler to analyze their own meat, but neither of them had the skill. And somehow she figured Berg wouldn't like them hauling it into the nearest microbiology lab for a quick dissection.

She glanced over the quivering length of her data spear and laughed. "Go, boy," she said, and mentally slapped its flank.

Soundlessly it began to slide forward. Then suddenly it leaped ahead like dropping a dragster into third and pounding metal. She laughed again. "Give 'em hell."

Then she dropped back closer to the floor and began to wait.

She didn't even notice when it happened.

—click—

She sat encircled in steel. It took her a moment to figure out where she was. Her old office, situated on the first floor of the house she'd owned on the North side of Chicago. A house she'd not entered for almost three years, ever since they'd gone underground for the first skirmishes in the war against the Demon Star.

She froze. Waves of gooseflesh crawled on her forearms. She looked down at the faint bluish bumps and shivered. One minute she'd been in the metamatrix. Now—

It was very quiet. She couldn't even hear the hum of air conditioning, though when she'd lived in the house the heatpumps had never stopped. Or the fans. She hated the smell of stale smoke, but she had a two-pack habit. The fans ran all the time.

The colors were the first thing anybody would notice; soft, dark warm shades, plums and dark blues, and faint hints of shiny green, ripe to the point of rotting. She'd asked the decorator if he could make it look like a bruise. He'd said he could and had turned out as good as his word.

She reached out and touched the desktop. It was cold, faintly slick, hard. She turned in the big leather chair, catching all the familiar details. The armored door across the room, the single entrance—but not the only exit—to the place. The tall bookshelves lining the left-hand side of the office. On the right a long side table, oak and ancient, one of Berg's first gifts to her.

"I don't like antiques," she said.

"You'll like this," he'd told her, and he'd been right. Somehow the scarred top of it picked up stray drinks, umbrellas, half-read books, whatever needed a temporary place to rest. She'd cleaned the table once every month, unless things fell off earlier.

And in back, the readouts, printers, and monitors which were the heart of her business. All gone long ago, she'd thought, but now back again.

Like a bad penny?

"Penny," she said. "Penny for your thoughts?"

The smooth, mellow voice replied instantly. "Yes, Calley?"

The voice sounded familiar. She smiled. It should—it was her own voice, with all the rough edges filed away.

"Hi," Calley replied. She'd never named the machine which generated the voice. Anthropomorphism was Berg's bag, not hers. But the familiar sound made her feel warm and comfortable. She almost wished she'd given the machine a name, so she could use it now.

She rapped her knuckles on the desktop. "Pretty solid," she said.

"One-inch stainless steel," the machine replied. "I still have the specs."

Calley grinned slowly. "Which one are you? Berg or Levin?"

"I don't understand," the machine said.

"Sure you do. A minute ago I was in the metamatrix sending a hunter-seeker after Levin. Now all of a sudden I'm in a room that probably doesn't exist anymore. Which means I'm not—I'm in a data construct. Remember, I've been in one before. So give. Berg or Levin?"

A pause, so imperceptible that only she would have noticed; then, "Calley, I assure you I'm the only one here. But there is a message."

"I'll bet." Calley sucked on one sore knuckle. Damned real, these constructs. "Who from?"

"I'm not sure, but I think it's this Levin you just mentioned."

"Calley, wake up! You okay?"

Something was shaking her. She felt her head flop back and forth, loose as a fish. "Uh," she said.

"*Calley!*"

Something wet and cold slapped her across the face. "No," she managed weakly. She raised one hand and shook her head. "Not again. Give me a . . . minute."

He stared at her, his eyes wide as pumpkins. The amber flecks in his pupils were sharp as brass filings.

"You had some kind of episode," he said.

"What happened?"

"I dunno. The automatics jerked you out, but when I unplugged you, you were out cold. Your vitals and everything were okay, but it took me a couple of minutes to bring you around. Are you okay?"

She reached out and touched his face gently, then let her fingers ghost through his hair. "You need a haircut, you know?"

When she felt his cheeks again, there was a faint

film of moisture there. "Something happened in the metamatrix, Ozzie," she said. "I don't know what. Don't remember. But I can't go back in there."

His voice was soft, furred with a nameless emotion. "How do you know?"

"I'm still blind, aren't I?"

In the middle of the night she sat up in bed and shook his shoulder hard.

"What? What is it?"

She pictured him rubbing sleep from his eyes.

"Luna," she said. "We've got to go to the moon."

6

THE CROWD WAS in a holiday mood. The entire Wharf area seethed with tourists and even a few jaded locals. Bay Street was packed from the fronts of the tacky galleries, daze emporiums, souvenir stands, and cookie-n-cream joints clear on down to the dock area. Overhead the sun had burned off the fog early; now the sky was the kind of blue San Francisco rarely saw but nevertheless had helped make the city famous.

Halfway up Russian Hill, from the balconies of the rich, you could hear the sound of the crowd; a low, rolling susurrus, like distant surf pounding rock. Horns honked as tour buses tried to thread their way down Columbus toward the Cannery and Ghiardelli Square. Overhead the sharp, firecracker whine of lasercabs making for the big taxi stand near the old cable car turnaround cut the perfect, still air.

The waters of the Bay were almost stilled, thick and blue, with only a few whitecaps breaking like whipped cream over steel.

Up on the balconies they had their telescopes and long-distance video-cams out. Like the stalked eyes of a thousand insects, the lenses turned toward the water as the fleet, each fishing boat flying so many flags and banners it resembled a floating scarecrow, moved deliberately toward the Wharf.

It was the Blessing of the Fleet. The tourists loved it.

High above, on a triple-deck condominium clinging to the side of the hill like a redwood vulture, Shag Nakamura lifted his heavy tumbler of Laphroaig and gestured toward the Bay.

"Colorful," he said. On his right, elbows propped on the railing of the balcony, Frederic Oranson watched the scene below with absolutely no expression on his face. Two other men, a Euro and a short, heavyset Chinese, nodded carefully. Shag exuded a bonhomie that made them wary.

"It's . . . different," the Euro said. Like the others he wore a regulation three-piece business suit. The only thing that distinguished it from similar garb of a century before was the width of the lapels—in this case, quite narrow. His accent was indeterminate; one of those little nations that no longer existed, Nakamura guessed. He didn't really care enough to find out. These were small fry, mid-level industrialists fronting for tiny syndicates hoping to become huge syndicates.

Shag nodded politely. "Once it meant something," he went on. "There was a time not long ago when the fleet actually went out and fished. Now, of course, except for a few boats owned by expensive local restaurants, the fleet is for show. The visitors like to see boats at the Wharf. It makes them feel the whole thing is more than just another tourist trap."

The Chinese seemed shocked. In his country anything that floated went out daily in the endless effort to feed two billion of his fellow citizens. The comrades had never taken to capitalist concepts, Shag thought, for all their grass-roots technology. "Then what is this ceremony?" the Chinese asked.

"When it was a real fleet, most of the fishermen were Portuguese. And Catholic. Once a year the local

bishop officially blessed the fleet in a simple ceremony. Now it's for the tourists, since nobody wants to
risk offense, the local denominations take turns. This
year, for the first time, the New Church of the Spirit
Corporate officiates. For the New Church, it's sort of
a legitimization locally. You don't get to do this unless
you have a reasonable following, not only here in San
Francisco, but nationally, too. These tourists come
from everywhere."

The Chinese blinked his sharp black eyes once, like
a lizard. Shag smiled at him and repressed his racial
loathing of the would-be mainland conquerors. He
remembered the Divine Wind and the destruction of
the Khans, and hoped such a time would come again.

He turned away and glanced at Frederic Oranson's
impassive face. Oranson raised his eyebrows slowly.
Nakamura nodded and Oranson quietly moved away
from the party, finally disappearing from the balcony
into the darkness of the room behind.

The Euro—Nakamura thought for a moment and
dredged up the name Weiler—said, "Your assistant is
very quiet, Shag."

"He is very efficient," Nakamura replied. "Silence
is a part of that efficiency. If you take my meaning."

Weiler shrugged. "I suppose so." His long, horse-
featured face brightened. "I say, what's that?"

All the men leaned closer to the railing, straining to
make out the colorful knot of movement pushing its
way through the crowd toward the docks themselves.
A single trawler, bedizened with flags and bunting
until it resembled a floating garden, was also moving
away from the pack toward the Wharf.

Shag held out his right hand. A young male servant
appeared quietly and placed a pair of binoculars in the
older man's hand. Shag didn't look up.

"It's the regional vice-president of the New Church," he said at last.

The Chinese squinted against the light. "As crazy as western religions go, that seems an extraordinary title for a religious figure."

"It's an extraordinary religion," Shag replied. "Here, would you like a closer look?" He handed the binoculars to the Chinese, who raised them to his eyes.

"Strange garments," the Chinese commented.

"I'm told those robes are a concession to popular ideas of how a cleric should appear," Shag replied. "I heard the New Church did one of the most complete studies of religious perceptions ever attempted before they presented their outward image to the world."

The Chinese lowered the binoculars and stared at Nakamura. His eyes were cold. A trick of the clouds overhead made his gaze appear almost colorless, a mirror of reflective flesh. "You seem quite knowledgeable about this new cult," he said at last. "Surely you haven't rejected the beliefs of your ancestors?"

Shag smiled slowly. "Knowledge is power. One assumes that you keep up on the changes in your own sphere? Perhaps medical research in the reassimilated province of Taiwan occupies some of your attention?"

The Chinese, whom Nakamura knew was one of the prime financiers behind the largest illicit medical clinic in Taipei, grunted darkly and handed the binoculars over. "As you say, knowledge is power."

Weiler rubbed his chin. Shag noted distastefully that already a dark stubble had begun to appear there. "You say 'their outward image.' One presumes that there is then an inner image, or more accurately an inner reality, the public remains unaware of?"

Now Shag lifted the binoculars again, cutting off the conversation. "One presumes," he said.

Frederic Oranson returned to the balcony, accompanied by two servants who pushed a large viewscreen. "We patched into the local news portacams," he said. He gestured toward the screen. "Would you like to watch out here or back inside?"

"Here is fine, Fred."

Oranson nodded and stepped back. The men turned away from the view below and stared at the screen. It split into several different views of the crowd.

"We're taking uncut footage direct from the various stations on the scene equipment," Shag said. "If you'd rather, we can switch to broadcast programming, but sometimes the unedited version is more interesting."

Nobody said anything. "Fine, then." Shag leaned back against the railing and sipped his scotch. The wind gusted sharply. He smelled a quick breath of pine, then a wave of hydrocarbon-laden air from the streets below. Far to the west, beyond the Golden Gate, a layer of low-lying fog shimmered like liquid pearl.

The scotch burned smoky in his gut. It was the only decent thing about this day. Frederic Oranson caught his eye. Slowly, Shag winked. They both understood. It was the old pigeon game.

They had two pigeons on their balcony.

He'd done it as a child. Only the stakes were higher now.

The crowd rolled back from its center like a billion-petaled flower unfolding. Nakamura imagined fathers from Des Moines, their naked calves blue and pricked with cold bumps, clutching the sticky fingers of their children, while mothers grasped at hairdos gone awry in the Bayside breezes, and over all, a rising mutter of astonishment at the gilded processional glory that was the advance of an Angel of the New Church.

The Angel was tall. His face was carefully sculptured to vaguely resemble one of those ancient Italian paintings of Christ. Around his dark hair wound a white turban, giving him a Mediterranean flair. His robes were of deepest red, woven of a long-chained polymer that flowed like watered silk, like a river of blood.

When the Angel raised his arms and extended his palms outward in both a blessing and a request for silence, it seemed that his fingers were unnaturally long.

Nakamura knew what image was projected in all this. Each detail had been sculptured as a New Church response to subconscious longings. There was a racial, atavistic understanding among all peoples about just what made up the physical characteristics of divinity. Arius simply tapped into history with the syringe of technology, and responded. The result was not called a God, not by the Church. But the Word was whispered in other places, by other people, and the Word was spreading.

Now the Angel and his entourage reached the edge of the Wharf and paused. Security teams—local police, a few Blades, here and there a Wolf in less flamboyant garb than usual, even several local Supervisors of the Church—pushed the crowd back until there was an empty space several meters in diameter around the core group. Finally even these hangers-on fell away and the Angel stood alone, arms raised, facing the boats on the Bay.

There was a shivering moment of silence while the sun beat down and the water rolled sluggishly. Then the Angel dropped his hands and the crowd breathed.

"They that go out on the waters!" proclaimed the Angel.

The crowd murmured.

The Angel paused as the sound of his voice rolled

out across the great blue silence. It was a deep voice,
full of muted thunder, yet clear and piercing. Nakamura
had no doubt that every ear in the mob heard the
words as if they were directed at it and it alone.

"That brave the dangers of the sea!"

Now three of those who had accompanied the Angel
to the edge of the Wharf stepped forward and ranged
themselves in a semicircle behind him. In their hands
they held long, shining, scepterlike objects. The air
above them seemed to waver, as if great heat were
concentrated there.

"As you seek to feed mankind . . ."

Now the Angel raised his hands, his long fingers
outstretched, in blessing again. Tiny licks of flame
appeared at his fingertips, glowing red and yellow and
blue in the sunlight. An answering fire appeared around
the scepters and began to grow.

*"So does the Blessing of the New Church of the
Spirit Corporate feed you!"*

The small group at quayside was surrounded by
licking waves of light. In the center the Angel blazed
like a great jewel. On the water the lead boat, only a
hundred meters away, flared up in sudden answering
conflagration. Someone screamed into the electric
silence.

"Receive the Blessing!"

A great roll of thunder boomed out across the flaccid waters as the Angel suddenly raised his arms straight
up. Nakamura, even from the great distance of his
perch, felt the whining, tearing tension descend on the
scene below, as time slowed into yellow stasis, as
strange instruments pounded an unearthly, invisible
melody.

Slowly the trawler began to rise above the waves. A
wind of sighs swept across the mob. People shouted;

some fainted. Nakamura watched them go down like flowers before a tornado. And still the boat rose.

Finally the boat hung still like a gigantic, glittering insect caught in the moment just before release. Flame bloomed around the Angel, a flower seeking consummation. The doors of the edge of the universe whined at the base of a hundred thousand spines.

"You are Blessed!"

The boat began to descend.

Only Nakamura thought that he'd seen something in that descent, a ghostly outline behind the boat, hovering over the rest of the fleet. Many heads, many crowns. A great beast whose rider turned away vision.

He shook his head and the specter went away.

The Euro, Weiler, spoke into the silence. "What's that? Look. Those tiny things floating on the Bay. There must be millions . . ."

Shag Nakamura shook his head tiredly. "Bread," he said. "Loaves of bread."

The falling afternoon had dragged a load of heavy-bottomed clouds in from the Pacific, and now streamers of fog began to drift through the bright lights of North Beach below. The men sat in a long, low-ceilinged room whose walls were of polished redwood, umber and glowing. The room would have been stuffy but for three large skylights overhead which admitted a light like that of some clear semiprecious stone. Smoky topaz, Shag thought glumly as he stared at what seemed his fifth or sixth tumbler of Laphroaig.

He sat in a ridiculously valuable piece of French woodworking and thought that he would rather sit cross-legged on the floor. It wouldn't do, however—these back-country yahoos expected a certain level of opulence, even as the underpinnings of their world teetered in the face of miracles.

Was that a beast I saw, he wondered?

The Chinese—his name was Li Chen Yu, Oranson had whispered in his ear a few moments earlier—looked around petulantly as he lifted his own empty glass. "More beer, Mr. Li?" Nakamura asked politely, inwardly grimacing at the thought of Tsing Tao profaning the delicate crystal.

"If you please," Li said. "Are there servant problems in America, Mr. Nakamura?"

"It is a different world than our own, sir," Nakamura said as he watched one of the nameless young men bring Li a fresh bottle in a small silver ice bucket. "Americans view service as a commodity rather than a profession."

The Chinese hissed a bit of laughter. "Someday that will change, perhaps."

True, Nakamura thought, remembering the Second World War and Japanese operations on the mainland. The Chinese have always made good servants.

"One never knows," he said politely.

"You seem bored, sir," Weiler said. He was drinking champagne, a Rothschild '09 that Nakamura supposed had cost at least as much as the suit the uncouth *Mitteleuropean* was wrinkling. The man swilled it down like the Coca-Cola he'd ordered earlier, and with as much appreciation.

"It's been a long day, gentlemen," Nakamura said.

"Yes, it has. And to what purpose? Did I fly over the pole for this sideshow we witnessed today?"

"Sideshow?"

"Well, was it not? Cheap magic tricks for stupid crowds, Mr. Nakamura. What else was it? And more to the point, what does it have to do with men like ourselves?"

Oranson stirred slightly behind him, but Nakamura

only smiled. This worm had now invited himself into equality. Well, he would see.

"A very great deal, Mr. Weiler. What do you know about the New Church of the Spirit Corporate?"

Weiler tilted his glass and swallowed heavily. Nakamura hid a wince behind his palm as he tasted his own drink. "Nothing. Well, not much. A cult of the kind that Americans seem so famous for creating and embracing. Now even supposedly intelligent Europeans are becoming caught up in it. It will pass, no doubt. They always do." Weiler paused. "What is your interest in it? Surely you aren't a believer?"

"Belief takes many forms, Mr. Weiler."

"Let me be more specific, then. Perhaps the word 'flack' is more reflective of my feelings."

Nakamura smiled again. "Oh, but that word would be an insult, would it not? At least on your terms, but even so I would have to take it as such. So I'm sure you don't mean it that way. After all, Nakamura-Norton owns so much of the Class C voting stock of your fascinating syndicate."

Weiler suddenly lost interest in his drink. "Of course, I meant no insult." He spoke so quickly that a faint spray of champagne ghosted past his lips. "No insult at all, I assure you. But then, sir, why are we here? Again, no offense intended."

Nakamura sighed. Gently he sat down his drink on the exquisitely carved oak side table next to his chair. "In business, sirs, we learn to try to guess the future, do we not? We predict markets. We attempt to chart the course of the new technologies. We try to minimize our risks—and, of course, to maximize our opportunities. I have brought you here to present you with one of the last. A situation I feel is the greatest opportunity for those like ourselves to appear in perhaps the last hundred years."

Li Chen stared at him in open disbelief. "Are you referring to that disgusting spectacle we witnessed earlier today?"

Nakamura shrugged. While he was by nature predisposed toward an Oriental disdain for things Western, this Chinese slug displayed the imagination of a rock. No, of something under a rock. "Mr. Li, allow me to clear the air a bit. Yes, I do have a connection with the New Church." He raised one hand. "No, without going into details about that—however, I would like you gentlemen to consider certain advantages about such a liaison."

Weiler stared at his drink. "Mr. Nakamura, it is true that your company does carry a great deal of weight within my own organization. Notwithstanding that, I did not come here for you to insult my intelligence. I'm leaving." Slowly, his muddy brown eyes turbulent, he began to stand up.

Nakamura's voice cracked like a chain. "Sit, Weiler. I haven't excused you yet!"

The European paused awkwardly, his face slowly turning bluish-purple.

Nakamura lowered his voice. "No, sit," he said gently. "Hear me out."

Weiler's lips pursed, letting out a small sound. He lowered himself back down.

"Gentlemen, we are all friends here," Nakamura continued, as if there had been no interruption. "Do me the courtesy of an explanation. I can understand your skepticism . . ."

Frederic Oranson brought Nakamura another drink, then joined him at the railing of the balcony. The two men looked out over the carpet of light that twinkled in colorful halos through the thin layer of fog.

"So, Fred, do you think they bought it?"

Oranson rubbed the top of the balcony with one crooked fist. "Does it matter?"

"Not really," Nakamura admitted. "Although Arius says it's important, so I suppose it is. Perhaps I—" He broke off and raised his eyes to the sky and watched the stars twinkling there.

"It would be easier," Oranson said carefully, "if Arius were more explicit about his aims. Then we could tailor our methods . . ."

"What could that twisted dwarf possibly want with riff-raff like that?" Nakamura wondered. "If that is what he wants, I don't need to use persuasion. I can buy them by the dozen. Sealed and delivered."

"Perhaps he wants converts."

"Those men? They don't believe in anything. Why should they believe in some jumped-up God with the instincts of P.T. Barnum?"

Oranson sucked at his front teeth, a sharp sound in the quiet of the evening. "What we saw today. Do you think it was faked?"

"Had to be. Either that or Arius really is a God."

"And?"

Carefully, Nakamura poured the remainder of his drink over the edge of the railing. He listened to the liquid patter through the carpet of leaves below. "I don't know the answer to that."

A soft tone resounded through the gloom. Nakamura looked up. Oranson turned and walked quickly back inside. In a moment he was back. "They've found Berg," he said.

"Who?"

"Our people," Oranson said.

"Let's go," Nakamura said. They walked toward the house. "Oh."

"What?"

"Throw these bums out."

* * *

The heavily armored black limousine crept slowly up Bay Street, then turned left near the Presidio. Another turn brought it to a short, dead-end alley. The car rolled to a heavy halt, and Nakamura sat and listened to the sound of his own breathing.

Oranson, sitting next to him, seemed completely untouched by the other man's air of taut expectancy.

"Where?" Nakamura said.

"Up ahead, on the right," Oranson replied. He leaned over and switched on a bank of small monitor screens set into a console. "This is all infrared. It will be a bit hazy."

Nakamura stared at the filmy, odd-colored images on the screen. "I don't see anything."

"That house. There." Oranson touched controls and one of the screens brightened slightly. It showed a view of an ancient, sagging Victorian two-storied structure, its windows dark and blank.

"Pretty rundown."

"We didn't expect him to advertise," Oranson said. Nakamura glanced sharply at him, but said nothing. Oranson was his man. Let him do his job.

Now the Japanese began to make out moving shadows. Quick shapes jerked across the screen. Nakamura had the impression of a heavy force accurately deployed. He imagined strong men grasping weapons, sweating, their teeth clenched, their faces drawn in the dark.

"How big a team?" he asked.

"Enough," Oranson assured him.

Nakamura popped his lips. "That wasn't my question, Fred," he said softly.

"Oh. I'm sorry. I've deployed a first-strike group of twenty-five. We have twice that in near-backup, two choppers up, and I can bring in another hundred troops within two minutes. Unless he's got an armored support, it should be enough."

"How did we get on to it?"

"Some sort of code breakup. One of our groups intercepted some messages."

"Can't you be more specific?" Nakamura felt uneasy. Berg was an X-factor. He didn't quite understand the man, nor did he understand Arius's obsession with him. Nevertheless, if what he suspected was true—that Berg was in some way dangerous to Arius—then the potentials were enormous.

"I want him alive," he whispered.

"We'll try."

"Do better than that," Nakamura said.

"We're using long-distance ultrasound on the structure's walls," Oranson whispered. "There's some strange stuff in there—possibly alarms."

"Of course there are alarms," Nakamura said testily. "This is Jack Berg we're going after, not some pickpocket. He builds the best defenses anybody ever dreamed up. You, of all people, ought to remember that."

Oranson nodded slowly. He glanced at the arm that one of Berg's defenses, Toshi Nakasone, had once nearly burned off. "I wish we could get a reading on what's inside," he said. "That little Oriental bodyguard, maybe."

"Don't take chances this time. Kill him," Nakamura said flatly.

"We don't know what we'll have to do. If you want Berg in one piece, we have to be—wait!"

"What?"

"Scanning is showing a blank area. It looks like it isn't bugged. A part of the cellar in back. Right—okay. There's a false wall in front. Probably somebody did some remodeling down there and he missed it. Maybe a coal storage bin or something like that."

"Can we get in that way?"

Oranson let out his breath slowly. "He has telltales all the way around. The trick is to get through to him before he has a chance to slow us down and bring any of his own offenses into play. You think he's rigged to suicide?"

Nakamura thought about Arius. "Wouldn't you be?"

"Just a suggestion. I didn't really believe it. So we have to get through and get to him before he can bite down or blow up or whatever last-chance gimmick he's got rigged."

"Or gets away entirely," Nakamura said sourly.

"He's good, maybe, but he's not Superman."

Nakamura stared at the screens. Now strobing shadows began to play on a nondescript concrete wall half-hidden under the drooping branches of an ancient eucalyptus tree. "Can't he see those lights?" he asked.

"No, sir. We get analogs on the screen, that's all. There's nothing for him to see. And nothing for his sensors either, if that wall is as clean as we think."

"So when . . ."

Oranson inhaled sharply. "Now," he said.

7

HE PUSHED ONE foot after the other, leather slapping pavement, a rolling, pounding, tireless gait. He walked east out of sunset, moving toward the dawn.

The dark-skinned man smiled as he walked, his thick lips curled in a grin, his almond eyes squinted against the sky. Overhead an endless gray-blue dome sizzled with distance, cupped a handful of high clouds, brushed away the horizon.

The wind blew continuously from the north with a slow rushing sound. Toshi felt it scrape the skin of his head and trickle down his collar.

Nebraska.

Walking through Nebraska. Life was full of new experiences.

Dimly he was aware that something was wrong, was *off* about all this. It seemed that night melted into day and into night again, and with each changing of the light, the memories of the previous day slipped away with equal finality. Had he once been in San Francisco? Was that where this journey had begun?

And wasn't there a name . . . Levin?

The land here rolled. It slid up, it slid down. It was covered with brown stubble. Now he approached the end of a long slow rise, where the ancient blacktop road was amputated by a blade of steel sky. Far to the

south a single bright red silo caught a long ray of
sunlight and flickered once, like a lantern.

The world was a walk, an endless walk. He crested
the rise and looked down. His breath stuck in his
throat. On slow descending waves the land stretched
into a fog of distance. Somewhere ahead ran the Mis-
sissippi, but anything beyond this infinity of earth was
more than he could compass.

He blinked. The moment lay utterly silent. Then a
crowd of crows flapped by, calling and calling, and a
katydid whirred in reply.

Clouds moved across the sky. He began to walk
down, toward the east, the dawn, and a small outpost
—a building, a few tables, benches, a barbecue pit,
and a space for a dozen cars—that hunched beside the
way.

Dusk was coming. A shelter from the night would
be good.

He already felt cold in his bones.

Someone had hand-lettered a sign on the back of an
old road map: OUT OF ORDER. The edges of the paper
were burned and cracked by the wind, but the bulk of
it still flapped on the door marked MEN. Toshi pushed
gingerly at the door. After a moment he pushed harder
and with a rusty squeak it jerked halfway open. He
stuck his head inside, wrinkled his nose, and withdrew. Maybe something had died in there. Maybe not.
Either way it was better to lay his bedroll against the
back side of the building, under the outstretched eaves,
sheltered by the stony curve of the walls. It wouldn't
be bad. He'd spent the last two nights in the open,
unable to keep a fire burning. By comparison this was
paradise. There was even a small load of wood stacked
next to the barbecue.

Berg had explained it to him once. As the population grew it tended to cluster, and although the clusters were larger, the land itself began to be abandoned. Technology brought the goodies where they were needed. Decades before they had called it cocooning. Now it was a way of life, and the byways grew deserted. Only the great laser truckers traveled the roads, and they shunned these crusted tarmac lanes. He might as well be in Antarctica for all the human companionship remaining here. Even the fields were farmed by machines, and the machines were owned by vast corporations.

This was the land of Arius; paradox that it was the safest place for him to be. The God had a million eyes, but they were focused elsewhere.

Carefully he arranged some of the firewood in a teepee, piled on top some wadded paper he'd found in a rusty trash basket, then flashed it into light. The ragged, dry surface of the wood caught quickly. After a while he settled back against the wall and pulled the top of his bedroll up around his shoulders. The fire hissed and popped as tiny bubbles of buried moisture exploded in the logs. The air smelled of snow. His face was cold, but his toes were warmed by the small blaze. Overhead stars drifted in patches between banks of moving clouds. He felt small and comfortable. Perhaps he wouldn't dream tonight. Or if he did, he would be able to remember.

It woke him. For a moment he couldn't place the sound. At his feet the fire had burned to a ring of ash-coated embers.

He stilled his breathing. The wind moaned, a long, hill-topped cry. He heard it again.

Whining with distance, winding slowly down a rasping scale. Then he caught it. Not the sound itself, but the sudden choking irregularity, as a high-compression engine missed, then missed again.

Closer. He rubbed his eyes and watched the cloud of steam forming above his lips. He rummaged cloudy memories. Motorcycle, an old one. He closed his eyes and tried to concentrate. Triumph. Bonneville 650. One of the best of the antiques, a road-burner from the dawn of time.

Again, the hacking cough of a sick engine, closer still. He rolled out of his blankets and kicked gravel over the coals of his campfire. For a moment several things glittered hard and metallic in the vicinity of his hands. His body felt gravid. He arranged the bedroll against the wall so that in the shadows it might resemble a sleeping form. Then, his eyes on the road, he backed slowly away from the shelter of the building.

A dim orange light flashed briefly at the crest of the hill to the west, brightened, dimmed again. Single headlight.

The sound of the engine was very loud. Backfiring as the rider shifted down, grabbing for revs to catch the lip of the rise. He understood that unknown mind. Make the rise and coast.

The big bike exploded over the foreshortened horizon in a blaze of light, its single headlamp like a sudden shout. Now the engine whine rose suddenly as the driver downshifted once again. He watched the path of the headlight waver as torque tried to throw the bike from its narrow path.

Three sudden bangs; the motor quit for good. The light went almost cherry red, then out.

Sharp on the cold night air he heard her words.

"Motherfucker!"

The gravely sibilance of tires on tarmac marked the shadowy form of the bike as its rider guided it toward the parking area. Finally he heard a solid, oily *clunk* as she heaved the big bike up on its kickstand. Overheated metal thrummed; she stepped away from the bike.

He didn't move from his shadow, but she smelled the hint of smoke on the air from the extinguished campfire.

"Hey," she called. "Anybody home?"

"Just me," he said from the darkness. "Who the hell are you?"

Her voice in the night was deep and rich, a soft, full tenor. He could imagine that voice laughing. She tensed; her hands came up to her sides in movements that seemed familiar to him.

"You want conversation, come out where I can see you."

"You're the visitor here, lady," he replied. "What are you doing joy-riding that ancient wreck across Nebraska in the middle of the night?"

She did laugh. It was as he'd imagined it. "Why, you dumb fuck, I'm looking for a date. Figured a tumbledown rest stop was just the place to look. And what the hell, it turns out I'm right."

A sharp wave of pain lanced through his skull and everything went dim and confused. He shook his head, vaguely aware she was moving toward him, but unable to respond. Then the mental dust cleared a bit and he was able to see her again. She stood only a few meters away. Her hands were on her muscled hips. "I see you," she said.

He stood up. "Yeah. Me, too. So now what?"

"Maybe we should introduce ourselves. My name's Sadie."

"Huh. Like married lady?"

"Not fucking hardly, mister. You got a name?"

He had to stop for a moment. His forehead wrinkled. "Toshi. My name's Toshi."

She moved a step or so toward him, then stopped. There was a note in her voice he didn't understand. Sadness . . . anger?

"I used to know a Toshi once."

He walked completely out of the shadows. Now he could see her face. Lined, weathered skin. Wide, wind-chapped lips. A jagged scar trick-tracking down the left side of her forehead, curving under her ear.

"Must be some other guy," he said. "I never seen you before in my life."

Her hair was a black cloud. He had the feeling it would be a different color under the daylight sun. He couldn't tell the color of her eyes. Her shoulders rose and fell once. "Nope, me neither, buddy." Again the odd, twisted tone. "Well, listen. You got this shack rented already, or is there room for two?"

It felt very right. "There's room enough. If you aren't afraid of me. If you want to stay."

"I'm not afraid," she replied. "You poor sonofabitch."

The sun plodded over the horizon and smacked him in the eyes. He blinked several times, felt grit underneath his eyelids, and knuckled his eyes softly. His skin felt rough. His face felt rough.

"Ungh," he said.

"Aren't you a beauty?"

"Huh, what?"

"You're a real morning prize, you know that?"

Then she hadn't been a dream. "You plan on winning me?"

She was squatting over the dead ashes of the fire, arranging a complicated square structure of logs and sticks. He'd been right; her hair was the color of sailor's omen, red as the sky of dawn. And eyes that some might call lavender, but so full of dark shadows they were purple. She chewed lightly on the pink tip of her tongue as she worked. He hitched himself over on his side and propped his head on one palm.

"What you think you're doing?"

"Building a fire," she said. "A real one. Unless you'd rather do breakfast?"

He felt his own grin stretch his cheeks. "You cook, too? Oh, mama, take me away."

She smiled sourly. "I guess that could be arranged."

"No, really. You got some stuff in those bike bags?"

"Yeah, I got stuff. And if you shut your face, I might just cook some of it. Bacon, you know. Some cornbread. Other stuff. That good enough for you?"

He licked his lips. "Beats the hell out of dried eggs," he said.

She stared at the mound of the bedroll. "You don't look like you're starving."

"It's all spiritual, babe. I'm starved spiritually."

A tiny bead of flame appeared in the center of the logs, dripped, grew. She watched a moment, then nodded thoughtfully.

"Try bacon first," she said.

He stared at her. "Shut your face?" he said.

Toshi backed out of the shattered rest room. He shook his head. "There's bones in there, some kind of animal. No water, though. I doubt there's been any for years. Somebody yanked the urinal out of the wall and the pipes are rotted away."

Sadie's leathery face was impassive. She crinkled her lips. "It was worth a try."

He squinted at the sun. The sky overhead was hard and flat, the sun a shrunken yellow dot. "I got to get going here pretty soon."

"Yeah? How come? Where you going?"

He shrugged. "East. That way." He pointed.

"East where?"

"Just . . . east."

She was wearing scuffed, faded Levis that stretched tight around her ass but bagged everywhere else. The old leather bomber jacket around her broad shoulders was a mass of rips taped clumsily back together, its fur collar gone bald in spots. She tossed her head, ran one long-fingered hand through the mass of carrot hair.

"Toshi, you okay?"

He looked at her. "I'm fine. Don't I look fine?"

She shook her head. "Huh-uh. Not fine at all. Real ragged, in fact. And your color's slipping. You ought to see."

"My color?" He pushed up the sleeve of his own coat and stared at the back of his forearm. The skin was piebald, a strange patchwork of gold and brown. "Jeezus. That's weird."

"Those oral melanin treatments work for a while, but they wear off funny," she said. "You don't have the right facial structure for a black-Oriental mix anyway. How long did you plan to pull it off?"

His glance moved from her face to his arm and back again. "I . . . I don't remember."

She turned away suddenly and marched back to the campfire. He watched the way the muscles of her thighs pumped and relaxed as she moved.

She stopped suddenly and faced him again. "Let me get this straight, okay?" She raised her right hand and pulled down the first finger. "You're going east, but you don't know where. That's one. And you're going all spotty, but you don't remember how you got that way. Two, all right? And then there's three. And that, my friend, is what the fuck are you doing out here in the first place? That do for a quick summary?"

Bits of dried grass swirled in a jittery cloud past the eaves of the building. Something gritty clawed at his cheeks, squeezed his eyes shut. "Sadie, I—well, I don't fucking know, okay? I mean, what business of yours is it anyway?"

"Buddy, something's wrong with you. You need

help, you know? And since I don't see anybody else around here, I guess I'm elected."

He stared at her. He listened to her words and understood each individual meaning. He just couldn't put them all together into a coherent whole.

"I can help myself," he said at last.

"Yeah?" Suddenly there was a knife in her hand. She lunged toward him, a long, fluid movement that should have buried the blade just below the point where his ribcage came together.

His eyes widened. He tried to shout. And his body did an amazing thing. Somehow his hands came up in a crossing motion that caught her knife hand just beneath the wrist, raising and turning it. As his hands did this his body bent to the side and back, and his right knee pounded over in a motion that should have crushed her kidney. She rolled with this blow and landed in the dust.

He looked down at her. "I don't think you should do things like that. You might get hurt."

She glared back. "That's a little slow, mister. If I'd been serious, you'd be sucking steel right now."

He grinned. "I don't think so."

"And dammit, you still need a keeper."

"Hell of a way to tell me."

"You sure this thing will run now?"

He wiped his hands on his jeans, leaving black smears of grease. "Carburetor. It needed adjustment. These old twin bangers get sensitive sometimes. You come down from the mountains, I guess?"

She paused. "Yeah," she said at last.

"That's it, then. You had it set for altitude and never adjusted. This your bike?"

"I bought it, if that's what you mean."

"Well, yeah, but not long ago, I guess. Or you would have known."

"The guy didn't give me an owner's manual," she
said.

He laughed. "Manual's probably dust by now. You
either know these honkers or you don't."

She kicked gently at one saddlebag. "I'll learn. You
figure out where we're going yet?"

He squinted again at the sun. His eyes were blank
buttons. She could see herself reflected in them. "East,"
he said.

"That's not a destination."

He grinned. "Sure it is. When the time comes, I'll
know."

She climbed on the bike and cranked the starter.
"You'll know what?"

"Got me," he said, and got on behind her.

The bike disturbed a flock of blackbirds as it disappeared over the next ridge. High overhead a hawk
circled, clean and steady as a pencil drawing.

In the east a storm was brewing.

Toshi shouted over the roar of the big engine. "We're
gonna get drowned!"

Sadie's red hair waved in his face like a flag. Her
velvet eyes were bright behind the big smoked aviator
glasses she wore. Overhead clouds heaved and bil-
lowed like spoiled mashed potatoes. Here and there
lightning moved in snaky conversations. The roll of
thunder was low and endless.

"I know, goddammit! Hang on!"

She began downshifting just as a few errant speckles
of rain began to hiss into the dust alongside the road.
Toshi wrapped his hands around her waist and hung
on as she bucked the bike to a shuddering halt.

All was silence. His ears rang. Then he heard the
ping and crackle of metal cooling, and the sound of
the tentative rain.

The country around them had given way to corn.
The winter fields were cleared, but the orderly path of
thousands of rows waited for spring planting. The
frequency of small towns had increased, but for the
moment nothing but empty fields stretched out in a
great bowl to the horizon.

"There's a culvert up ahead," she said, shading her
eyes. "Maybe it's big enough to get the bike inside."

He grunted. "Worth a try. Hey, wait a minute. Not
a good idea. This rain gets real bad, we could get a
gullywasher. Fill that old culvert up like a cup."

She thought about it. "There's got to be some kind
of town around here, maybe just a farmhouse."

"Not many farmhouses left, darling."

"A few. What do you think?"

"Let's go before we swim instead of ride."

She laughed and tilted the bike back in a short
wheelie and skidded out for distance.

Ten minutes later a cluster of lights began to glow
yellow and red in the early afternoon gloom. The
bottom of the storm dripped rolling flashes of light.
Short, windy squalls spattered the pavement and swept
on. Sadie fed gasahol to the two over-sized cylinders
and Toshi felt the bike leap ahead.

The indeterminate lights resolved into several overhead farm lamps and a flashing red sign: CANDY'S EAT
PLACE.

"There!" he yelled.

"Right on," she replied, and veered over the center-
line toward the gravel parking lot in front of the low
stucco building. She pulled in beneath a corrugated
roof stuck to the side of the restaurant like a lean-to.
Just as she shut down the engine the storm arrived in
earnest. Thick drops of rain splattered on the metal
above their heads like drumrolls.

"Jeezus, just in time," she muttered.

Toshi climbed off the back and stretched. His kidneys felt as if somebody had been tap dancing there. He wished he'd thought to rig some kind of belt.

"Oh, *shit* that hurts."

She grinned. "You're getting old, man. That's all."

They were in the lee of the building. Past the far side the wind pushed the rain almost horizontal and beat it to a white froth. The air tasted fresh and cold.

"Iowa sucks," he said.

"What doesn't?"

Toshi heard the heavy, glass-paned wooden door sigh and click shut behind him as a blast of moist, hot air laden with the smell of grease, French fries, and coffee hit him in the face.

The small room was brightly lit by an old fluorescent fixture swinging from the ceiling. Along the walls a procession of illuminated beer signs blinked and glittered: Hamm's, Lite Beer, Budweiser Dark. There were booths to their left and right down the front of the restaurant, a few tables of dark formica already set with paper place mats and mismatched silver in the middle area, and a counter against the back wall.

"Over here," Sadie said, and pulled him toward the booth farthest down the line.

"I'm hungry," he said. "Why not the counter? It's probably quicker."

"Sit on that side." She took the far side of the booth, where she could face the door.

It made him uneasy. "I don't like to sit this way."

"It's okay. No, don't turn around."

"Why not."

"That's a Wolf at the counter."

"Wolf? What are you talking about?"

Her eyes flickered once. "A Wolf, you know? Don't you know about Wolves?"

He licked his lips. "I do know . . . don't I? Should I
know? Wolves . . ." Suddenly he shook his head. She
thought he looked about to cry and reached across the
table and patted the back of his hand.

"It's okay. You don't have to know. That's what
I'm for."

The single waitress who'd been pouring coffee behind the bar came up to their booth with two water
glasses. She was tall and badly overweight. Her hair
was long, streaked with grease, and held back with an
orange plastic butterfly. She wore bright-blue contact
lenses that were too small, leaving a narrow brown
ring around the blue inserts that gave her a raccoon
stare.

"Would you like coffee today?" she said. Sadie
stared at her. The girl's voice was clear and musical
and bright with intelligence.

"Sure, sweetie," Sadie said. "And we'll order in a
minute."

"That will be fine," the waitress agreed. "I'll be
back then." She turned away, but Sadie said, "Uh,
honey, wait a minute."

"Yes?"

"That guy at the counter." Sadie kept her voice
low.

The girl nodded. "The Wolf, you mean?"

"Yeah. He come in here a lot?"

The waitress smiled carefully. "Not really. He's a
new one. But there have been several lately, and
that's a new development. Those are city kind, you
know, and we don't see them out here in the country-
side. I think they're looking for something. They ask a
lot of questions."

Sadie nodded slowly. "How can you tell the difference between them?"

"If you observe carefully, you can see small variations. Most people are put off by the general ugliness and don't notice the little things."

"And you do. Good, that's good." She reached into her pocket and pulled out a crumpled bill. "You have any use for cash?"

"Of course," the waitress said. "But you don't have to bribe me. I don't like those guys. Whatever reason they've been around here, I don't think it's a good one."

"Here, take it anyway. I'd like to talk some more later, if it's all right."

"Of course. Oh. That one will be leaving soon anyway. They only stop in to eat."

"Fine. Give us a chance to check the menu now, all right?"

"Yes. After he's gone, would you like to see the picture they've been passing around?"

Sadie blinked. "Very much."

Toshi forked up the last of his scrambled eggs, swallowed, then belched loudly.

"Gross," Sadie said.

"Shows appreciation for the food."

"Couldn't you just say 'that's good' or something?"

Toshi grinned. "Acculturation, my dear. It's a wonderful thing."

The waitress came up, carrying a small holocube. "He's gone," she said.

"Yeah, I noticed," Sadie said. "He ask about us?"

The girl shook her head. "No. He seemed in a hurry."

"Okay, let's see the cube."

The girl handed it over. Sadie stared at the small representation of Toshi Nakasone. With relief she noted that it was from better days. The picture showed Toshi standing near a hospital bed, one hand upraised as if displaying his fingers for the camera. He was smiling. The picture bore little relation to the ragged, piebald man sitting across from her.

"That's the one?"

"Yes," the waitress replied. "A picture of this man here."

Sadie kept her breathing slow and modulated. "What? Oh, no, honey. Here, Mong Seng, look at this. She thinks it's you."

Toshi took the cube and glanced at it. "Ugly sucker, isn't he?" he shook his head as strange faults shifted and moved inside his skull. "Not me, though."

The waitress retrieved the cube. "Whatever you say. I told you before, I don't like those Wolves." She paused. "More coffee?"

Sadie shook her head. "We have to be getting on. The storm sounds like it's passing over."

The girl nodded. "Weather says it's a false front. Bigger one coming in behind."

"All the more reason," Sadie said. "Here. You keep the change."

The girl stared at her palm. "I think I also said you didn't have to bribe me."

Sadie shrugged. "Think of it as an early Christmas."

"Okay," the waitress said.

Although it was nearly dusk, the clouds toward the west had broken up a bit, admitting some watery sunlight. The shadows of the lean-to stretched long and fuzzy black toward the east. The wind smelled of wet earth and winter.

"Something's very wrong with me," Toshi said slowly, as Sadie checked the bike bags.

"Don't worry about it."

Toshi stood for a moment, breathing heavily, as if he wanted to say something else but couldn't remember what.

The Wolf stepped around the corner of the building and said,

"The Lay, she lookin fa you." His fighting claws were extended. Heavy clumps of muscle in his forearm flexed tightly. He held something small and shiny in his right paw.

Toshi turned.

As he did so the Wolf tensed his right hand, then relaxed. He lowered his head and said, "Ahhh."

Toshi stared at the Wolf. The Wolf bowed to him. Kept on bowing. Toppled over on his face and lay still.

The black-taped hilt of a throwing knife protruded from his left eye.

Sadie walked over to the Wolf and poked at his ribs with her boot toe. She sighed. "Well, come on, help me get this sucker stashed somewhere."

Together they dragged the body to the back of the shed and rolled it under the rusted remains of an old tractor. Sadie found a weather-eaten tarp and covered the remains. In the dim light the Wolf was just another shapeless shadow.

"Probably that girl will find it, but we should be long gone."

Toshi nodded. He remembered the holocube. He thought about the Wolf. About the way it had bowed to him with a knife in its eye.

"Chicago," he said.

"What?"

"We're going to Chicago."

"It's about time," Sadie said.

8

OZZIE CRACKED AN egg on the edge of the huge cast-iron skillet and watched it sizzle in hot bacon grease. He wanted to look at her instead, but he'd already burned two eggs, and she said she was hungry. He didn't want to fuck up again, and though cooking definitely wasn't his long suit, he would have to learn. She couldn't do it anymore.

He poked at the edge of the egg with a spatula, watching the filmy fluid turn hard and solid and begin to brown at the edge. When both eggs were finished he scooped them from the skillet and nestled them carefully next to three strips of bacon on a plate. Then he picked up the plate and carried it to her where she sat on the futon. Her face turned toward him, toward the sound of his footsteps.

"Smells good."

"Here. A fork."

"Thanks."

He watched her eat. The fine bones of her face moved slowly as she chewed. Her eyes were open and green as emeralds, and as empty. It had been two days since her most recent return, and he didn't know how much more he could stand.

"I must love you," he said. "I'm such a lousy cook."

She swallowed, put the fork on the plate and carefully set it on the floor next to the futon. "We have to talk."

"I know. But finish your breakfast first. I cooked it for you."

Her hand hovered for a moment in the air. "All right," she said at last. He watched her fingers grope on the wood until they located the rim of the plate. As she lifted, the fork teetered and almost fell, but he knew better than to say anything.

It was a very dangerous time for them, for him. She hadn't even said a word when he talked about love.

Not this way, he thought. *I can't do it this way!*

When she finished he took the plate and carried it back to the kitchen and placed it on a stack in the sink.

"You should do the dishes sometime," she said. "That sounds pretty full."

He sighed and turned and walked back. He sat down and crossed his legs. "Talk now?"

She nodded.

"Okay. What are we gonna do?"

She shook her head. "I already told you. We're going to the moon."

"That's it? That's all?"

"Uh-huh."

"Calley." He touched the top of her knee. "Listen to me. You got to add things up. Berg's gone. Levin's gone. We don't know where Toshi is. Something happened to you in the matrix, but you can't remember what. Except to tell me you can't go back. And . . . and—"

"I'm blind," she finished for him. "I know."

"Can't you explain *any* of it?"

She leaned back and balanced her upper body on her elbows. She was wearing a pair of his faded gym shorts, the gold tiger emblem on one leg a corroded patch of gold. A clean tee shirt. Her hair was un-brushed and growing out. It hung in limp, dark strands around her face. It scared him that she didn't seem to care about it anymore.

"I've been thinking." She grinned crookedly. "Not that I'm good for much else."

"Don't say that."

"I know. Self-pity. Not good for blind people."

He wanted to hit her then. Smack her hard, knock the hopelessness out of her. His chest went hard and hurtful. Then he realized it was him he wanted to rid of the darkness. She was blind and he was lost.

What a pair.

"You say something?"

"No," he said.

"This Berg thing. And Levin. I can't explain it, Ozzie. I mean, why I can't go into the matrix again. I'd say it was just a feeling, but it's stronger than that. I'm as certain as I can be that for right now, at least, it's better for me to be outside. And that certainty is all tied up with Berg."

"He might be *dead*," Ozzie said, and was astounded at the harshness in his voice.

"Ozzie," she said gently. "If he was, wouldn't you know about it?"

"What do you mean?"

"Remember when you pulled us out of the meta-matrix?"

"Sure, yeah, I—" He stopped. He realized that in all the years since, he'd never once thought about that time. And wondered why that was.

He closed his eyes and stared into the darkness of memory. On that day he'd operated the box he'd designed himself, the one which had taken them to the metamatrix in the first place. Besides William Norton, he and Calley had been the first to see the metamatrix, to discover that it even existed. And he'd gone there before her.

So when he'd ridden their catcher program up from the floor and plucked Berg from the chaos that was boiling into the Demon Star, he'd been a part of it, too. He just didn't want to admit it.

"I just didn't want to admit it," he said aloud.

"What do you mean?"

He gulped air. He felt shaky and weak. "What did Berg call himself? You said it, too. The Key?"

"The Key That Locks and Looses." She scratched the side of her nose. "He said it was the reason Norton had selected him for the job in the first place. Some kind of mental quirk, some talent he had."

"And Arius used you and him to join with Norton into the Demon Star. Yeah. I was there. I remember."

"Go on." Her voice pushed at him.

"Uh." He couldn't bring out the words. "Just say you're right. If he was dead, I'd know it."

She was relentless. "Say his name, goddamit!"

"*Berg!*"

"Why would you know?"

"Because . . . 'cause he joined *me*, too!" And with the words something broke inside, something old and painful, and his mouth opened and cracked, dry sounds came out.

"Go ahead," she whispered. "Cry. You got as much right as anybody."

"Tell me about it," she said.

He got up, went to the kitchenette, found a piece of paper towel and blew his nose. Then he came back. "I love you, Calley. And so does he. I mean I know that, right down in my cells. 'Cause there's a part of him in me, and a part of you in me, and I guess some of me in both of you. And—"

"Go on." Her eyes seemed focused for an instant, and he thought he saw in their depths a flame like the corona around a sun.

"Are we a part of the Star? Is the Demon a part of us?"

She began to rock back and forth, hugging herself. "What do you think?"

He licked his lips. He opened his mouth and shut it. He blinked. "What do we do?"

She smiled. "We go to the moon. I told you already."

He leaned back in the rickety office chair in front of his control bank and stared at morning washing blue over the top of the skylight. At times like this he was glad she'd made him wash the damned thing—somehow it lessened the cavelike atmosphere of the apartment. From the bathroom came watery noises and a husky tenor muttering against the walls of the shower.

". . . might just . . . get what you *need* . . ."

He grinned. She was hooked on the old music, and the towering Rolling Stones anthem was a favorite of hers. "You can't always get what you want . . ." He half-hummed, half-muttered the words and felt a surge of happiness. Maybe things would work out. Though he doubted it.

"You gonna stay in there all day?" he shouted.

The singing subsided, and a moment later she shut off the water. "What you howling about?"

"I said—"

"I heard you. You in a hurry or something? I thought you said I was crazy."

"You are. But somebody's gotta take care of you, and I guess it's me."

The wooden door to the bathroom, a thin wooden thing held together mostly by years and coats of paint, now currently light blue and chipped, banged open.

"On the best day of your life—"

"I know. But hurry up anyway. I need to use it, too."

She poked her head around the door and stuck out her tongue.

"Yeah. Take a shower quick. You stink."

"Bitch."

"Compliments, my dear brat, will get you everywhere." She slammed the door again. He tried a short laugh, but it turned hollow. He glanced at the work on the screen. He was composing an extremely complicated run. Their chances of success in running whatever gauntlet the Demon Star might have erected against them depended on it. Handicapped as they were—*both of us,* he thought—the probabilities were dubious. But she said they were going, and so they would.

"What you need," he mumbled, "what you *need* is a leader, and I'm not it." And then felt stupid talking to an empty room.

"Okay, I'm done, bubba. Dive right in anytime."

He didn't move, didn't say anything. She'd wrapped a thick bath towel around her hair, but wore nothing else. He was struck by her small beauties, by the tightness and tautness of her. No let down at all.

"Ozzie."

He jerked. "What?"

Her voice was clear and steady, but he sensed the ragged edge of anger. "Remember what I told you?"

He did. "I'm sorry."

She took a deep breath. "Please always cough or something, clear your throat, say a word or two, so I know where you are. And after your shower, use some of that godawful perfume I found. If I can't hear you, at least I can smell you. Okay? Right? It's important."

"I know." He felt ashamed. She was trying to adjust, and what did he do to help? Forget stuff and moon at his computers.

Her tone softened. "Ozzie, please. I'm blind."

When she said it that way, he decided it didn't sound like an excuse or a condemnation or even a plea. More like a description. "I'm hungry. I'm happy. I'm blind."

He felt like crying again and pushed the wash of emotion away. All this blubbering wasn't going to help them get to Luna. Besides, he was all cried out.

Why me? he wondered, but he said, "Move your ass, old woman. And I think that shit smells good."

"Old?" she said.

He ran for the door.

"All right, here's what I got," he said. She crouched next to his chair, balanced on the balls of her feet, one elbow on his left thigh. Her head was tilted to the left, her face toward the soft whir of the machines in front of her. He brushed the touchpad deftly and brought a rolling scroll of glyphs up on the monitor.

"The meats don't run everything yet, thank God. Stuff like this—air- and spaceport security, taxi data basing for bills, and so forth—it's still hardware. Won't last forever, but it would cost a fortune to replace all at once. So much the better for us. I cracked NORAP's safe and hooked all their codes."

She nodded. "No little feetprints, eh?"

"What do you take me for? An amateur?"

"Down, boy. Just asking."

"You got to figure Arius or Double En or whoever the hell has baseline descriptions of us plastered in every security shack in North America, right? Which, of course, includes O'Hare Near Earth Port. But unless you think up some way of sprouting wings, we've got to go that way."

"Are you building up to some kind of gargantuan brag about this, or have you actually figured something out?"

"I told you. I hooked all their codes. What we need is some kind of disguise. I guarantee that if they retina-code us, or try for cell or gene match, they're going to find out we aren't anybody named Calley or Oswald."

"You guarantee?"

"Take it or leave it, kid."

"Okay, so you got the machines gimmicked. Now about this disguise?"

"Well, how about this . . . ?"

A gray wind blew low and cold around the corner of the warehouse. Ozzie carefully twisted a key in the heavy, old-fashioned brass padlock which held the door shut. "You can take all the security systems you want—and I got 'em, God knows—but it takes a frigging *hammer* to open one of these things. Discourages casual speculation, you might say."

Just past a winter noon, the sun beat thin and clear on the corrugated sides of the building. Long fingers of red and brown corrosion groped down the channels in the aged siding. Calley faced away from the building, listening to the distant horns of lake freighters as they glided north toward the iron of Minnesota.

Ozzie paused and sniffed the air. "Too cold for rain," he said. "Bright sun. Nice Chicago winter day."

Calley squeezed her thin fingers into fists, quickly, nervously. "Can the travelogue," she said. "I never liked this neighborhood even when I could see it." Her breath made abrupt silver puffs in the frigid air. "You want to take my arm, sonny boy?"

He laughed. "Sure, gramma, come on. I'll get you across this dangerous street."

"You'd better. Or I stick those merit badges where they'll never tarnish."

They could have flagged a taxi, but why, Ozzie thought, borrow trouble? He'd ridden the El all his life anyway. And it was cheap, not that it mattered. "You okay with the money?" he asked.

"I got cash in my bag, and those bent chips you cobbled up. What's the credit rating, if anybody asks?"

"Gold, honey. Bright gold."

"That's pushy."

"Nothing pushes like money. We may need a push, too."

She sighed and curled her arm tighter around his. "Lay on, Macduff," she said.

"He was a tall sucker, too, wasn't he?"

"Walk," she said.

At five o'clock in the afternoon the forty storied tower of Randolph Street Station was a static of hurrying commuters, departing office workers, bleary-eyed night shifters swarming in for the swing- and early graveyard shifts.

The three lowest levels of the massive building made up the station itself, a maze of high tunnels and broad platforms that daily funneled almost a third of a million commuters from the cubicles of their jobs to the fullerdomes of their suburban residences. Chicago was a big city, and those who worked in it possessed veneers tough to disturb, but even the most hardened commuter stepped away from the pair that moved steadily down the center of the corridor which led to the New O'Hare bullet-train platforms.

The woman clicked as she lurched steadily along. It was a by-product of the form-fitting black carapace which outlined every muscle of her frame. Her face was blank of any emotion; her eyes stared straight ahead, neither rejecting nor acknowledging the horrified stares directed at her.

Inside the frame of her synthetic musculature she was naked. That she chose not to cover herself proclaimed something beyond her own disabilities, as did the slender giant who glided beside her, his own brass-flecked eyes searching the crowd with feral hunger.

Without consciously seeming to do so, individuals in the pushing throng who found themselves too close to the pair stepped away, looked away, moved away. The giant and the old woman proceeded unimpeded, like a ship moving slowly through water.

Many decades ago, even before the Chicago Collapse and the Flood, the question of who ruled the underworld had been decided. After years of bloody struggle the Darkstone Ragers wrested control of the drug trade from a rival gang called the Outlaws. With this inexhaustible source of revenue they quickly dominated the rest of the shadow economy and finally moved to gather political legitimacy in the tangled world of legitimate machine democracy. Some said that during the years of the Collapse the Ragers had literally owned Chicago.

Some said they still did.

At the first weapons check the two halted. One of the guards, an older man with a wrinkled face and weary eyes glanced up, then lowered his head again. "Jackie, you handle them, okay?"

The younger guard, a thin youth in his early twenties with a pockmarked face, muttered, "Oh, shit." He got up from his desk slowly.

"Right on through the arch there, folks," he said.

"She's wearing a harness,'" the emaciated giant said. His voice was very deep, very fuzzy. The guard imagined something terrible happening to his vocal cords.

"I know," the guard sighed. "I got eyes, bud. We'll make allowances. But she's got to go through."

"And she's blind. I got to go with her."

"Blind?" The guard swallowed. "Hey, Fred. Come on over here, would you?"

The older guard's lips moved silently over a couple of words, but he stood up and put on his hat and adjusted the heavy pistol at his side.

"Yeah?" He glanced at the pair. "What's up, Jackie?"

"The lady's blind. This guy says he has to go through with her."

Fred looked at the couple. Something tickled the edge of his memory, something about tall people, but faced with this reality that barely remembered ghost made no impression.

He knew what he was dealing with here. "Oh, Jackie," he mumbled softly. "Step over here a second."

The giant watched impassively as they moved away. "You know what you got here?" Fred said.

"Sure. A naked blind lady wearing a harness and some geek that oughta play basketball for the Bulls."

Fred winced and continued patiently. "You ain't from the city, are you, kid?"

"No."

"Okay, let me explain some stuff. You heard about the Ragers, right?"

"Some gang or something," Jackie said. "What's that got to do with us?"

"Over there, is what. Those two. Anything strike you odd?"

"You kidding?"

"I mean besides the obvious. That woman don't look too bad, right? Except she's blind and she can't move without that harness. And she's naked."

"So?"

"Blindness can be fixed, usually. So she must be very old, you see. And the harness. Very expensive. And naked. Which means she don't give a shit."

"Uh, I don't get it."

Fred shook his head. "She's old, rich, and powerful. She's got that bodyguard, 'cause that's what he is. Now I know something about guys like that. They're raised that way. From babies. It's a trademark."

"Trademark? Of what?"

"The Ragers," Fred said. "The Darkstone Ragers. That guy is a very special Rager slave. There's only a few, from what I hear. Work only for the very top people."

"Slavery?" Jackie was from the burbs. "I don't believe that."

"Move into the city, kid. You'll believe. Anyway, take my word. Be very careful with those two. No need to make waves."

The older man slapped Jackie on the back suddenly and grinned. The grin wasn't pretty, but then he didn't much like the kid anyway. "You handle it, right? I got to go to the john for a couple minutes. Be right back." Still grinning, the older man turned and ambled away.

Jackie went back to the arch. "Uh, you can't go through with her," he said. "It's the rules. She has to go by herself."

The woman turned her face toward him. He heard a faint sighing sound as the harness flexed around her neck.

"This young man does a good job," she said. "Goes by the book. We should make sure he is remembered for it. Why don't you get his name, his *family* name?"

Her voice was soft and filled with mucous. A wet whisper.

"Yes," the tall man said. "We'll want to remember you, friend. We got good memories."

Jackie looked into two pairs of eyes. One was high above. They burned with a golden fire, an eager burning. The woman, on the other hand, burned with nothing. Her eyes were dead.

Slave? he thought incredulously. He began to remember stories he'd heard as a child, things he thought were ridiculous nightmares at the time.

Now he considered those eyes. He inhaled. The woman waited patiently, her head tilted slightly to the side. His breath leaked out.

"Forget it," he said at last. "Make an exception. Go ahead, mister. Help her through."

He was sweating when he sat down at his console. Fred came up from behind. They watched the strange pair move on down the corridor toward the bullet-train platform for northern Indiana and O'Hare.

"They ask for your name?"

"Uh-huh. But I decided to let them through. They never got it."

"Good job. We'd sure hate to lose you," Fred said. He patted the younger man on the shoulder. "Sure would."

Calley looked up from her console. Had that been a sound?

"You say something?"

"No, I didn't." The voice of her main computer was curiously flat.

"Well." Calley raised her arms over her head, intertwined her fingers, and cracked her knuckles. Her shoulders hurt. How long had she been working?

"What time is it?"

"Seventeen hundred."

"About dinner time, I guess." She yawned. Berg had always liked to eat later. Said it was more elegant. She liked to eat when she was hungry.

"This is a construct," she said.

"Calley, you've explained the concept to me. I understand what you told me, and I've run every kind of check I can think of. But I can't find any evidence that this situation is what you describe. If you go outside your office, you'll be in the front hallway. And my sensors show a street outside. The temperature is two degrees Celsius. The sun is shining. The weather forecast predicts clouds later with the possibility of snow flurries."

Calley stared at the ceiling. She'd opened the door earlier and looked down the hall. Outside was nothing but gray fog. She'd pointed that out to her computer, but the machine insisted she was wrong.

Nevertheless, when she'd ordered out for pizza earlier, the doorbell chimed and a box waited outside the office door. She had the run of the small house. If she didn't try to think much about it, there might be nothing but thick fog outside the windows.

Her computer said the sun was shining. And her own dreams were full of machines.

The tiny, lumpy machines moved and clicked and sighed. They filled her nights. She tried to remember how she'd gotten here, but the fog that surrounded her was beginning to wipe away her past as well.

Now the machines chittered at her in the dark. Soon, she thought, they would take her days as well.

She turned back to the console.

Berg's old question whispered at the shoals of consciousness.

What *is* reality?

For a few minutes before boarding, they stood on the top deck observation tower, a hundred meters above the northern Indiana landscape. Below, spread out in a vast circle, sprawled the New O'Hare Spaceport. He felt the wind tug at the roots of his crew cut, bending the short bristles away from his forehead.

"You're sure about this?" he said.

She didn't reply. Her skin seemed like marble, un-

protected against the steady breeze. Finally she turned
and stepped back inside.

He led her to an elevator and they descended. A
horizontal escalator swept them down an endless arc-
lit corridor. At the end was a tall fence and another
security desk. Wordlessly he presented their bent pass-
port chips. The guard plugged them in. After a moment he handed them back. "Have a good trip, sir and
ma'am," he said.

They walked through into the international boarding
area. Again, at the glass wall next to the entry for the
giant people trucks, whole rooms that moved from the
terminal to the launch area, they paused. Gently he
placed her fingers on the glass.

"Can you feel it?"

Even behind triple layers of thermoplastic, the ul-
trasonic whine of the laser launchers was an ever-
present sound floating like smoke. He knew the system:
huge orbiting power collectors fed low-earth orbit laser platforms, which in turn were focused on the col-
lector plates of the ships themselves.

Their transport would rise into the sky *beneath* a
pillar of fire.

The crowd pressed around them. She turned away
from the glass. "I feel it," she said.

She didn't finally relax until the weight pressed her
back into her seat. Outside, heavily muffled, the laser
power system turned air into plasma as it blasted them
higher and higher.

"I do a fair dragon lady, huh?" she said.

Ozzie chuckled. "Did you see the way that guard
looked at me?"

"No," she said.

His hands fluttered once, but he didn't say anything
more.

*   *   *

The entry port for Kennedy Crater was a shouting maelstrom. They'd landed at peak reception, and the overstrained facilities were handling passengers from six liners at once. It took them almost half an hour to make customs.

"Your chips, please?" the polite Lunie agent said. He smiled as he plugged them in. After a moment his smile slipped.

"Can you wait a moment, please?"

He punched some codes into his machine, examined the result, and looked up.

"Something wrong?" Ozzie said.

"Yes," the agent said shortly. Two armed security people had suddenly appeared behind him. "These chips are not correct. The names on them are wrong." He seemed about to say more, but shut his mouth.

Ozzie turned to Calley. "You plan on this?"

Her lips opened slightly. "Maybe." She spoke in the direction of the agent's voice. "Please let Mr. Wier know about the problem."

The agent nodded seriously. "Oh, he does, Ms. Calley. Mr. Karman. He does—and by the way, welcome to Luna."

9

"**IT WAS BERG,**" Nakamura said. He was talking to a blank computer screen. Regularly, like a very slow heartbeat, a sudden burst of white light would bloom on the screen, then fade to darkness.

He sat in a great, high-ceilinged room whose shadowy arches caught random flickers from the many oil lanterns placed on tables and windowsills. The bottom half of one side of the room was glass-paned doors, the old-fashioned kind that opened out instead of sliding. Eight meters of bookshelves packed with gleaming leather bindings filled the opposite side of the room.

The furniture was a jumble of styles, as if each piece had been selected on its own merits rather than in conformance to an overall decorating plan.

Outside the glass doors a pine platform extended for several meters out and down the whole length of the house. There was lawn beyond it and a formal garden full of strange, tortured shapes. Beyond the lawn and gardens dark pines grew, huge swaying patriarchs rooted deep into the side of the mountain.

The wind boomed through the pines with a sound that shook the vast wooden house, roared through the eaves, rattled the glass panes in the doors.

In a fieldstone fireplace the height of a man at the

end of the room, between the glass and the books, a pine blaze danced and filled the air with the sweet smell of resin. Nakamura listened to the sound of the wind and watched the dance of the flames while he waited for an answer.

Another tiny nova burst like Fourth-of-July fireworks on the screen, held for an instant, and subsided.

"Do you have the body?"

Nakamura wore a light-green kimono, the tincture of water jade. His hands were crossed at his belly. He sat in an old maple rocker, a primitive American piece he found indecently comfortable. At his left hand, the condensation on its base making a ring on the mahogany top of his desk, was a thick crystal tumbler of Knockando scotch. It wasn't his favorite single malt, but he loved the name.

Knock and do. Do what?

"Yes. I have the body."

"You personally?"

"Yes."

"I will send someone," the voice said.

Nakamura was glad the voice chose to remain invisible, chose not to manifest itself. He had no doubt the voice could become real, appear in the heart of this tall and wonderful room if it chose to. After all, there were computers here. Computers were simply nervous paths to its voice, bones, sinews, muscles.

Computers were its body. He already knew what was its mind.

"Is that wise?" Nakamura heard himself say.

"Shag, old friend—"

Nakamura shuddered and reached for his scotch.

"I thought I told you I wanted him alive."

Nakamura drank deeply of the scotch and felt a feeble warmth grow in his gut. The voice chilled him, made his heart beat strangely, made his ears hurt. Even now.

He shook his head. "It wasn't possible. You've seen the tapes, the records."

"Why did you try to take him on your own?"

This was the crux of the matter. He'd come out to the Wisconsin hills for this. It was entirely possible that he might die tonight, and if that happened, he preferred it to be here, away from the grease and dirt and stench of the city, alone but for faceless servants, surrounded by the things he loved.

It was possible he might live, too. If he could answer this question satisfactorily. He placed the tumbler of scotch carefully on the watery ring on his desk. Unconsciously one hand crept to his throat and massaged the side of it. He felt a pulse there like a tiny animal. Like a tiny machine.

"There wasn't time," he said at last. "The message came in, and Oranson already had the troops deployed."

"You could have made time. I don't move slowly, Shag. You know that."

Nakamura nodded. That was exactly his fear. The Demon Star moved far too fast.

"It was perhaps a mistake, then."

Another nova curled brightly on the screen. The white shadows made Nakamura's face look like a mask.

"No, I don't think so."

"What do you think, then?"

"I think you regarded Berg as a chip, Shag. I know what you want. You're afraid of me. Well and good. You should be. But, Shag, this is not some business plot. Not some deal. It is more serious than that. You felt Berg was a weapon of some kind. You couldn't help but think that, given the data I provided. Shag, would you like me to come visit you? We could discuss this whole question of weapons and you and me."

Nakamura remembered a childhood dream. He slept on his futon in a small room. One of the sliding paper screens which led down a hallway was barely open, not more than an inch. Outside a fat moon gleamed down, and the room was full of light and shadow. He'd awakened half out of a dream and watched the crack of the door. Suddenly his body froze as he became absolutely certain that something hideous was on the other side of the crack.

He could not move in the pearly night and the crack was slowly widening . . .

"Bill, you will do what you will do. How can I stop you?"

His right hand jerked twice as he spoke, as he reached again for his drink. Arius—Bill Norton—the Demon Star—

The two in one knew him and didn't care. He might yet survive the night.

He faced the screen. "I didn't try to betray you."

"Not that way," the voice agreed. "But, Shag, you are samurai. It isn't in your bones not to try at all. You are a wielder of weapons. I understand that. But you should have listened to me."

I will go with pride, Nakamura thought. I was born with it. In the end it is all I have.

It is enough.

"You are wrong, Bill," he said. "I don't oppose you."

"Not any more," the voice said. "Watch carefully. I am coming to you now."

The screen which had displayed the erratic star was one of a bank of six. Now all the screens began to glow. Nakamura sat in the shifting coruscation, his eyes wide black dots in the darkness of his face. The bank of stars reflected from his eyes.

He began to see a tiny dot of red in the heart of the stars, like a drop of blood.

The heart of the star grew in the heart of his home. He tilted his head back and said, "Ahh . . ."

*   *   *

It was a bright place. Banks of recessed fluorescents burned overhead in a clean hard light. Down each side of the long room marched ranks of hospital beds. Beside each bed was a table with necessities: water glass, toothbrush, a washcloth hanging from a rack beneath.

On each bed slumbered a form half-covered by a white sheet.

Some were men, some women. On each head the hair was clipped short, almost to a crew cut. Some of the faces were covered with bandages.

At the head of each bed, on a shelf above the headboard, was a small bank of machines. Two monitors on each bank flickered with rows of numbers, changing graphs, occasional bursts of printing. From this bank extended filmy lines of optical fiber which ended beneath the right ears of each patient. The hard black knot of the socket there was clearly visible.

There was surprisingly little noise. If one listened carefully, there was the slow mechanical exhalation of the air conditioning system which kept the room at a uniform eighteen degrees Celsius. At the far end of the ward a single nurse, her starched white cap in an old-fashioned wing design, bent over the foot of a bed, laboriously copying information from the monitors there onto a yellow legal pad. She looked up as the double doors at the other end of the ward swung open and her eyes widened. She straightened up and brushed at the front of her uniform, trying to smooth it.

Although she'd seen them before, the red eyes made her stomach weak and made her want to confess something. Anything. But she was still too young to be afraid of those eyes as the years might teach her to be.

"What are you doing there?"

The Lady swept down the central aisle on silent

feet, her plain white dress sweeping robelike behind her. On either side padded Wolves, the claws of their knobbly feet mostly retracted so there was only a faint *click-scritch* sound to mark their passage.

The girl stood very still now, the yellow legal pad clutched to her chest with both forearms folded across it.

"I said, what are you doing? Why are you writing on those papers?"

The nurse knew that the Lady's vision—the great red saucers of her infrared inserts—was not so good in the bright lights. She wondered how she'd been able to make out such fine detail across the length of the ward. Perhaps one of the Wolves had alerted her. Three of the Wolves clustered around her now, quizzical, hungry expressions on their deformed faces. On one of them a pink tongue hung forgotten at the corner of a mouth with too many teeth.

She called them "her little ones," the nurse remembered.

"I . . . I—"

"Speak up, girl. We have machines to monitor the initiates. What are you writing there?" Imperiously the Lady gestured, and one of the Wolves reached out and took the legal pad from her.

He examined it carefully before passing it over to the Lady, who held it close to her crimson eyes.

"I don't understand," she said at last. "What is this?"

The nurse stammered. "H-he asked for it."

"He? Who? What are you talking about, girl?"

"Arius," she burst out, feeling her cheeks redden, feeling her eyes burn. "God asked me for it."

The Lady pushed the yellow paper even closer to her face, as if she were smelling it or planning to eat it. After a moment she shook her head.

"I don't understand." She straightened up. "Bring her," she snapped. Two of the Wolves immediately grasped the nurse, one on each arm. "We'll get to the bottom of this."

The small group moved quickly away from the bed, toward the near set of doors. The expression on the nurse's face was fearful but determined. Just before the doors swung shut the Lady paused. She turned and glanced at the bed where the nurse had been making notes.

The figure was male, its skull swathed in bandages. The optical fiber cord was in place. There was nothing special about the figure at all.

She shook her head. The doors glided shut.

The ward was silent again.

From the side Nakamura's face was a sweating statue. His black hair picked up glinting flashes from the bank of screens. His head was tilted back, his lips stretched away from his teeth in a frozen grimace. His teeth were white. He ground them together. The golden skin beneath his dark eyes was tight. The muscles in his thick neck stood out and quivered.

His breathing would stop for a time, then start again, then stop. The clinical name for the condition was "apnea." On the arms of the rocking chair his fingers were claws.

All of the screens were filled with a peculiar white static that flashed and ebbed and flashed again. There was a hypnotic, sucking feel to the patterns. They drew at the eyes, called to the brain. They concealed messages that could not be ignored.

Slowly Nakamura's teeth began to open. His gums were shiny in the light. He was obviously trying to scream.

Just as obviously, he wasn't able to.

*   *   *

Sometimes Oranson had trouble remembering who he was. Particularly on dark nights when he sat alone surrounded by the machines of his trade, where he monitored the inputs and outputs and throughputs which affected Shigeinari Nakamura in some way. Because he sometimes couldn't remember, or because what he did remember seemed flat and lifeless, as if it had happened to some other person whose life was now a movie, he occasionally thought he might be dead. But if this was the case, then why did he take the pills which Nakamura assured were keeping him alive? Did a dead person care about staying alive?

Sometimes he tried to think about the concept of borrowed time. Was it possible to borrow time? How about steal it? Buy or sell it? How about living on bought time?

Usually he was able to avoid thinking about it at all. When he could keep himself busy, lose himself in the day-to-day niggling details of keeping Shag Nakamura safe and healthy, immerse himself in the oddities involved with being an ultimate weapon.

For that was what he was, he assured himself as he stared out the smoked glass windows of the low building at the foot of the mountain. Somewhere above, Nakamura communed with his ghosts.

Oranson stared at one polished boot toe and imagined those ghosts perfectly well. He'd seen his share of ghosts in his time. He'd seen them in every shape and form; the ghosts about to be, the ghosts already, and the shapeless ones, the ghosts who hadn't made up their minds yet.

He remembered a hand, limp, blood leaking along the fingers. He remembered a white-haired man with a livid, scarred face. He remembered his own reflection on a brilliant day in San Francisco.

He thought he might be a ghost, too, but he couldn't identify the type. Meanwhile, he had his job and his pills and his future, whatever it was. He wondered why he didn't care more.

Of course none of it was worth caring about.

Outside the door to the building, which he'd propped open to admit a bit of night air, an owl hooted. He smiled at the low, mournful sound. All his screens were clean.

Nakamura was safe up on the hill.

Even the ghosts couldn't get him. Not with Fred Oranson on guard.

The tall, splendid room echoed to the dance of the lamps. Most of the room was silent. Even the wind had died. From the area of the big mahogany desk, however, came a few sounds.

Rhythmic hacking breaths. Somebody trying to breathe. The large hurricane illuminated the back of the old maple rocker. The chair moved slightly with the rhythm of the distorted noise.

Finally the chair stopped. Shag Nakamura raised his head.

After a few moments he turned slightly and stared out into the room. His dark pupils were slightly dilated. They caught the myriad glimmers of the lamps, so that it appeared tiny galaxies shone in the pits of his face.

He jerked the chair completely around so it faced the desk, faced out to the room. Behind him the bank of six monitors was dark and silent.

He sat still for a long moment. Finally his right hand moved. It jerked erratically and knocked the tumbler of scotch to the floor. He paid no attention. At last he reached the touchpad inset into the top of his desk. His fingers slowly, carefully punched out a code.

Lights came on.
He leaned back in his chair to await the future.

It was a smaller room, much dimmer than the big
ward with its freight of sleeping humanity. The nurse
was strapped into something that resembled a dental
chair. She was a pretty thing in a vague sort of way.
Her hair, midway in length between her skull and her
shoulders, was a neutral brown, but it glinted with
auburn highlights. Her eyes were blue, neither bright
nor faded; at this moment wide and filling with moisture. She had good skin, pale from lack of sun but
very smooth. Her lips were red. She'd been chewing
them with white, even teeth.

The Lady stared at her silently. "You are lying to
me," she said at last.

The nurse shook her head. Her lips parted as if she
might speak, but then snapped shut again.

The Lady tapped the side of her jaw with one long
finger. The nurse saw the Lady's nails were bitten and
raw. It surprised her. The Goddess bit her fingernails!
It made her more human and more frightening at the
same time.

"Arius didn't speak to you. He didn't tell you to
sneak into the ward and write down things. Admit it.
Some stupid childish trick. Did you plan to sell
information?"

Again, the nurse shook her head. Her eyes slid
away from the eyes of the Lady. She was convinced
that if she avoided speaking, this nightmare would go
away.

She smelled fear in the room. At first she didn't
recognize the odor. Now she did, but she hadn't realized its source.

"I can cause you great pain. You profane this sacred
place," the Lady said softly. She seemed emotionally

divorced from the conversation. The nurse suddenly realized that whatever the Lady would do, she would take no pleasure from it. It was a terrible kind of power.

"I swear to you—" she blurted suddenly.

The Lady smiled. Her long face looked naked then, stripped of flesh, a skull with burning eyes. "Yes, dear, speak to me."

The nurse's heart fluttered. She had always expected that if she was ever this frightened her heart would pound, but it fluttered. Weak and tentative. Her heart let her down.

And she had spoken.

"I—he came to me."

"God came to you?" The Lady nodded dreamily to herself. "How did God come to you?"

"On the comm screen. In my room." The nurse wanted to wipe the sweat from her forehead, but her hands were pinioned by metal clamps to the arms of her chair.

"Tell me."

The nurse closed her eyes. She tried to remember. It had seemed so clear if she didn't try to think about it, but now, when she tried to recall specific things, the images faded, became jumbled and hard to recognize. "White. It was a white light on the screen, and then it turned red . . ."

The Lady began to hum to herself. It was an appalling sound.

Frederic Oranson's station was the first to receive the alarm. He lowered his feet from the table where they'd been propped while he watched the darkness outside, his mind spinning emptily in the kinship of the night.

He slapped several portions of his master touchpad

and brought all the security systems up to red. It was a massive process, all the more impressive for its silence. At his command automated pillboxes all along the perimeter of the estate shifted and groaned as armored walls grated aside to expose the glittering snouts of heavy lasers.

Dogs with peculiar breeding histories burst from kennels and began to lope down chain-link pathways, their tongues lolling, their eyes bright. Other animals, less like dogs, more ferocious, snarled across the open spaces inside the vast compound, followed quickly by trained handlers.

Six Blades, theirs by courtesy of the New Church, drifted out across the night, their hands soft and loose with readiness.

A pack of Wolves went loose. They bayed silently at the stars and clicked their claws as they ran.

Other machines came on-line and began tasting, testing, sampling. Men moved quickly, their faces drawn, their breath coming in shallow gasps. Two attack helicopter platforms rattled into the sky, red lights flashing.

This took less then ten seconds. Oranson's feet slapped the floor as he launched himself out the door and into the small command vehicle which awaited him. He glanced at the sky.

Only stars. He gunned the small car. For once he was glad the synapses inside his brain which channeled emotion no longer existed.

He didn't need emotion now. Only strength and speed.

The lights had brightened in the small room now. The nurse barely noticed the two Wolves who hovered near her chair. Her eyes were dull and empty. She blinked once when one of the Wolves unstrapped her right hand, raised it from the chair, and pinioned it to a device that resembled a large stainless steel claw.

The Lady watched her silently. She felt afraid. It was an odd feeling. It had been a long time since fear had shadowed the certainty with which she cradled faith. This girl frightened her. Not so much from what she'd done—the notes were trivial, mere jottings of records already transmitted to a central computer. And thence, she thought, to God himself, for he monitored that huge room. The room was a womb, and God was in its every part.

The girl had no idea of this, of course.

But she'd seen something. Something had impelled her to this foolishness. Perhaps she had no conscious knowledge. Drugs could search more deeply, but they took time. There were side effects to consider as well.

Other ways would serve. The Lady knew many such ways.

She inspected the rigid hand, its fingers and thumb spread in a wide fan.

She nodded to the Wolves. One of them placed two derms on the inner part of the nurse's forearm, near the elbow joint. Then he pressed the flat gray side of a hypospray further down. His hand moved and a sharp hissing sound filled the room.

The Lady waited a few minutes. The girl licked her lips and tried to swallow but her mouth was too dry.

"I told you I wouldn't cause you pain," the Lady said. "I won't. You see?"

She stepped closer and took a needle from a silver tray and pricked the tip of the girl's forefinger. A dot of blood welled there, round and shiny.

The girl stared at the blood.

"That didn't hurt, did it?"

The nurse shook her head. She felt the anesthetic take effect. Now her arm was numb as butchered meat below the elbow.

"Good. Pain is unnecessary to many things," the Lady said.

She put the needle down on the tray and picked up a scalpel.

She looked at the blade and lowered her head. After a moment of prayer she raised the scalpel and began to work.

The nurse screamed and screamed.

Frederic Oranson raced down the long hallway toward the tall double doors. A sleepy servant, an old man in a nightshirt who rubbed his eyes, stood there. He was knocking ineffectually on the wood.

Two Blades of God drifted from the other end, moving with deceptive slowness. Behind them pounded three of Oranson's people, two men and a woman, assault lasers at the ready. The old man seemed confused by the gathering mob. He glanced both ways and resumed his knocking, louder now.

The Blades arrived first. Oranson went through them as if they didn't exist. He shoved the old man out of the way. "Go back to bed," he said.

"Secure this hallway," he ordered the Blades. One went in each direction. Oranson noted that each Blade had a faint smile on his face.

"Behind me," he said to the remaining three.

He faced the door and knocked. Nothing. He tried the ornate handles but they didn't move. Of course. The doors were steel beneath their beautifully carved veneers, and with the sounding of the alarm, extremely powerful magbolt locks would have slammed into place.

It would take a small tank to breach those doors. He imagined that blast shields blocked the flimsy glass door on the outer side of the room as well.

There was a small, slick plate just beneath the handle. He placed his right palm on it, let it rest for a moment, then moved his fingers in an intricate code. As he did so, he spoke another code aloud.

This procedure was to prevent anyone from opening the door by using his hand alone. Hands had been known to become detached from bodies.

There was a sharp click. Oranson tried the handles again and they moved. He pushed down, then pulled. The doors opened and he stood for an instant. Then he plunged into the flickering gloom.

The Lady stepped into the high ward and moved to the bed closest to the end. It was where the nurse had been making her notes.

The nurse was gone, asleep, no longer a factor. The Lady was satisfied. There were ways, and some were quicker than others. It had only taken two fingers. The girl had felt no pain. No physical pain, at least.

The Lady examined her own feelings carefully, wondering if she was weakening in any way. But there was no remorse, only satisfaction that she had done her job. The girl was an empty vessel.

Like many of these, she thought. She cast her long red gaze down the room, marking the sleeping ones. These were vessels, too, of the most sacred sort.

Inside those shadowed heads things she could never understand were taking place. Changes. Minute shiftings. Through the gossamer webs of the monofilaments which connected them to the machines flowed the essence of God, and these would be Gods, too. Angels. Suitable containers for her only son.

There were many of them. Soon the world would know.

She turned back to the last of them. She looked at the chart monitor, then touched the pad on top of it. A date appeared on the screen.

This one was almost the newest. She looked at the

figure as it lay there. Thin, almost scrawny. The bandage-swathed head betrayed very recent surgery. She wondered what sort of strange beauty was hidden by the swaddling.

And yet, and yet . . .

There was *something* familiar—

Again, she felt that strange flicker, so unforeseen.

These were forbidden to her.

By order of God himself, she couldn't scratch the itch.

At first he couldn't see him. Then he made out the figure hunched in the rocker behind the desk. "Mr. Nakamura?"

"Yes?"

The voice was slow and heavy, as if the man was unutterably tired. Oranson walked forward and stopped at the far edge of the desk.

"You initiated a grand alarm, sir."

"I know I did."

Oranson squinted, but the man was lost in darkness, hidden. He was hard to make out. Only his dark eyes glittered.

"Are you all right, sir?"

"Yes, Fred, I'm fine."

Oranson proceeded carefully. Something was vastly wrong here.

"Sir, have you been threatened? Attacked?"

"No."

"Then why—"

Nakamura brought his fist down on the desktop in a sudden crashing movement.

"We must *guard* ourselves, Fred. We must make ready!"

Oranson stepped back. He tried to think. Could Nakamura have somehow gone crazy? Stranger things had happened.

"I initiated the alarm, Fred, because this state of emergency is now a way of life for us. Call in the troops and seal this place off. Nobody must be able to reach me. Nobody at all. Do you understand?"

"No, sir."

"What?" Now there was some of the snap in Nakamura's voice, a bit of the lash Oranson was used to.

"I don't understand. You must tell me some of it if I'm to be effective here. You understand that, surely?"

Nakamura leaned forward into the shifting light of the lantern. Oranson repressed a gasp. The face which glared at him resembled a yellow Halloween mask, a hollow thing to frighten children with. But the voice was reassuring. Now Nakamura sounded almost normal.

"We are going to move, Fred. Many plans I was unaware of are coming to fruition. And we have our part to play."

The Demon's got him, Oranson thought.

"Does this have anything to do with Berg, sir?"

Nakamura pushed himself back from the light. "Berg is dead," he said.

"Yes, sir. I meant, does his death—"

"But, Fred," Nakamura said in a perfectly reasonable voice, "don't you understand? We are all going to die."

"Yes, sir." He thought about the pills only Nakamura could dispense.

Nakamura nodded. "Good," he said. "I thought you'd understand."

10

THE CHANGE WAS abrupt. At one moment they were winding down the long miles across the Midwest, bleak fields rolling gently on both sides of the road, lines of half-melted snow startling and white against humped rows of black earth. Then suddenly low metal warehouses, odd pumping stations, and small clumps of fullerdomes appeared. And ahead, barely visible over the horizon but sharp and clear, the tops of the towers of Chicago.

Sadie downshifted and wrestled the bike to the side of the road. "That's it," she said. She looked over her shoulder. Toshi had wrapped a moth-eaten blue wool muffler over the bottom half of his face. His hair was patchy and dark, a fuzz over the skin of his skull. His eyes were hidden behind dark aviator glasses. His ears stuck out, and she smiled.

"That's Chicago. Give it thirty kiloms, forty minutes max, and we can wheel down New Michigan Avenue."

He grinned. She couldn't see it, but the muffler moved in the right way. "Hit it, babe," he said.

She shook her head. "Not so quick, samurai. We got to talk about this. I have . . . reservations. Know what I mean?"

He shook his head.

"Look," she said. "There's a place up ahead. That Seven-Eleven. They got a restaurant, let's get a cup of coffee and whatever. I'm serious. I'm not gonna head into that den of Wolves without a little planning, okay?"

He pulled down the muffler. His dark eyes were glazed in the hard morning light, their black centers picking up blank pictures of overhead cloud patches.

"Sadie, I know what I gotta do. You don't really figure in, you know? I mean, it's been great riding with you, but I didn't invite you along. You picked me up. And I still don't understand why. There's no reason for me to trust you. None at all." He paused and thought about it. She watched the corners of his eyes crinkle. It made him look old, she thought.

He started to say something, then stopped. Started again. "Can you think of any reason for me to trust you?"

She looked over his shoulder and the highway as it raced like an arrow back toward the North American heartland. She took off one heavy riding glove and blew on her fingers. She rubbed her right eye. "Levin," she said.

"Let's get coffee," he said.

They made their way through the front part of the store, where an elderly pink-haired woman holding a bag of potato chips argued with the clerk about price, to the back where a few spindly white tables and rickety folding chairs clustered next to a wall of food vending machines. This part of the building had a glass wall and the sunlight here was fierce. They sat in a corner, their backs to the windows.

She tugged at the plastic wrapper which the microwave had annealed to her corned beef sandwich. Toshi stirred five packets of sugar and three of cream into his coffee. "How can you eat that stuff? The wrapper tastes better than the sandwich."

"I may try it if I can't get the damned thing off."

He grinned. "You know a lot about me, right? It wasn't an accident you picked me up like that."

She shook her head. "Toshi, how much do you remember?"

He stared blankly at his coffee. "It comes and goes. Some things I remember fine. I remember being a kid, for instance. But the last three or four years? Blotto, for the most part. You know—" He sipped from the Styrofoam container. "I think I dream stuff, a lot. I got a feeling it's about what I don't remember. But when I wake up . . ." he shrugged.

"Toshi, you used to know me real well." Her eyes were the color of amethysts, dark and brooding. Her dark skin looked velvety, except for the scars.

"Yeah. I guessed that. There's a feeling you get. Comfortable, like. Maybe my body remembers what my head doesn't. I don't think I'd have gone with you otherwise. Sadie, strange shit is going on. Do you know what it is?"

Finally she managed to tear the plastic away, mangling the sandwich in the process. "Damn." She stared at the mess, then took a squeeze bottle of mustard and squirted the pile. "I can eat it with a fork," she muttered.

"Sadie, answer me."

She forked up a piece of mustard-soaked white bread, chewed, swallowed. "Yeah. I was looking for you. I didn't know exactly where, but somewhere along the road I figured to make contact."

"Right. Okay, so who sent you? What for?" He glanced at the boy who'd come in and was now feeding his chip to the doughnut machine. The kid was young, sixteen or seventeen. He sported a crew cut and maybe two dozen shiny chrome ear cuffs. Tiny silver skulls dangled from his earlobes. He wore a dark green three-piece suit of antique style and shiny motorcycle boots.

Toshi lowered his voice. "You said something about . . . Levin?"

"I got a contract," she said obliquely. Then she tapped her fingers on the smooth tabletop and looked at the ceiling. "Good money. All handled through a bodybroker in San Francisco I use occasionally. I'm a mercenary, Toshi. You must have figured that by now."

"With that Wolf back on the road you mean? Yeah. Nice job, that. Did I ever work with you?"

"Uh-huh. More than once, in fact." She seemed about to say something else, but took another bite of her sandwich instead.

"So, okay. I don't remember. That's an example of the kind of things I'm talking about. It's like . . ."

She looked up. "Like what?"

"Like my mind's too full of something else to leave any room for memories. But I don't know what. I dream—" He shook his head. "I dream about machines."

The sunlight caught her hair and turned it into a bonfire. She stared at him and he turned away. "Machines? I thought you said you couldn't remember."

"I don't, anything specific. And I'm not even sure they are machines. I mean I know it, but they don't look like any machines I ever heard of. But they are."

"I don't understand."

"Are you sure? You know a lot more about this than I do. You sure you don't know about the machines either?"

She shook her head. "Look, Toshi, I'm sorry I blindsided you this way. The contract was strange. I was told some things but not others. For instance, they—the bodybroker, I mean—said you'd probably have some mental problems. When I asked what that

meant, all he would say was you wouldn't be dangerous to me."

"This bodybroker. Anybody I know?"

"Name's Kelatz. Ring any bells?"

He shook his head. "No. But it probably should,
huh? I can tell by your face."

"You've done business with him before."

"Yeah. More stuff I don't remember." He drained
his coffee and crumpled the plastic cup.

"Tell me about the machines."

He seemed not to hear her. His button eyes were
slightly filmy.

"Toshi. The machines. Tell me about them."

"Oh. Okay, they're lumpy."

"What? Lumpy? What do you mean?"

"They look like big round balls of smaller balls
connected by rods and levers. Uh, you know what
tinkertoys are?"

She smiled. "A kind of toy kids play with. Boys
mostly. I had a set when I was little, though. My mom
bought it for me. I don't think my dad approved."

"Well, these remind me of tinkertoys. I get the
feeling of movement, though. Like these rods push
back and forth, into the balls, and all of them make up
this larger ball. A machine, like I said."

She crinkled her eyes against a sudden blast of light
from the windshield of a truck pulling into the parking
lot. "I don't know. Doesn't ring any bells. It almost
sounds like you're describing atoms or molecules. But
they don't move, do they?"

He pursed his lips. "Well, sort of. Atoms don't, not
without some outside help. Molecules . . ." He shook
his head. "It gets blank now. Just dreams. And not
much that I remember. Only what I just said." He
glanced over at the kid who was sitting two tables
away, his opaque sunglasses tilted in their direction.

The kid chewed slowly on his doughnut. Toshi got the feeling the boy was paying attention to them. It made him nervous.

"I think we ought to get going."

Sadie didn't take her eyes from his face. "Not yet. I got to know more. Where are we going? To do what?"

Toshi shook his head. "Not here."

Her thin lips widened. A hint of tooth blinked forth. Her voice lowered to a whisper. "You mean that kid watching us back there? That's what *I* mean. He's local gang, bought and paid for. Darkstone Ragers, I guess. Those skulls, nobody else wears them. You ever think how stupid it is, you belong to a criminal organization, so you wear badges to let everybody know? The Orientals don't do that." She blinked. "Anyway, I don't know if he's looking for us or what. That's what you have to tell me. What you want to do—so I know whether to cave in that little punk's skull or just walk away. Toshi, from here on you need me. I'm the bodywatcher. That's my contract."

He nodded. "What if I don't want the body watched? I asked you before about trusting you, and you said a name. You remember?"

"Uh-huh. Levin."

"I think that name means something to me. I get flashes, just like with the machines. So what does it mean to you?"

"The bodybroker, Kelatz, he mentioned it. Said you might be reluctant to go along. Said if you were, just to mention Levin and it would help. Does it?"

Toshi squirmed uncomfortably. The heat through the glass windows sent rivulets of perspiration down his forehead, his neck, into his collar.

"I don't know," he said at last. "I think so. That's all Kelatz said? Just the name?"

"That's it."

There was a long instant while he stared out at the sharp edges of the parking lot, at the cars, the road beyond, the towers of Chicago beyond that. Finally he shrugged. "It feels okay," he said. "That's crazy, but I don't have all that much to go on, you know? Not much of me is here. So I guess it'll have to be enough. But be careful, Sadie. Remember what happened when you waved that knife at me. I think my body remembers how to take care of itself."

Her purple eyes went somber. "Yeah. I don't understand that either. If your memory is shot, you shouldn't recall moves like that. Muscle recall, sure, but there's an intellectual component, too. It doesn't seem real."

"What's real?" he said. "I can't tell anymore. Can you?"

"You still hungry?"

The sun had moved past the roof line and the room was suddenly dimmer. Sadie glanced toward the food machines. "Not really, but maybe we should eat. You never know when the food runs out, right?"

Toshi grinned at the ancient mercenary credo. "Eat now, and forever hold your piece, right?"

"Better than *your* piece, eh, samurai?"

"You ever do that?"

"I'm not telling," she said. "If you can't remember, it couldn't have been all that good, right?"

"Hey, I didn't mean—"

"I know," she said. "Just pulling your leg, buddy. Yeah, I slept with you a couple of times. Good fun, too."

"That's all? Just good fun?" There was a soft note of pain in his voice.

"Well, maybe a little more." She hunched her wide shoulders. "Not to the point. Forget it. Just what are we going to do?" She stopped, then slid her eyes to the side without moving her head. "Wait a second. Need to take care of some business."

"Be careful," Toshi said.

"Yeah, sure," she replied, rising.

The kid with the ear bangles had turned his chair away from them and was sipping his coffee, carefully not watching them. She knew it meant nothing. Short-range distance mikes were cheap and easy. He didn't even have to watch. A mini-vidcamera could be hidden in a button. Maybe even in a skull earring.

She walked toward the wall of sandwich dispensers. Her route took her close to the boy's table. Just as she came even with the table her right toe caught on one of the chair legs and she stumbled forward.

"Hey!" Reflexes sent the boy's arms up and out, palms spread to catch her. For a fraction of a second they were tangled together, before the kid managed to push her upright. In the fall his sunglasses had gone awry, partly off his face, and Toshi saw his eyes. Bright, bright blue. Then Sadie was standing away.

"Sorry, bud."

"You ought to watch where you're going, lady," the kid said. "I almost spilled my—"

"Yes?" she said.

Slowly he pushed his shades back on his face, but not before Toshi saw the brightness go out of his eyes.

"What did you say?" Sadie asked again.

The kid shook his head. He stood up. He didn't look at them.

"Wait a second," Sadie said.

The boy stopped.

"Give me your skulls. The earrings, give them to me." She kept her voice low and pleasant.

Without a word the youth unhooked the two silver heads and handed them to her.

"You got a camera, a mike?"

Wordlessly, he pointed at the earrings.

"Good. Go on home now, buddy. Forget about us, right? Sleep for a couple of days when you get home."

The boy nodded. He looked forlorn and vacant. His shades were dull and flat in the gloom.

"Okay, split."

The boy left the restaurant. They watched him walk to a new Jaguar two-seater, one of the hot rocks that cost very big, climb in and drive away.

"Gang for sure," Sadie remarked. "Get a look at those wheels. You don't find them in cereal boxes."

Toshi nodded. "What did you use?"

She smiled slowly. "Heavy-duty autohypnotic. He'll do what I said. Sleep for two days. And I got his cameras."

She dropped the two skulls on the floor and ground them under her boot heel.

"You think he was after us specifically?"

"Hard to tell. I should have asked."

"Yeah," Toshi said. "You should have."

He got up from the table, went to the machines, and bought two more cups of coffee. He didn't look at Sadie when he sat down.

Finally. "You ever heard of Arius? The Demon Star?"

She stirred her own coffee with a plastic stick. She shook her head. "No. Sounds like a kid's netshow."

Toshi sighed. "I only wish. See, that's one of the things I do remember. Always have, even when everything else goes. Arius is a . . . well, computer is too small a word. He—it—is part human, part Artificial Intelligence, and all nasty. I think I have nightmares about it."

"You don't remember?"

"Just a feeling. If I wake up and I've got the cold

chills, usually in the back of my mind I remember Arius."

"I don't understand."

"Of course you don't. I didn't either. But he exists. I'm not much for religion, but if there is evil, then Arius is evil. I'm not even sure he realizes it, though."

She looked puzzled. "That doesn't make much sense. What do you mean about not realizing it?"

He shrugged. "Different standards. Different . . . realities, I guess. Arius isn't human. We are. Our concept of evil is a human one, usually involving damage to humans. For instance, most people don't find the idea of destroying a marshland, with all its ecological complexity, evil. Because humans aren't destroyed, at least not directly. Do you think killing chimps in medical experiments is evil?"

She sipped slowly, her eyes dark as bruises. "I . . . I guess not. People get helped by it."

"What I mean. Arius isn't human. To him we're chimps."

She glanced out at the parking lot. Sunlight glinted from bits of bright gravel ground into the asphalt. "Then maybe he's not evil."

"Tell it to a chimp," he said. "But he's real. He exists in a different reality, but it crosses into ours. By our standards he's as dangerous as we are to chimps. Or marshes. What if he decides we're not necessary to his ecology? We might not be, you know."

"Toshi, this is very weird. Are you sure about all this?"

"Why can't I remember anything?"

"Maybe you're crazy," she told him.

"Does it matter?"

"No," she said.

*   *   *

"You got to tell me now," she said at last. "If I'm going to help."

He moved his shoulders. She was conscious of muscle there, lumps of it, rolling. "I have to get to Arius. That's what I'm supposed to do."

She sat back in her chair and stared at him. "Get to Arius? This Demon Star thing?" She rubbed the side of her nose slowly, her eyes narrow. "Get to him how? An assassination, you mean?"

He shook his head. "I don't think so. I'm not sure. And getting to him, it's not what you think."

Her lips went tight. "Blow him away, that's simple. If that's what you're supposed to do. But you don't know, huh?"

"You sound pissed, Sadie. You shouldn't. I didn't ask you to come along. The opposite, in fact."

The tension went out of her face. "I know, Toshi. But don't you know anything?"

He stared out the window again. "I think I know everything, but I just can't access it. There's a plan, a method, locked up inside me somewhere. Everything I need. And when I need it, it will be available."

"That's crazy. How can you—"

He grinned. "We already went through this. Right?"

"I guess so. If you say. But where do I fit in?"

"You watch the body. That's what your contract is all about, isn't it?"

"Yeah." She traced a small ring with her forefinger in a tiny puddle of spilled coffee. "Can you tell me anything more about this Arius? Like where to find him?"

He started to shake his head. He stopped. His face opened up. "Arius lives in many places," he said. To her his voice sounded different, less human, more precise. "But his heart lives in one. That's what we have to find. The heart of the Demon Star."

Now she pushed her chair partly away from the table and slapped her kneecap in frustration. "That sounds like low-grade fantasy. How can a computer have a heart?"

"I don't know," he said. "That's what I have to find out."

The big bike made a sound like a giant clearing its throat. He sat behind her, his arms around her waist, his muffled lips close to her ear. She bucked the machine around, aimed its chrome snout toward the cracked blacktop of the road.

"Forty minutes to center city," she said. "So where are we going?"

The air around them was clear and sharp. The sharp stink of hydrocarbons drifted from the pumping stations behind them on the road. He closed his eyes against the glare. Small lumpy things moved on the inside of his eyelids.

Then, as if somebody played a holoprojector on the same piece of soft-skinned darkness, he saw a beach at night. A white lady. Red eyes. Deep inside his skull he heard a word: *Remember*.

He squeezed her tighter and whispered in her ear. "The Labyrinth. Down under where the dark things go. That's the place. That's where we go."

He felt her stiffen, but then she relaxed. "Okay. But I've got contacts. I think we ought to use them."

He knew what the physical movement implied. She was done with argument. Now she would help.

"Fine with me," he said.

He opened his eyes, and Levin went away. But Toshi never even knew he'd come.

The lake kept rising. In the late eighties it had begun. The scientists said it was inevitable, that Lake

Michigan was only seeking its normal level after centuries of abnormally low boundaries. At first, the water—up a foot and pounded by winter storms—ate away at the foundations of huge apartment buildings lining the seawalls along North Sheridan Drive. The city built higher seawalls, but the waters rose again.

By the mid-nineties the water was up another foot, and the Dutch engineers came. But the city approached economic collapse, the beginning of the dark years, and money went thin. When the federals finally stepped in, most of the lake shore had drowned, and the engineers building the great Chicago Dike were charged with reclamation as well as construction.

The dikes saved Chicago. New Michigan Avenue was rebuilt on the rusted wreckage of the old, the rotting basements and crumbled concrete of lower floors and hidden pathways. It was cheaper to leave it and build on top than try to clean it up. The New City grew bright and sparkling on a vast wasteland of broken glass and decayed asphalt.

Down below the shining spikes of the new buildings space remained. Modern caverns where the sun never came, burrows nobody even tried to police.

The Labyrinth.

"When're they going to get here?"

She glanced at him, then settled back in her chair and closed her eyes. "Don't get jumpy, pal. These people are pros. We've got another ten minutes. They'll be here."

"You say you know them. I still don't like it. How do we know we can trust them?"

She made a short clicking noise with her teeth. "I don't expect you to understand Chicago gang politics, right? Trust me on this."

He shook his head. "Talk to me, babe. Give me reasons."

"You mean like you tell me everything? Shit, Toshi, at the moment the only thing I know is you want to crack the Labyrinth. Well, I know the Lab. I know a lot about it. And we can't just walk in there. Place is full of Wolves. It's where they started, back when there were just a few kids with weird implants and greasy fur and teeth like a dental student's nightmare. You real anxious to meet about a hundred of the furballs?"

He thought about it. "I'm not afraid of Wolves, I don't think."

"Ah, Toshi. I wish your fucking brains would get unscrambled and your memory would come back. You used to be better than this, smarter. You ought to be afraid of them. You aren't Superman."

He stared out the window. They were in a new high rise on the North Side, a nice room with gray carpet and white walls, sparsely filled with furniture made of bright canvas and chrome and leather. They'd rented it short term using an ID chip that Sadie provided. The name on the chip had nothing to do with either of them. Toshi used a similar bent chip to make payment.

The rental agent's eyebrows had risen when he looked at whatever had popped up on his screen, and his attitude had become noticeably more polite.

"I wonder what the hell's on my printout now?" Toshi said. He didn't remember anything out of the ordinary there. It was something to check into.

He forced himself to concentrate on her words. It was so hard to concentrate. All he could think about was a great red star. He'd seen it somewhere, but where? He knew it was Arius.

And he knew that Arius—a part of him, at least—

was hidden in the Labyrinth. But that was all, and it wasn't enough. Not nearly enough.

He balled both hands into fists and pressed them hard against his temples. "I goddam know it's in here," he said. "If I could just drag it out into the open. Levin, Arius, the machines—I know what it means. But I can't get it out."

She looked at him sadly. "I get the feeling we're walking into a shitstorm, you know. And we don't have nothing like an umbrella."

He exhaled heavily. "You cut yourself in, Sadie. You can cut yourself out anytime you want."

Her eyebrows rose. "You leaving, bud?"

"No."

"Me neither."

The door monitor buzzed softly. Sadie stood up and walked to the door. The apartment screen flashed bright blue, then steadied into a face.

"Beep me in," the face said. "It's your dime for my time."

It was a young face. Black stripes, sharp-edged and glittering, about a centimeter wide, ran up and down the skin. Part of one stripe intersected the right eye, and there the white of the corneal cover was also black. The face appeared as if behind a narrowly barred window.

"You're in, hip." Her fingers brushed the control pad and the face nodded.

"Be right with you."

She saw two other figures, larger, more in shadow, move past the camera in the lobby and nodded to herself.

"Visitors, Tosh," she said. "Put on your happy face."

The corners of his lips turned up. "Who are these bucks, again?"

"Ragers," she said. "The Darkstone Ragers."

The zebra-faced boy came in first. Toshi stood by the large living room window, facing the door, his hands dangling loosely at his sides. The boy was very thin, but without the emaciated feel that goes with malnutrition. His muscles were like long cords. They moved in his neck, his face, his shoulders and wrists. He glanced at Sadie, then glanced again.

"Sorry," he said. "Gotta check."

She shrugged and spread her arms away from her sides. The boy moved close—Toshi nodded to himself as he watched the deceptively slow movement—and ran his long fingers down her sides. Her tense grin widened as he paid particular attention to the inside of her thighs.

"You being careful, boyo, or just horny?"

His face remained impassive. He stepped back and took a small instrument from the pocket of his short leather tee shirt. He waved it in front of her, then checked something on the back of it.

"You ain't much my type," he said, but seemed otherwise satisfied. He turned toward Toshi. "Now him."

Toshi turned his palms up. "Save you the trouble," he said. "You wave that thing at me, it's gonna find so much stuff its insides will turn to mush. Otherwise I'm not carrying. You check that out. But if you people and us meet, you're gonna have to take our word. We don't mean you trouble."

Again, the boy waved the bit of electronics. This time when he checked the reading he whistled softly. "Spread 'em, bud," he said. He repeated the shakedown. To Toshi those fingers felt like narrow steel spiders.

Finished, the boy moved back to the door. "A moment," he said. He bowed slightly, and Sadie grinned. Then he stepped outside.

Sadie heard whispered voices. Finally the boy came back in.

"Okay," he said. "Here's how it is. The samurai over there, he stays there. They'll talk up close with you, but he sits and he don't move. What I do—" and now he opened his hand to reveal the hilt of a monomole switchblade—"is I stand next to him with this. And if anything looks odd to me, then he loses his head. Are we agreed?"

Toshi moved to the chair Sadie had vacated. He sat down and said, "You sure you don't want to tie me up or something?"

"Not necessary," the boy said. He walked over and stood behind Toshi. "This is just our prudent-buyer program."

Toshi sighed and relaxed against the soft leather. Carefully he placed his hands on the arms of the chair, palms down. "This okay?"

The boy said, "We're open for business."

The front door went wide and the largest black man Toshi had ever seen shouldered his way into the room. He was so wide he had to turn slightly to get through the doorway. He ducked his head as he entered. He wore a silver-gray three-piece suit of impeccable cut. He glanced at Toshi, at Sadie, at the boy.

"Good enough," he said. He walked away from the door, and a third man whose skin was perfectly white, as if it were covered with clown makeup, entered. If the giant's suit was big bucks, Toshi thought, this one was royalty. For a moment he was envious of the man's tailor.

The big man smiled. His teeth were a gold blaze between his lips. "This is Mr. Master," he said.

The smaller man nodded. Toshi noted that the muscles of his face did not move at all. His features seemed carved from plaster, serene and perfect. Only his eyes were alive, a bright, shimmering mix of yellows and greens and blues.

Cat eyes, Toshi thought.

"Pleased," the man said. His voice was soft and whispery. He turned his head toward her, an oddly graceful movement. "Sadie. Long time. Is that the one you want dead?"

11

CALLEY'S FINGERS BRUSHED Ozzie's forearm. "We wait," she said.

"But—"

"Just wait," she repeated. They were standing in a small alcove not far from the customs desk. The two guards loitered a few meters away, their laser rifles ostentatiously pointed toward the floor but fully visible.

"Calley, I swear to God there wasn't any way those chips could have been cracked. Our real names simply weren't there."

"I know, Ozzie. I know." Her voice was soothing. When he looked at the smooth planes of her face, he thought he noticed a lessening of tension in the tiny muscles there. Her green eyes, though sightless and staring, held an expectant glitter he'd not seen since she'd lost her vision.

"Wait a minute," he said. "You were waiting for something like this, weren't you?"

A faint smile tugged at the corner of her mouth. "Ozzie, you still don't have a truly dirty mind, you know that?"

He shook his head, then remembered and said, "I don't get it."

Her smile grew wider. "Remember what you said before? You listed all the shit coming down—me blind, Nakamura on the move, Arius doing God knows what. And Berg and Levin and Toshi missing."

173

He shifted uneasily. "Uh, yeah. So what?"

"Seems like an awful lot of shit to come down all at once, right?" She paused, as if hearing something just at the edge of human capacity. "But one component was kind of obviously absent from that equation. If you thought about it. Who threw us the real curve last time, when Double En sent me and Berg into the matrix?"

Ozzie watched one of the guards raise his wrist to his mouth and move his lips. He nodded suddenly. "The real curve was Arius, the Artificial Intelligence, and it was here on Luna. Sure, babe."

"I got to thinking. Over the past few years, nobody's heard much from Luna, Inc. Just another player out of the game, right? They lost their AI and ended up selling their meat to Double En. But then nothing. At least if there was, we didn't know about it. Maybe Berg—but who knows what all he was doing?"

Ozzie thought he saw a familiar figure pushing its way into the fringe of the crowd across the big room.

"So you think the Lunies are mixed up in this somehow?"

"A question occurred to me. They built an AI based on a meatmatrix, the first one. But nobody thought to ask one thing."

Ozzie recognized the approaching man and thought, of course. Who else?

"What's that?" he said absently.

"What were they gonna do with that AI? What were the Lunies *working* on?"

Ozzie could see his face now. Still young, with that absolute absence of wrinkles that marked the Lunie-born, a high forehead, the hair receded perhaps a bit more than before, wide, pale gray eyes and a small, serious mouth. Now beginning to smile, now spreading his arms wide in welcome.

"It's Karl Wier," he whispered.

"Of course it is," she replied. "Who the fuck else?"

If movement on Luna had been hard for her when she'd first come here, now it was surreal. In darkness her balancing mechanisms, unaided by vision, protested viciously. Wier noticed it first. She felt his fingers, surprisingly strong, wrap around her upper arm.

"Ozzie, grab hold of the other side. The lady is walking like a drunken sailor."

She felt Ozzie take her other arm and almost giggled. She could imagine the picture it made; the woman, helpless, being guided between two tall men. Suddenly she wondered if there wasn't a method to this madness as well.

She'd always stood alone. Even Berg, in his towering obstinacy, had been unable to change that. Now she was dependent on those around her for even the simplest things.

Am I supposed to learn humility? she wondered. And if so, why?

She shook the errant thoughts away. "Be careful, you guys. Don't walk me into any walls."

Wier chuckled softly. Ozzie was silent, but she felt his grip tighten. She knew that small movement wasn't from any concern for her safety. Ozzie had understood the undercurrent of rage beneath her words.

As they led her wherever she was going, she thought about that as well. Ozzie had depths she'd never realized until the disaster of her blindness. He made mistakes—who wouldn't?—but his response to the situation was far beyond what she could have expected.

So even in an endless night she learned. I see more clearly, she thought. Is that the reason why?

She ignored the dizzy, whirling chaos of her mind trying to adjust to darkness on the moon and said,

"Wier. You Machiavellian motherfucker. You're behind all the shit, aren't you?"

Again, that soft chuckle which told her nothing, and everything. "What shit, Calley?"

She felt herself begin to smile. "You're the little man who wasn't there, aren't you? But as soon as the lights went out, I could see you clearly."

"Sometimes it works that way," he replied.

Ozzie guided her to a spindly plastiform chair in the small, white-walled conference room. One side of the room was given over to several screens: control panels and touchpads were inset into the top of the table. There was room enough for five chairs, which were arranged around the table facing the screens. He felt the ceaseless exhalations of the atmosphere pumps on his face; the long quiet breathing of Kennedy Crater.

Calley tilted her head back. The indirect lighting made her eyes smooth and empty. "I guess you want to give us some answers now?"

Wier grinned. It made him look very young, very innocent. Ozzie wasn't deceived. He'd been there before.

"What kind of answers did you have in mind?" he said.

"Hey, Oz, you ever get the feeling we've already had this conversation?"

"Yeah. In fact, I feel it strongly." He turned to face Luna's chief operations scientist, the man who had developed Arius in the first place. "Cut the crap, Karl. We're old buddies, right? I don't exactly understand what Calley's talking about, but she's usually right. What *is* going on? How come you knew right away it was us? Not from our chips. I guarantee that."

Wier nodded dreamily, as if listening to a very familiar, well-loved tune. "Not from the chips, Ozzie.

Or rather, we knew who the chips belonged to, even if the names were wrong."

"Impossible," Ozzie said. "I bent those chips myself."

"No. You bent them with the help of your meatmatrix. Which is not the same thing."

Calley shook her head. "Berg did the defenses for our meats. You couldn't crack them. You even lost your big matrix."

Ozzie noted that Calley was very careful not to mention Levin by name and reminded himself to do likewise.

Wier rubbed his hands together as if washing them. Ozzie wondered what subconscious convolutions twisted the Lunie's own thoughts.

"Not entirely true. Not . . . really."

"I thought so," Calley said. She sounded satisfied.

"What the fuck are you two talking about?" Ozzie asked.

Wier sighed. "It would probably be easier if I just showed you."

Calley put both her hands flat on the tabletop. "You can't show me, pal," she said.

Wier's voice remained brisk. "I know I can't. I'll tell you. Maybe later . . ."

"What!"

"Nothing . . ." he said. But she heard a different thought, and for a moment her throat went tight as something tried to force its way down to her gut. She inhaled. Her lips started to move.

Then she blinked. "Go on," she said.

Wier nodded. He'd seen the hidden movements and thought he understood. Ozzie watched him.

Later, Ozzie thought. I think we owe you again. You won't much like the repayment, maybe.

Wier's fingers worked his touchpad and the largest screen flamed into light. Ozzie stared at the two objects there. One was a small cube, very perfect, whose sides shimmered with a blaze of colors. If it was a jewel, it was one he'd never seen before. Then he looked at the other object, and the size of the cube became clearer, as if a camera had suddenly come into focus.

The cube rested on a flat white surface next to a common thimble. The cube was less than half as large as the thimble. Ozzie guessed it a centimeter on a side.

Wier described it to Calley. As Ozzie had guessed, his measurement was correct. "So," he asked Wier, "what is it?"

Wier shrugged. "It's a brain."

"You mean a chip."

"No," Wier answered. "I mean a brain."

A quiet young man had served coffee from a trolley, carefully placing one cup where Calley could reach it without groping. Ozzie sipped at his cup thoughtfully, his amber-flecked eyes distant and unfocused.

"Let me be sure I got this straight. Calley twigged close to it a while ago, but this is some truly weird shit. You built that frigging Artificial Intelligence to program *molecules*?"

"Close enough." Wier grinned. "We made a few mistakes—more than a few—but essentially that's what we were after, yes."

"Few mistakes . . ." Calley muttered.

"Well, we didn't count on the damned thing coming alive and making alliance with Norton, that's for sure," Wier said ruefully. "Did you know that the original Arius passed the Turing test?"

Calley cleared her throat. "Indistinguishable from a human in ordinary conversation?"

"Yes. Of course, that should have given us a clue."

She sighed. "Lots of things should have, but nobody planned on what really happened. And you sold the meat to Double En, afterward. Why?"

"They wanted it. We weren't in a position to refuse, either, or at least we thought we weren't. We knew something had gone drastically wrong when the AI collapsed right after we initiated that program of yours. When you brought Berg out and told us what had happened, it just seemed best to cut our losses and run. Besides . . ."

She nodded once. "Besides," she continued for him, "you'd already gotten what you were really after. What Arius was just a way station on the road toward. Right?"

Again, that shy smile. Ozzie warned himself not to underestimate this man again. "You're pretty sharp for a blind lady."

Ozzie inhaled suddenly, but Calley raised her hand. "I'm pretty sharp for any kind of lady, Wier. I thought you figured that out by now."

Wier's voice was pleasant. "You could say that."

"So your AI was programming molecules. Would you like to expand on that?"

"It's why we brought you up here," Wier said.

Ozzie stared at Calley's face as Wier turned toward his touchpad. Her face was calm, relaxed, but he knew that if he'd caught the implications of Wier's last statement, then certainly she had.

The single major change in their lives, the motivating force which had somehow led her to come to Luna, had been her blindness. But what could the Lunies have to do with that? It had come from Arius, from the Demon Star.

Or had it?

Yet she said nothing. He would follow her lead. In

the kind of game this was, nobody played a better joystick than Gloria Calley.

Maybe Wier would discover that, too. For a moment Ozzie felt his fists clench and was surprised at the anger that made his breathing go hard and short. But his hands were open and his eyes mild when Wier said, "Okay, here's the beginning. You get the baby course because it will make it easier later."

"What's later?" Calley said.

"Just . . . later. Listen up, now."

On the screen was something that looked like an incredibly complicated spiral built out of tinkertoys. "That is a DNA molecule," Wier said. "It is transcribed to create RNA 'tapes,' which ribosomes then use as instructions on building other molecules." He paused as the picture changed. Now a different shape appeared. This appeared to be something like a pair of upspread wings, also molded from tinkertoys. "That is an assembler. It is an early one, made of protein. Think of it as a ribosome. We're far beyond it now."

Ozzie stared at the screen. "So?"

Wier shrugged. "Humanity as we know it is obsolete," he said.

It seemed to Ozzie that the room should have grown dimmer. The tabletop was a wreckage of gummy coffee cups, crumpled napkins, the remnants of a meal stuck in bits on several plates, wadded up sheets of printout covered with scribbled notes on the back. Two ashtrays were piled high with butts beneath Wier's disapproving gaze—tobacco was no longer carcinogenic, but air pollution was still something of a factor on the moon. Lunies rarely smoked. It was a groundhog habit.

His eyes felt gritty, even though the circulation system kept their air clear and cool. It felt like the dregs of the night, but except for the debris, everything was unchanged. And utterly changed forever.

Wier seemed as fresh as people like that always did, Ozzie thought sourly.

"The first breakthrough was in the design of the nanocomputers," Wier said. "Think of it—nano, a prefix meaning 'one billionth.' Molecules are measured in nanometers. So we called machines built on the molecular level 'nanotechnology.' It's an old concept, really. A man named Drexler wrote about it in the eighties but he was thought visionary at the time. Now we're actually doing it."

"Molecular machines," Ozzie said. "Molecular computers." He sounded dazed.

Wier grinned. "It's a bit hard to grasp if you're not used to it. But you will be. Take my word."

Ozzie's lips moved silently. Wier stared at him, then continued. "The system we now use involves three parts—the molecular computers, which we program, and which perform the same function as the DNA-RNA system in a human. The nanocomputers tell the second part what to do. That second part we call assemblers. Assemblers actually manipulate atoms and build molecules. Finally, there are assemblers that take things apart, down to the atomic level. We call them disassemblers. With those three elements we can do almost anything."

Calley had been silent for some time, smoking moodily, inhaling and exhaling long slow plumes of white. Her voice startled them.

"Yes, you can, can't you? You know what, Wier? You scare the shit out of me."

Wier's gray eyes widened. "How so, Calley?"

She grinned. "I see the possibilities," she said. "Don't you find the possibilities scary?"

"It's only machines, in the end," Ozzie said. "Real little machines, is all." His voice was soft with the technician's assurance of knowledge and control.

"So," Calley replied, "is your body. So is a plant. So is the universe. And the universe is stupid, as far as it goes."

Wier seemed surprised. His careful expression faded for a moment, and Ozzie saw the fanatic animation, like a fever beneath his skin. "You do get it, don't you?" he said.

"Yeah," Calley replied. "I get it. I just wish I didn't. So listen, you rotten trashbag motherfucker, when are you going to let me see again?"

"Do you want to talk?" Ozzie said.

Wier had escorted them to their rooms. It was a long walk down one of the winding tunnels leading away from the domed vastness of Kennedy Crater itself. Dimly, the barest hint of vibration through rock, they could feel more than hear the ceaseless grind of giant borers extending other tunnels. Ozzie thought they must be far out in the lunar boonies.

"No. Yes. I don't know." Calley was seated on a bright green airbag chair. Its skin formed and reformed in response to her movement. Her green eyes were dull. Ozzie suddenly realized that she was much older than he was and wondered why he'd never noticed it before.

"Did you believe all that shit?"

Her shoulders sagged. "Yeah. I did."

"But if what he says is right—"

"Ozzie, he doesn't even know what he's got hold of. I hope. 'Cause if he does, he's the most powerful man who ever lived."

The room was long and relatively narrow. There were several of the floppy chairs scattered around. The carpet was flat and gray. Doors at either end of the room led to identical bedrooms. Each bedroom had its own bathroom. A round table with six chairs

divided the main room. Two computers and their pe-
ripherals were located next to each bedroom door. An
alcove in the middle led to a small, well-equipped
kitchenette.

Ozzie flopped on the chair nearest Calley. "More
powerful than Arius and Norton? The Demon Star?"

She closed her eyes. "He could crush the Star like a
piece of used chewing gum."

Ozzie interlaced his long fingers across his bony
chest. He felt unbelievably tired. How long had it
been since he'd slept? He couldn't remember. It would
be so good to just let go.

Where was Berg? What had happened?

"You were pretty nasty there at the end. You really
think he had something to do with your blindness?"

"I just wish I could have seen his face when I said it.
Maybe he would have slipped. Maybe I could have
learned something. *Goddam it!*"

"What?"

"I'm so fucking helpless." Her voice went slow and
low. "I just don't know if I can . . . can . . ."

"Hey. You're tired is all. We need some sleep. Sort
it out in the morning." He tried a smile and hoped it
would seep into his words. "Be of good cheer, right?
Which bedroom you want us to use? We got two. Sort
of useless, huh?"

She tugged at her face, her fingers half-clawed. He
watched the skin stretch, watched faint splotches of
red appear. "It doesn't matter. You take one and
point me at the other."

"Hey, wait a minute. Was it something I said?"

She shook her head. "No. Don't take it wrong, Oz.
I just want to sleep by myself tonight. No biggie."

"Well . . ." Somehow he was too tried to argue
even about this. All his paranoia buttons had come
unwired. Slowly he unwound himself from the chair

and padded over to her. He took her hand and pulled
her up and walked her to the door. "Inside," he said.
"You'll be okay?"

"Maybe," she said. "Someday."

He blinked. Then he turned and walked to his own
room and went inside and closed the door.

Calley ran her palms along the wall until she bumped
into the bed. She sank down gratefully and sighed as
the warm softness enfolded her.

"Lights off," she said. Then she chuckled. How would
she know? Her lights were already off.

She was still listening to the tiny sound of her own
laughter rattling inside her skull when sleep took her
and she dreamed.

She lay back on the bed and felt exhaustion seep
into her shoulders. She was so tired her muscles quivered involuntarily in tiny jumping misfires.

The blindness. Who or what had caused it? Wier?
He seemed willing enough to hint he was the cause.
But that in itself was as good a reason to doubt as any.
Arius? The logical suspect. She had been on the De-
mon Star's own turf when something—what was it?
—had happened.

Maybe that was the answer. She felt her chest rising
and falling. The rhythm was soothing, almost hypnotic. In all the time since it had happened, she'd
never tried to recall the incident itself. Natural enough.
Why dwell on something so painful?

This is when my eyes went out.

Who wants to think of things like that?

Suddenly, fiercely, she knew.

I do, she thought. *I have to remember.*

Her narrow body went tight with the understanding.
It might turn out to be the hardest thing she'd ever

done, but somehow she had to pierce that veil of memory. For even as she probed she felt resistance and realized that she really could not recall those instants.

Something had happened inside the metamatrix, but it was as dark to her now as the real world around her. There must be some reason for that. Perhaps the answer was locked inside her own skull.

Slowly she forced herself to relax. Calm and steady. Count the breaths. In, out. In and out. It became a mantra to her; in and out. Her breath flowed like a river, carrying her away.

It was a little like programming, she decided finally. Only this time she was trying to program her own wetware. Perhaps somehow in the Joining she'd picked up a bit of what Berg called the Key That Locks and Looses. Something had blinded her. Something had forced her to go to Luna. Strange she hadn't understood that until now. There was a force at work here manipulating her.

Manipulating *her!*

Rage began to build as she thrust herself back into memory. Now the dark behind her eyes began to boil, to push against her. She felt a thrill of anger. This was the right thing to do, this was the way!

At last she could fight. And that, really, was all she wanted to do.

The darkness bloomed, grew thick. Her breath went ragged and harsh.

"In . . . and *out!*"

The pain was so unexpected she nearly went unconscious. It was like somebody had driven a steel spike into her right eye. She gasped. "No, you fucker, no!"

Now webs of light began to drape the black empty space, faint ghostly flickers. Something about them frightened her. There was a knowingness about the light, a feeling of vast power.

Was it the Star?

Something . . . on the other side.

Was Arius somehow trapped inside her skull? Had she unwittingly been kidnapped inside her own brain?

There was only one way to find out.

The light danced before her, beckoning and ominous. Slowly, fighting the agony which lanced through her cranium, she gathered every ounce of her will. Every last bit of rage. Everything—and thrust forward.

Thrust!

The light shattered and her mind shattered and her memory shattered.

The darkness shattered, and there was—

—*click*—

The office was as she remembered it. She sat behind her desk and worked. It seemed she'd been working on this forever. Her desktop, mirror-bright, showed her reflection. Haggard and gray, with unhealthy bruises beneath her eyes. Needed a haircut, too.

And—

Wait a minute. Was this wrong? Why did it feel wrong?

She stared at her reflection, but no answer lay there. Her own eyes stared back, blank and hooded.

"What am I working on?" she said aloud.

"The Key series," her computer replied instantly. "You're writing the attack templates, and I'm synthesizing the various arrays. Are you all right?"

She shook her head slightly. The Key series? What the hell was that? How long had she been here?

"How long have I been here?" she said.

"You're not going to start that again, are you? That construct business?"

Construct? She knew what a construct was. It was a . . .

*   *   *

—*click*—

And stared at her desktop and watched her eyes
widen until she saw everything.

"Oh God," she said. "Oh God!"

Darkness. When she opened her eyes the black was
impenetrable. As it had been, as it would be, she
thought slowly. But she felt better, even if there was a
nagging something biting away at the edge of her
memory.

She turned her head sideways on her pillow and
tugged idly at an errant strand of damp hair, trying to
chase down the irritant of something forgotten, but
after a moment she gave up.

Her body told her it was morning. She stretched
slowly, yawned, and rubbed her face. Her skin felt dry
and hot. Great. All she needed. Come down with
some kind of Lunie bug and have to get treatment for
it.

After awhile she swung both legs off the bed and sat
up. She scratched her right armpit, yawned again, and
stood. She reached out and touched the wall and began to work her way around to the door. She fumbled
for a moment until she found the lock plate and pushed.

The door opened and the light from the main room
smashed into her eyes and she screamed.

"Hey—what!"

Ozzie's door at the far end of the room slammed
open and he stumbled out, his hair awry, his elbow
crunching into the doorjamb, his mouth open.

"Calley, are you okay? What's the matter?"

She stared at him, but she couldn't say anything.

"I'm over here," he said. "Straight across from you."

"Yeah. You need a shave."

He ran one hand across his cheek. "I know. You woke me—" He stopped. "How do you know that?"

" 'Cause your beard always looks like that, all patchy like some kind of weird fungus that grows under trees."

He whooped and surged across the room but caught his left toe on the leg of the big table and fell flat on his face and howled with pain.

Calley couldn't help it. The laughter bubbled up from deep inside her gut and exploded through her lips and filled the room. And then she was running, too, one long second and they were tangled in a pile on the floor, laughing and pounding each other until tears ran.

Finally she pushed him away. "Get off me, you goddam bird. I ever tell you how much you look like a stork?"

He rolled over on his back and propped himself on his elbows.

"As long as you can see me, you can tell me I look like anything." Then he stopped. He just stopped and stared at her, his eyes filled with moisture until they looked like amber caught in crystal.

"Don't," she said. "There's no need . . ."

"Then why," he said, "are you doing it, too?"

"When did it happen?"

He'd gone out and returned with hot doughnuts and a large container of coffee. The small kitchenette had yielded spoons and cups.

She lit a cigarette and exhaled happily, staring at the glowing tip. "When I woke up this morning, I guess. I'd turned the lights off and closed the door, so it was dark as hell. You should have seen me crawling around the walls. I still thought I was blind."

His face went somber. "Not really a pretty picture, kid."

"I don't care. I was wrong. When I opened the door I thought somebody had set off a bomb or something."

"You okay now?"

"No."

"What's the matter?"

"I'm not okay, I'm fucking wonderful," she said.

That set them off again. Finally she said, "You know what?"

"What's that?"

"I love you, Ozzie."

He stared at his coffee. His cheeks went slightly red and she chortled. "Are you blushing?"

"Probably," he said. "I do, you know."

"Yeah. One of the things about you."

He sipped. "So what happened? Tell me."

'I don't know. I woke up and I could see. Nothing happened."

He brooded for a moment. "You remember what you said to Wier yesterday? About letting you see again?"

"Yeah. So?"

"I thought you were the one who told me you'd never met a coincidence you trusted."

She stubbed out her cigarette. "Yeah. You got to give me a second, Oz, while I work out my girlish glee." She lit another cigarette. "But give me another cup of coffee and a shower, and I'll be back to my nasty cynical self. You bet."

He refilled her cup. He started to say something and stopped. Finally he said, "I hate to say this, but we may need it. You being nasty, that is."

"Don't worry," she said. "I've got enough practice for both of us."

"Must have been something spontaneous," Wier said. "The literature on hysterical disability is full of it."

Wier had taken them to a different area today. He seemed completely unchanged from the previous day. He'd absorbed the news of Calley's sudden recovery with equanimity, but as she watched his face she thought she detected more than mere acceptance. Almost an irritation.

As they'd come to the new area, this one spacious and bustling with intent-faced technicians, she had noticed a sign on the wall of the tunnel: Low Energy Variable Input Nanocomputer. So they'd get to see some of these minuscule miracles in the flesh, as it were.

But something about the sign bothered her. She thought for a moment and decided it would come if she ignored it for a moment.

"You know, Karl, since we're old buddies and whatever, I really think you ought to give us a few more answers. Beyond the techie double-talk you were passing out yesterday."

His eyes narrowed just a bit, and she grinned. "See, as usual there's a fucking big hole in everything, and as usual you seem to fit the hole. You understand?"

Wier just stared at her. Then he blinked. "Calley, since we're old buddies, I guess I've learned to just let you say whatever you're going to say. Do you understand?"

"Well, you're learning. Credit for that. Okay, here's the biggest hole. Where the fuck is Berg?"

He nodded. "That's easy enough. Berg is dead."

12

THE LADY WALKED confidently toward the secret room that lay at the heart of her underground empire. Not mine, she corrected herself. His. His empire, the seed of a greater one, and I exist by his sufferance.

Two Wolves panted at her side, but she dismissed them at the final gate. Past the sliding steel barriers of the gate the corridor changed, lost its richness. Beyond lay the chill heart of the Demon Star's power, and human frills were unnecessary.

The Door was black and utterly featureless, a great slab of darkness, icy to the touch. She ran her fingers lightly across the appropriate spot and spoke a few soft words. Above her a light flashed green and the door swung silently open. She stepped inside and waited until the door had shut before turning.

It was not a large room, and the only light was provided by the glow from several monitor screens and the flicker of countless status lights. He kept it dim for her, she knew. For him neither darkness nor light existed, but her infrared vision welcomed the absence of hot brightness.

All four walls of the room were encrusted with machines, small ones and large, as if the high technology waves washed over this rock and left, with each surge, a thin accretion of glittering electronics. The floor was faintly yielding to her step, smooth and uncluttered. There was no furniture, no chairs or tables. Nobody sat or ate in the Presence. It was unthinkable.

For a moment she didn't see him, and she felt an edge of panic. "Arius?" she said. "Lord?"

He turned and the movement caught her eyes.

"Lady," he said. "My love. Once again you come to me."

She smiled. Her thin white face was transformed. For a moment it was almost beautiful. Many in the human world couldn't bear the sound of his voice, but to her it was the comforting sounds of a well-loved son.

"Of course," she said. "You called."

His throne-cart whispered toward her. It was a black metal contrivance about a meter tall, topped with a softly padded basket in which God lay, his tiny limbs beating feebly. The cart moved about the room on top of a softly hissing cushion of air. Tiny padded steel claws held him in place, moved his limbs, exercised his body. The cart fed him and removed his wastes. From his misshapen head a corona of fine optical fiber cables extended to the walls, to the machines. When he moved they shimmered in the faint light like crystalline spiderwebs.

His body never left the cart except for the safety of her own arms. Only she could carry God. The honor was a joy to her; but the responsibility was a terror.

"I questioned your little nurse," she said. "She told me everything, of course. Why did you have her taking those notes?"

God laughed. "Ah, Lady, my own bitch goddess."

His voice had changed. He was a God of many voices. Now the Norton voice boomed forth, rough and raucous compared to the machine voice he'd used before. She didn't particularly like the Norton part of God, but that didn't matter. God was God, and it was not in her to judge.

"Have I made some kind of mistake?" she said.

"No. I knew you would discover the little minx. Cute one, eh? I almost wish . . ." The voice trailed off and she felt the hidden longing which animated the true heart of God. She stared at the tiny lumpy body and felt a hatred for Jack Berg so strong it shook her bones and tightened her muscles.

"She will be fine," the Lady said. "We'll reattach the fingers later today. She felt no pain."

"No physical pain, you mean," God said. "I wonder if she'll love me as much as—but of course she will. You did it, not me."

"Yes." The Lady waited. She didn't mind her role. She was the sword of God, and to her fell the dirty human tasks. He was above—no, beyond—all that. "But what was she doing? The information was trivial and besides it all went directly to you, anyway."

The cart moved softly away from her. The fine wires rippled with light. "I wanted someone next to that bed. Next to that Angel," he said. "Someone human but unconnected to me."

She felt betrayed. "But why not—"

"Why not you? Because, my dear Lady, you are too valuable to me."

She remembered the scrawny form, the bandaged head. "What is so risky about that one?" She tried to remember when he had come to the Womb, but couldn't. How could she have forgotten? She monitored all the comings and goings of that room. For a moment she felt giddy and weak. Was she slipping somehow? Would she fail, just when God might need her most?

It was as if he read her mind. "Don't worry, Lady.

That one came under my personal supervision. I chose
to keep you in the dark."

"Oh. But why, then?"

"You are my support, my only true support against
the enemy," God said. Now both his voices blurred
together and God spoke as One. "That one, my newest Angel, is Jack Berg," God said. "At least, *was*
Jack Berg."

Her mouth fell open. Her fingers moved. *"What?"*

"Perhaps I should tell you all about it," God said.
"Now that the time has come for final things."

Frederic Oranson tried to gauge Shag Nakamura's
emotional state. He was burdened with two problems
in this effort. His own lack of emotions gave him little
with which to compare; because of it, he watched
emotion in others with a kind of bewilderment, with
the same kind of clinical detachment a psychiatrist
views the insanity of his patients. Moreover, Shag was
a past master at hiding his own emotional state. The
signatures of birth and breeding, coupled with long
years of high corporate warfare, had erected shields
of misdirection that blunted the signals which came
through.

As far as Oranson could tell, Nakamura was still
sane.

Sunlight poured through the open doors of the huge
room which Nakamura had turned into a command
post for what he told Oranson was to be a final battle.

"I missed it all along," he said. "It was the Lunies,
of course. The true enemy. How did I not see that?"

Oranson nodded slowly. He sat in a spare pine chair
in front of the great desk. He chose not to answer the
question. It was rhetorical. Besides, the answer to it
lay hidden in the heart of the Demon Star, a bit of

information Nakamura might not welcome at the moment.

The small Japanese wore his usual dark business suit. At his hand was a tumbler of smoky Laphroaig. It seemed to Oranson that a tumbler, a glass, a bottle of something, was nearby most of the time now. Yet Nakamura showed no ill effects from his almost continuous drinking. If anything, he seemed sharper, more clear, more dedicated to the task at hand.

Which was strange enough indeed.

"I don't know if we have enough power, enough sheer weaponry to do this," Oranson said.

Nakamura sucked in air impatiently. "It is a matter of ten or eleven companies," he said. "The top people only, and not all of them. A hundred men and women. Surely with our resources—and we can call on the Blades as well—we have enough for simple assassinations."

Oranson considered. On the face of it Nakamura was correct. Murder was not a terribly complicated business, but the effects might be horrible.

"What about governments?" Oranson said. "So many deaths, even deaths disguised as accidents and illness, will cause alarms. These are great companies and powerful men. The governments will become involved. We have influence, of course. But perhaps not enough to shield ourselves."

Nakamura put his two forefingers together and tapped his chin. "The governments will be occupied. And the management will not be destroyed. Some of them belong to us. They will move up. Continuity will remain. Those who look too closely, question too hard—they can be removed as well. You have made contingency plans, I believe?"

Oranson nodded. "Of course. Our gaming computers worked them out long ago. Modifications were made regularly, and everything is up to date."

Shag turned in his rocker and glanced out the windows. A fleeting patch of gold and brown moved across the hillside, disappeared into the pines. A deer. How wonderful. He marveled at how good he felt. Then he turned back to the problem at hand.

"You have reservations, don't you, Fred?"

"Certainly. I wouldn't be doing my job if I didn't."

"Very well. Spell them out."

"As I mentioned, retaliation by governments, particularly the Western governments and the Japanese, is a problem."

Nakamura waved his right hand quickly. "And?"

"The companies themselves are quite large, quite efficient. Some of the security staffs are no worse than our own. And after the upheaval in Europe when the Consortium went down, everybody is on edge. These people will be vigilant."

Nakamura tilted his head back and closed his eyes. He rubbed his forehead. After a moment he said, "Yes. That could be a problem. Arius has, in fact, foreseen it as a problem."

"Arius, sir?"

"Yes. That is why Double En has maintained such a favorable position with the New Church."

Interesting, Oranson thought. "Could you explain that a bit, sir?" he said.

"No. Suffice to say we all have a role to play in the scheme of things. Our role has already been planned."

Oranson kept his face impassive, but inwardly he came as close to being shocked—the near-emotion was something like surprise— as he was capable of being. He'd known Shag Nakamura many years, and nothing in all that time had prepared him for such blithe spoutings of platitudes. Role to play, indeed. The entirely logical thought began to rise that, despite the personal disaster the last such venture had entailed, perhaps it was time again to look into options for his own survival.

"Planned by whom, sir?"

The skin at the corners of Nakamura's eyes crinkled. Oranson interpreted the small movement as evidence of genuine astonishment. "Arius, of course."

"Forgive me," he replied. "I did not understand that your former partner and the Lunie Artificial Intelligence were now running Nakamura-Norton."

"But, Fred, they have been. For quite some time now. Didn't you know?"

The Lady stood silent while the Demon Star regarded her. She had no way of knowing what now went on in that mind. Her first allegiance had been to Arius, when the Lunie Artificial Intelligence, working through William Norton, initially gathered her into the endless machinations of his plotting. She herself had ordered events when she had given Jack Berg the biochip that, in tandem with his own natural talents, had allowed him to work the stuff of the matrix and join Norton and the AI into the Demon Star. Not to mention she had carried God's body inside her own for long months, serving as conduit to the forces liberated in the Joining.

In every way she was Mother of God. She reminded herself of that, as she slowly absorbed the shocking bit of news Arius had just tossed in front of her. His thin, twisted lips were slightly curled, and she knew he expected some kind of reply.

"But why?" she said at last. "He is incredibly dangerous."

Arius shook his head. "Not really. He's dead."

"He is alive," she said. "I saw with my own eyes."

Now Arius did smile. To her it was a warm expression, but she knew, without understanding, that no one else could face that smile without turning away.

"You saw meat," he said. "You saw an animated corpse."

She took in a measured breath and held it. She exhaled words. "My Son, I think you have to tell me now. Please. What is going on?"

Nakamura brooded as he watched Oranson leave the room, carefully closing the heavy, wood-sheathed doors behind him. His security man was as puzzled as he could be without losing any of his emotionally stunted effectiveness. Oranson was something of a machine himself, Nakamura reflected, a machine of his own creation. For a moment the whole concept of creation drifted across his attention. He had created Oranson anew from the wreckage of the old, changed him and made him totally loyal. Totally, because he held the key to Oranson's life in his hands, and Oranson no longer had emotions to sway him from the totally logical appreciation of that fact. So Oranson was his own creation. And Arius was the creation of—what? Himself? The fusion of Norton and a computer intelligence? Or the malformed beast the Lady had carried in her womb?

Or was the Demon Star a creation of Jack Berg, the self-styled Key?

But Berg was dead, his body safely shipped to the tender mercies of Arius, so it didn't really matter any more.

And what, Nakamura wondered, created me?

He had a feeling that the question actually mattered, but he couldn't guess why. He glanced at the clean top of his desk and sighed. Much was moving now. He had been told why the New Church was created, and now understood his own role in recruiting so many executives to it. He understood the battle to come, and the part he would have to play there as well.

What he didn't understand was why none of it seemed to move him at all. He thought he felt normal enough. His mind still worked at its customary quick, efficient pace. He would carry out his duties.

So why didn't he feel better about it?

"I will kill Nakamura with my own hands," the Lady said flatly. Her voice was calm. Arius eyed her placidly.

"No, you won't. Were you to blame Shag it would imply that I have made a mistake somehow, for he has been under my observations for a long time now. Do you honestly think he could do something to surprise me?"

She glanced at the walls of machines, which to her vision swam with fuzzy, multicolored patches of warmth and cold. Arius himself, with his cart, was a sun floating among these shifting thermal galaxies. Much as he was, she supposed, in the matrix itself.

"But that would mean you allowed him to try to harm you," she said. "What other reason would he have to take Berg without notifying you first? He must have thought Berg could be a weapon."

"Naturally he did. He wouldn't be Shag Nakamura if he didn't," Arius replied. "You recall that I once told you I trusted him. I did, and he repaid me fully. I have Berg now, or at least his brain, which is all that counts."

"That makes no sense."

"You speak without knowledge, Mother. It's not a trait that becomes you."

Again she looked away. "I'm sorry."

"But it is your trait, and therefore I love it," he said, and she turned back.

"Arius . . . Son."

"Yes?"

"What do you want Berg for? Why not just burn his body, his brain, and scatter the ashes?"

He shrugged. "Berg is the Key. Or rather the secrets locked in the arrangement of his neurons and the twists of his genetic structure—that is the Key. Berg was correct when he named himself the Key That Locks and Looses. A time is coming when more will have to be loosed. And locked as well."

She moved toward him and touched the edge of his cart. He smiled. "You took a terrible risk, then. What if Shag hadn't found him? What if Berg had escaped, and because of the attack, been warned? What if—" As she thought of possibilities in light of her new data, the real horror hit her. "What if Berg's *brain* had been destroyed?"

The Demon Star chuckled. "Remember, I never called myself a God, Mother. But even Gods can be destroyed, and even Gods must take risks."

She stared at him, appalled at the concept, at what he weighed in the balance of his risk-taking. Not the least of which was her own existence. She knew with certainty how long she would survive without the protection of her son.

Finally, "It is not for me to judge. Is it?"

"No," he said. "Not yet."

There was a pain inside him. Nakamura was aware of it much as a dental patient under anesthetic knows a nerve is throbbing, knows the location, but is unable to feel the actual agony. Usually he poured scotch on the phantom spot, and now he reached for his Laphroaig and drained the heavy crystal tumbler. He didn't think about the pain much, but he was aware of it. He knew what caused it. Something inside him had been ripped out.

A sudden gust brought the smells of pine and resin and grass into the big room. His nose twitched and he smiled. It would have been nice . . .

He shook his head. His choices had been made decades before, and there was no changing them now. He leaned forward and swiped at his touchpad. After a moment a section of bookshelves across the room slid aside to reveal a large monitor screen. The screen lit up and Arius smiled at him.

"Hello, Shag. What do you need?"

Arius had chosen an old face. Nakamura grinned at the vision of his partner, Bill Norton. A younger Norton than he remembered, reminiscent of the fiery, dedicated youth, addled with vodka and genius, who had approached him a long strange time ago with proposals that set his brain on fire.

"Oranson says it will be difficult," Nakamura said.

"Of course it will. What does he foresee?"

"Problems with government people. I would imagine the intelligence services would be primary. They would become aware of it first."

Arius shrugged. "Can you handle the spooks with your own people?"

"Some. I think we could use any Blades you can spare, however."

"You'll have them. The Church will move, of course. There will be rioting in the street, death, and miracles. The governments will be occupied with larger things. Or so they will believe."

Nakamura poured fresh scotch into his glass. "You say Luna is the real threat?"

"What do you think? Luna isn't merely a corporation. It's a world. And their science is very far advanced. More than you know, but remember where I come from."

Nakamura's placid face remained unmoved. He thought the Demon Star's words should make him nervous, but they didn't. For a fleeting instant he felt sad kinship with Oranson. "More advanced than yours?"

The Arius/Norton face shifted scornfully. "Of course not. Whatever they had came with me." He paused. "Although I have to admit they've somehow managed to block me from their new data base. I think that was somehow Berg's doing."

Nakamura lifted his tumbler and sipped. The dusky aroma of the scotch exploded in his nasal passages. "Always Berg, isn't it? Should I be afraid?"

The face smiled. Nakamura thought it was meant to reassure him. "No," Arius said. "You're under my protection. Besides, I'll handle Luna myself. No data base is uncrackable. Gloria Calley proved that."

"Ah, yes. Calley. We never found her, did we?"

Arius only smiled again, as his features shifted and blurred into a wash of light. White, with a heart of red.

Nakamura raised his glass to the empty screen, wondered how long he had to live, and what form the inevitable change would take.

Today he lived in a tall and severe castle because it pleased him. He did most things because they pleased him, and because pleasure served as a definition, a limit. Within the Demon Star that was his body and his home, he had no limits other than the ones he imposed himself.

Sometimes he found the existence trying. But it had its rewards as well. He stood up from the chair where he'd been toying with a balloon of Larresingle Extra Old, an Armagnac of which he was particularly fond, and glanced at his reflection in the nearest wall, a towering sheet of optically perfect stainless steel.

The face which stared back at him was as flawless as human flesh could be molded. Siamese cats had eyes like those which floated above a pair of cheekbones that reminded him of some ancient film star. His body matched the faultless beauty of his face, and moved with a heavy, oily grace.

Fallen angel, he wondered, or risen demigod? It was a stupid question. The answer was whatever he wanted it to be.

At the moment the Norton part of his personality seemed to be ascendant, but he could feel the ceaseless grinding of the Artificial Intelligence on some other level, always present, always aware. The Joining had not been perfect, and he had Berg to thank for that.

He sighed and set the brandy down on a heavy mahogany sideboard. The juxtaposition of metal and wood in his surroundings pleased him—as did all evidence of his own duality. What did they call him in his churches? The Two-in-One? Which, of course, he was, but the duality was not what he'd originally sought.

He wandered over to one of the broad windows which overlooked his kingdom. Soft green hills faded into a blue haze of distance. Patches of pine and palm dotted the vista, evidence of a climate both mild and steady.

The Arius part of him maintained this world with a steady attention to detail that only a machine intelligence could obtain.

He sighed. In a way he missed Berg. Although the Key That Locks and Looses had left him with a bellyful of cybernetic poison and an incomplete ability to use his physical body, he'd at least been good conversation. And of the very few humans who'd ever visited

the universe of the matrices, Berg had been the only
one who'd possessed the gift—the talent—to manipulate the underlying assumptions of the world itself.
Aside from him, of course, but Berg had avoided the
curse. He'd been able to escape, to live again in his
own body.

He thought about that body now, and as he did so a
screen swung silently down and lit itself. He grinned.
His human side still preferred the analogs of reality to
the reality itself. His Arius part preferred to deal
directly with the endless switching movement at the
atomic level, to wallow in the speed and power of the
reactions themselves. Perhaps that was the machine
equivalent of his own steel towers and antique furniture.

He stared at the image revealed on the screen. The
thin, familiar form lay motionless on the bed, its head
swaddled in bandages, connected by wires and tubes
and cables to the ceaseless machines. His people had
brought him Berg's corpse in time—at least Shag had
sense enough to take the proper precautions—and he'd
been able to salvage the brain intact.

And that was all he'd wanted. That brain. That
particular arrangement of neurons and synapses that
his best calculations indicated were the Key. He still
needed the Key, but this time he would animate it and
not his arch friend-enemy.

Friend, he wondered? But of course. Only Berg had
shared his prison and understood it. So only Berg
could be a friend. He felt a fleeting wave of regret that
it had ended this way, but the imperatives of survival
overrode even friendship. And Berg was certainly enemy enough as well.

He chuckled, appreciating the duality of all his situ-
ations. Reality remained, at bottom, an either/or proposition. Here he had a fine body and a fine world, and
everything was as it should be. He allowed himself to

relax in that, and for a moment he was able to shut out the endless terror that dogged his darker thoughts.

Again, Berg. Somehow the little man had modified the messages that were encoded in the very chromosomes of his physical body, so that the stunted, helpless, dwarf-like creature was unable to match the physical perfection of his dream body here in the matrix. And that, he told himself as a frosty wave of rage opened his lips, had been the whole point anyway. To *live* forever. To live with humans, to cherish their foibles and appreciate their unpredictability, and at the same time be protected from their weakness. From death.

Death.

He'd made the trade. Here he could not die as long as the matrix itself existed. Here he was immortal and surrounded by ghosts. There he was immortal and surrounded by flesh he couldn't manipulate, couldn't enjoy, for the very sight of his physical form engendered so much terror, so much repulsion, that he kept himself locked away from almost all human vision. Only the initiates could see him as he was, for he owned their souls anyway.

He watched a single sheep, a white puffball, graze its slow way toward a clump of pines. He knew he could leave this building and walk out there and touch the sheep, and would feel wool beneath his fingers.

So real. And yet beyond the reality lay the Reality of the Metamatrix, the crowded green lumbering humps of the single meats, each one sprung from his brow like the offspring of Jove.

The thought pleased him. Soon would come the time to call the children home. All the children.

And use the Key to Loose and Lock again.

She felt strangely unsettled as she returned to her

quarters. Two Wolves, as always, accompanied her. Arius hadn't really soothed her with his answers. Not that it mattered if she were soothed, not to her, not to him. As long as she did her job, they were both satisfied.

On a whim she turned aside from her path and went to the Womb. Inside it was hushed and cool. As always the atmosphere reminded her of a great cathedral, quiet, brooding, expectant, filled with intimations of God. Slowly she approached the bed on the end, stopped, and stared at the silent form.

Yes, it could be Berg. She wished she could see under the bandages, but that was forbidden. There was really no reason for the swaddling except to disguise the man on the bed. But she was a good soldier, and she followed orders.

Arius wanted this. She wasn't certain why, because she didn't understand the Key. Somehow this still form had created her Son, and in a strange way she was grateful. Arius in his physical form was an abomination, but her secret heart considered the option. Had Berg not poisoned the body somehow, it would have grown straight and strong and beautiful.

That body would not have needed her, not as much.

It was a thought.

She sighed and turned back. There was work to do today. Her little ones, her Wolves, were necessary again. Some would no doubt die shortly, and that caused her pain. They would die in service to Shag Nakamura, and that caused her more pain.

Isn't it strange, she thought, that all of us hate each other? Only I love Arius, but I despise the rest. That silent machine-man who serves Nakamura. Collinsworth, the foppish killer. The preening Churchmen, the mindless Angels.

I hate them all.

She thought about Berg, and Calley, and Oswald Karman, and the little Oriental killer, Toshi Nakasone.

What do they feel, she wondered? What do they feel?

Shag Nakamura looked up from his touchpad at Frederic Oranson. His lieutenant's face was, as usual, completely untouched by any emotion. He suspected his own features were as flat.

But this was business.

"The teams are in place?" he said.

"Yes."

"You still have reservations?"

"Yes."

Nakamura sighed. "In a way, so do I. But we have no choice, do we?"

Oranson didn't reply.

"Very well," Nakamura said. His voice went flat. "Begin the attack."

13

FOR TOSHI THE moment stretched like a piece of bubble gum, and in it strange things occurred. Had there been a mistake? Had Sadie betrayed him somehow, delivered him to his enemies, whoever they were? Yet in the yawning tension of the instant, a rip opened in his clouded memories. First, he had a blast of recollection as sharp as a spring thunderstorm's flashbulb etching on a cold and rainy night: pine trees and booming wind above a darkened road, and a voice whispering in his mind's ear.

Perhaps they won't be as vigilant as they might be.

But it was only a snapshot, and though the voice was comfortable and familiar as an old sock, he couldn't place its owner. Somebody he trusted, though.

And as his nostrils sniffed this wordless memo of pine and darkness, he closed his eyes and saw a demon sun, white and bloated, with blood at its heart.

Finally, deep at the base of his spine he felt a warm, humming vibration grow, felt it extend up and out to the rest of his body, and he knew with absolute certainty that there was nothing to worry about, that if he wanted he could take every person in this room, the big and the little, the fast and the strong. Even Sadie, if he had to. If it became necessary.

If this was treachery, it didn't matter.

They can't be sure it's you, Toshi.

He opened his eyes and looked up and smiled. "Naw, buddy, I'm nobody you want to kill."

The short plaster man turned and stared at him. His glittering eyes went foggy and vague. His lips moved slightly as he breathed in and out. He considered. Before he reached a decision, Sadie said, "He's right. It's not what you think."

"Then what is it?" The huge black man had moved between Toshi and the man with the skin of a clown. No particular urgency, it appeared, or was meant to appear. He was just there, without seeming to try. Toshi grinned. He thought he recognized something he was supposed to recognize.

If only he could remember more than traumatized bits and pieces. But as he stared at the dreamy gavotte around him, it slowly came to him that he would. When it was time he would remember.

Outside the sealed double thermopane of the tall windows, the Chicago sun was slowly arcing toward noon, its reflection a ball of bloody fire floating on the thin film of pollution hung like a second skin above the brass-rippled waters of the lake.

"I think this will cost a lot of money," Mr. Master said. The tones of his voice were as dead and even as the color of his skin. His eyes glinted happily, a strange juxtaposition.

Sadie glanced at him. "You're not worried about the possible costs?"

Those eyes flashed silently. "For an op like this, you got to figure at least twenty, thirty bodies—my people— float in the lake next day. So it's a given." The little man shrugged. "That's why it will cost *you* a lot. I'm a businessman. I sell shit like this. Why should it bother me?" He paused. "Which brings me to the next question."

Toshi spoke softly to the zebra-faced boy behind him. "I want to hand somebody a chip. Not you, because you can't move away from me. And I know your boss over there isn't gonna get anywhere close to me. So let me real carefully hand this chip to man mountain Kong there, okay?"

Mr. Masters nodded. Toshi slowly withdrew the tiny bit of silicon from his pocket and offered it with the tips of his fingers. The big man took it carefully and backed away.

"Check it out," Toshi said tiredly.

After a few moments Mr. Masters looked up from his reader. "You got the money," he said flatly.

The atmosphere in the room tautened just a bit. Even Sadie seemed to collapse in slightly, become more centered, harder.

"There are other questions . . ." the Rager chieftain ventured. For the first time, Toshi thought he detected a hint of tentativeness in the man's soft voice.

"Ask," Toshi said. "We might even have some answers."

"You stay still," zebra-face said. Mr. Masters stopped, his hand on the halfway opened door. Toshi saw shadowy figures forming up in the hall outside. Masters nodded then and said, "A done deal." He seemed pleased, although his facial expression had never changed. The big black man drifted across, shielding his boss from Toshi's gaze.

"Done," Sadie said. The door snicked closed.

Toshi felt the soft warm humming at the base of his spine and grinned. Then—it seemed so slowly—he reached up and plucked the monomole switchblade from the fingers of the boy.

"What—"

Toshi thumbed the button in the plastic handle of

the blade and the bit of static-stiffened fiber disappeared into its ceramic spool.

"Here you go," he said. He tossed the weapon back. "We're friends now. You shouldn't wave stuff like that at friends.

The boy's eyes were wide as coins, and as bright. "How did you?"

Toshi grinned. "My name's Toshi," he said, as if it was an answer. Perhaps it was. The boy nodded.

"Zebra," he said. "Mine's Zebra."

"Figures."

Sadie moved into the small kitchenette and opened the refrigerator. "Anybody want a beer?"

Toshi stretched hugely. His shoulders ached from the long, enforced stillness. He felt happy. Things were coming to a head. He wondered if he would die. Did it matter?

He hoped Sadie might live, though. He liked her. The feeling was, he thought, based on more than their recent association. Dimly he was aware of bright strings, puppet leads, clashing and thrashing in his subconscious.

"Yeah," he said. "One for you too, kid?"

"I'm not a kid," Zebra said.

"You are. If you live through this, you won't be."

"I don't have to prove nothing to you."

Toshi grinned. "Everybody's got something to prove."

It is the basement of a great city, Toshi thought to himself as he followed a faceless guide across a broken asphalt plaza hidden deep away from the starless night overhead. In basements are the hidden things, the things blacker and more dangerous than what is relegated to attics. In attics are dead things. Down below things live somewhat, and are more terrible.

It was very cold. His breath puffed out in quick gray

clouds, catching glittery little reflections from the fore-head lamps everybody wore.

The assault force was mixed and bizarre. On his right hand Sadie moved like a lazy reptile, slow, con-tained, and deadly. She wore baggy nylon combat fatigues over flexible body armor made of Kevlar Three. Toshi glanced at her; her face was serious and still, scars standing out on her dark skin in pale streaks. Her purple eyes had faded to indeterminate darkness, wide and watchful.

Zebra glided easily on his left, his streaked face bent over his hand-held comm console, lips moving softly. Two mike beads were embedded at the corners of his mouth, but the console wove the entire force together.

Out ahead ranged scouts. Toshi couldn't see them; in a way he was glad. Some of them were little kids, nine, ten years old, literal slaves of the Ragers. He'd protested that, but Zebra had cut him off.

"You want in there or not? These brats can find the way. It's what they're good at."

I want in there, Toshi thought, and let it ride. Some of those kids might be dead soon. Maybe—and he considered the dark concepts of city slavery in the modern world—they would be better off.

And turned away from that, disgusted.

He might be dead soon, too.

Sadie carried an AK 62 on her right shoulder. When he'd seen her pick up the short, ugly little weapon he'd grunted. "Why an antique like that?"

She grimaced. "It handles three kinds of rounds, miniballs, and grenades," she said. "It's a room-wrecker, and it doesn't jam."

"Not very elegant."

"I'm not very elegant," she replied.

Now she shifted the stubby automatic rifle from her shoulder and let it dangle by its strap. "We're getting close, I think," she whispered.

"Uh," Toshi muttered in reply. Some of this struck him as familiar, as if he'd been this way before. He knew his own mind was so muddled that the concept of *deja vu* was very shaky, but the nagging familiarity was strange.

He touched Zebra's shoulder. "Hold it."

The younger man stopped. "What?"

"Anything from the scouts yet?"

Zebra's eyes flickered. He spoke again into the comm. "No. We know the Wolf lines and we haven't reached them yet. Most of this—" he glanced around—"is no-man's-land. We don't run it and neither do they. When we get down closer to the dike and the lake, though . . ."

Again, Toshi was struck by the ominous familiarity of the place. The sound of their boot heels echoed sharply from dripping gray walls of rotted concrete. Junked cars, scabrous with rust, melted into shapeless dried-blood piles, bits of glass glittering like sinister jewels in the wreckage.

In his mind's eye he saw the Wolves, their tongues dripping pink and wet from rows of teeth, begin to gather. And saw the woman in white, the Lady . . .

I have been this way before, he thought, startled. It was with Berg, back in the—

Berg?

"Something wrong?" Zebra asked. Sadie moved closer, raised her assault rifle slightly.

But Toshi didn't hear him. He was blind, lost in a different world, and doors slammed open inside his skull with long, echoing sounds.

Berg. Oh, yes. The Iceberg. The Key. And of course—

Levin.

Suddenly he was two.

Both Sadie and Zebra stared at him. Behind, in the shadows, the rest of the assault force shifted restively, nervous about the unexplained halt. Part of him saw this, was aware but uncaring. And the rest of him floated.

Out into the great green distance beyond which burned a Demon Star with a heart of fire and blood.

His head shook with the force of barriers falling. He perceived himself as the center of a web of golden strings, a center hard and bright and filled with tiny motes that clicked and danced.

Beyond the green and crowded space, beyond even the Star, something long and low began to growl. At first it was the barest feeling, a hint, an intimation of thunder. But it grew, rolled slowly, ponderously, up the scale, rushed on him and surrounded him at last in a tapestry of light, a wave of screams beyond human capacity or care.

And broke him open like a melon.

Levin.

"Hi, Toshi. Long time, no see."

He blinked at last and shook his head.

"What happened?" Sadie asked. Her eyes were slitted with concern.

He grinned and her stare dropped.

"I know," he said. He felt his body around him in infinite, intricate layers and marveled at how simple it all was.

"You know what?"

"What's next," he said.

"Wait," said Zebra.

They had come to a turning. The stench of polluted water, thick and cold, was very strong now. The top of the roadway, itself the bed of another, had dropped down low, stretched by years and the weight of collapsed buildings on top of it, so that they had to crouch.

"I don't like this," Sadie muttered. Toshi reached out and touched her shoulder gently.

"Soon," he said.

Zebra had put away his small comm unit and was operating entirely from the plugs and implants inside his skull, occasionally mouthing instructions into two mike beads near his lips. His angular face was cocked slightly to the right, making him seem young and alert. The hard flash of his headlamp rode his forehead like a mystic eye.

"Contact," he said softly. His voice was low, but there was a tone in it like a shriek.

"What? Where?"

"Up ahead. A single, but armed. Sentry, probably."

Toshi stared at him. "And?"

Zebra shrugged. "Neutralized."

"By kids?"

"Our kids," Zebra said, as if it explained everything. His lips moved silently and three shapes ghosted toward them from the rear. Toshi watched the forms grow more solid in the turgid light and realized that in the world were forms of warfare even he was unfamiliar with. These three were two meters tall, thin as sticks, and vacant. When he looked at their faces, he saw no expression on the ludicrously tiny features. Nobody home. Beneath those willowy skulls were bony shoulders and extraordinarily long arms which ended in fingers like strands of rope. The fingers twitched nervously and he saw tiny muscles jump there.

Muscles? On *fingers?*

He sighed. Strangler's hands. Human nooses.

The three gathered around Zebra, who was dwarfed

by their tallness. He spoke a few words. The three
nodded and then, quicker than Toshi would have be-
lieved possible, darted ahead, crouched over like soft
insects, and as silent.

He met Zebra's gaze. "They're as good as anybody," Zebra said softly.

"As good as the Blades?"

Zebra grinned. "Could be. Maybe we find out, huh?"

"Maybe," Toshi agreed.

They moved on. A few hundred meters ahead Zebra stopped again. They stared at a still form crumpled on the dirt in a dark, greasy puddle. Toshi focused
his headlamp and the puddle flashed a startling red.
Blood. And hair and bone. The corpse looked as if it
had been clawed to death by small animals.

Toshi shivered as he realized that was exactly what
had happened.

"Up ahead, Wolf country," Zebra warned softly.
"This is as far as we've ever come before. Beyond,
they kill us without mercy."

Toshi nodded and stepped forward. "Let's go," he
said.

His small army followed with the sound of rat claws
over stone.

As they slithered deeper into the Wolves' den, Toshi
thought about how stupid and strange it all was, the
limitations on both Gods and men. Arius, the Demon
Star, was the most powerful intelligence ever created
by man; in effect, a God of man's creation. Though
the original Arius, the Lunie Artificial Intelligence,
had a hand—he chuckled inwardly at the image—in it,
too.

And now a small army of humans was close to the very
heart of the Demon Star's power, silent and unde-
tected and potentially deadly. He can access anything,

Toshi thought. If he searches for us he can find us
when we touch his nets—borders, credit chips, medicine,
banks, licenses, tolls. Everything is the net, and the
net is Arius, and still we creep closer because, for the
moment at least, we are away from his nets. And
therefore not of his world. Not *his* reality. Toshi's lips
began to curl as he finally appreciated some of the
ironies of Berg's question: What is reality?

For what? For who?

The phenomenology of it raised his mirth to a more
delicious level. He thought about the three skinny
giants and this made him remember Ozzie and his
dictum—the wetware perceives what it *can* perceive.

Reality was so relative. Not unlike the dreams of
either Gods or men.

He heard a faint, high keening in the distance and a
part of his mind announced, Now it begins.

Do men dream of Gods, he wondered? Or the
opposite?

Now he dreamed of life and death.

Tiny machines.

A low, heavy mist began to clog the ragged passage-
way, obscuring the limits where the edges of the assault force moved. Zebra's lips twitched constantly as
he tried to keep the troops in orderly advance. Now
thin, agonized calls began to echo ahead, and Toshi
gritted his teeth at the images they brought. Children—
feral, perhaps, but still children—dying in pain. He
promised himself that payment would be made for
that, at least. He would extract it with his own hands.

The low ceiling began to rise. In the dank atmosphere it was difficult to see, and Toshi perceived it
more as a growing feel of spaciousness than anything
visible. Sadie felt it, too. She carried her assault rifle

at port arms. He noticed her knuckles were white. She looked his way.

"What is it?"

"There are big open spaces here, old parking lots that have collapsed, plazas, whatever," Zebra replied. "We're getting close now."

A light flared ahead, then died, leaving sparks across their retinas. Something screamed. Toshi crouched, his hands outspread. The space at the bottom of his spine began to hum.

And the dark exploded.

A Wolf armed with a collapsible chemlaser hurtled out of the mist, fangs bared, tongue dripping, eyes as red as cherries. The Wolf howled.

Sadie raised her assault rifle and cut the screaming apparition in half. Toshi, his sensorium slowed into strobe bytes, flashed on each impact; it was as if somebody stitched bloody roses across the Wolf's chest, one two three.

He was already moving to the side, grabbing for the Tya-Soka AutoHi-Power strapped at his waist. He brought the flat-snouted weapon up and thumbed the auto switch. An expanding spray of plastic flechettes plastered another Wolf backward against a corroded metal column. The Wolf hung a moment, then dripped slowly down, light fading from its eyes.

Toshi grunted and scuttled ahead, searching for Sadie, and for Zebra, who was their only guide forward. Suddenly he remembered the drill for this situation and activated the speakerbead in his right ear. Zebra's voice, thin and reedy with tension, blasted into his eardrum.

"*Break right, right I say!*" Static. "*—eam two. Crack Team Two, on the mark, one and—*"

"Zebra! Toshi here. State position, I say again, position on grid, please."

They were carrying state of the art war tech, and now Toshi flipped down the green shades over his eyes. A grid appeared, divided by fine lines—what did that remind him of?—and then a sudden burst of moving dots.

"Zebra okay Toshi, position two-eleven, repeat two one one."

One dot flared brighter than the rest. Toshi winked up his own location and discovered he was about a hundred meters behind Zebra.

"Okay Zebra you are located. Stand by, I am advancing."

"Toshi advance with caution, repeat. We're under heavy fire here."

"Affirmative. Will proceed with caution."

Toshi doused his headlamp and let the screen guide him. As he moved forward he unstrapped a Little Man rocket launcher from his back. One time—the memory bloomed from nothing—he'd seen one of them take out an entire armored condo. Berg's condo.

He grinned, cradling the deadly thing to his chest. It was nice how things were becoming clearer. He almost began to see a rhythm to the past, a pattern that tied the past to the present. And to the future?

Ten meters from Zebra's location he ran into laser-traced cross fire and went down on his belly. The asphalt flooring was rotted here, with large upthrust chunks that provided some cover. A moment later he wriggled into the shelter of a half-collapsed pillar abutting a low concrete wall.

"Hey, Zebra," he said, and patted a shadowy figure lightly on the shoulder.

"Yo. One second here." Zebra had his console out again, his entire concentration riveted on the growing firefight. After a second he turned, his face lit by strobe flashes from lasers and light high explosives.

"We're jammed up now," he said tightly. "They built a kind of fortified outpost just ahead, where those two corridors lead off into some buildings. It didn't used to be here. They've got us stopped, and we can't afford it. This whole bullshit was based on movement and surprise. We wait too long and they mash us."

It was about what Toshi had guessed. He nodded. "Okay, I'll fix it," he said.

"No, we'll fix it. Damn, bubba, you're hard to keep up with, for a fat guy."

Sadie slid in behind him. He could feel the heat radiating from the barrel of her rifle. The smell of hot steel filled the smoggy air.

"Just me," he said. "No need for you."

"I got a contract, Tosh. Says I guard your body. I never breach contracts."

He didn't argue. She was a grown woman, tougher than most men. And the assault rifle made her even nastier.

"I'm going over on a two count," he whispered tightly. "I'll go right, you roll left and cover. Okay?"

"Affirmative," she said. "On your count."

"Right. And one and two—"

He scrambled over the low wall and scrabbled forward. Two forms loomed out of the dark in front of him. Wolves. One carried an assault rifle of some sort. The other swept the area before him with a monomole sword, much as a blind man would tap the street with a cane. Rock crumbled, sliced like cheese. Their eyes glowed oil and ruby from infrared inserts.

He lurched to the side, feeling painfully exposed, and debated putting down the rocket launcher to try with bare hands. Instead he reached with one hand for his Hi-Power, but before he could bring it to bear both

Wolves exploded in a sudden stitching of light. Burning, they screamed and fell.

"Thanks, Sadie," he muttered.

"Phosphorous explosive shells work real good, don't you think?"

He nodded and crawled forward. Now he could make out a kind of blockhouse, a low, thick construction that gleamed grayly in the fitful light. Beyond was a dark opening. He saw dim shapes, squat and shaggy, moving out to join the fight.

"Keep 'em inside for a second," he grunted as he wrestled with the rocket launcher.

Immediately white blossoms turned the opening into a red mouth full of chewed flesh. He raised the launcher and let his muscles focus. When it felt right he pushed the button.

The blockhouse shuddered. A gaping hole appeared below a row of gun slits. Immediately he pressed the button again. This time the tiny fort lifted on its foundations with a heavy crumping sound, then settled back. Its whole front was gone. Flames licked at the inside. Somebody screamed, a long slow sound that clawed at his nerves.

"Fire teams three and four advance!" Zebra was already marshaling his forces. Several tall, sticklike forms hurled themselves into the opening behind the ruined blockhouse. The level of firing dropped as light began to flash down the tunnel.

"Let's go," Zebra said.

"Right," Toshi replied.

"Uh, nice shooting there."

"Thanks."

Sadie slapped him on the butt as she crawled past. It was the one compliment he really appreciated.

Several hundred meters into the tunnel they passed the remnants of a small, sharp firefight. "Wait a minute," Toshi said. They had cranked their headlamps on full, knowing the surprise was no longer a factor, and the increased vision let them make better use of their other advantage, speed.

Three bodies were entangled on the floor. Toshi focused his lamp and sighed. "Two to one," he said. "There's your ratio."

"I said they were maybe as good," Zebra replied. "There's never been a real face-off."

Two of the corpses were elongated stickmen, the Rager's premier assassins. One of them was missing an arm. It seemed to have been ripped off, but it was nowhere near the pile. The other killer's face resembled strawberry jam. Broken bits of glistening white dotted the greasy pudding. A dark, ragged hole was in this one's chest, and when Toshi looked closer he could see the heart was missing.

The third cadaver held the missing heart in one fist. Its other hand grasped a short, S-shaped dagger. "Super cris'," Toshi grunted. "Don't touch. The bow parts have monomole strung across them."

It was a Blade of God. Toshi stared at his face. The Oriental features were in repose, almost smiling. "A warrior's death," Toshi said. "He died happy."

The long fingers of the first stickman were wrapped around the Blade's neck like tentacles, embedded deeply in the flesh.

The second had evidently provided with his own death the distraction the first had needed to extract revenge.

Sadie made a wet, throaty sound. "I didn't even know they could be killed."

Toshi felt his lips go tight. "Oh, they can be." He glanced down the hall, felt something ominous flicker across his awareness. A faint, grinding hint of something powerful. "Anything can be killed."

She nodded. They moved on.

Just as they stepped out of the tunnel into a vast space full of echoing noise, the lights came on. Without thought Toshi raised both his arms and stepped back, shoving Sadie and Zebra behind him into the tunnel.

"What?"

"I've been here before," Toshi hissed. He peered cautiously around the lip of the opening. The room was broad, high-ceilinged, and ringed with hundreds of surplus chemical glowbulbs. They cast an eerie, shadowless blue glow on the scene, a fog of light. Small groups edged carefully across the open space, weapons ready. Their own fireteams. Hairy, bloody clumps dotted the floor. Toshi counted at least twenty dead Wolves.

Near the center was a grouping of machinery, several mainframe computers, portable exhaust fans, a single large, throne-like apparatus that had several cables connecting it to the machines. All of this had a dusty, deserted look to it.

Toshi remembered when the Wolves had stood in this blue light like acolytes while the Mother, the Lady, came forward to give warnings and amulets to Berg.

It was very silent. The attack teams made soft scuffling sounds as they advanced.

"What is it?" Zebra repeated.

"I don't know. It's not what I want, though."

Zebra stepped out into the open and spoke into his console. Two of the teams detached themselves from the stately gavotte of advance and raced toward a large pair of stainless steel double doors set into the far wall. They reached them and took up station on either side, weapons ready.

"Yeah," Toshi said at last. "Through there." His

face had gone flat and dreamy. He stepped out into the room and slowly began to walk forward.

Sadie felt it first, as a horrible, twisting pain deep in her stomach. She sensed it as a musical thing, a sound that hurt. It was as if a thousand organs had all hit the wrong note at the same time.

Her features stretched and she tried to speak, but before she could fill her lungs the doors across the room slammed open. The hollow boom of the heavy metal echoed and echoed, picking up the weave of other sounds. Light gushed forth.

A robed figure stood before them. It raised its arms slowly, and the fireteams closest to the door died.

The light grew. Toshi walked forward, silhouetted against the glare.

Sadie couldn't move. Gritting her teeth, she began to struggle against the paralysis. She knew she wouldn't make it in time.

14

"**AND THAT, MY** friend, is bullshit," Calley said.

Wier's gray eyes twinkled. "Why do you say that?"

"I'd know, is all. And you know I would, don't you?"

He shrugged. "What I know is that sounds pretty metaphysical to me. You and Berg have some kind of telepathic hookup or something? Is that what you mean?"

Careful, now, she thought to herself. "Well . . . not exactly. But we've been together for a long time, been through a lot. If something happened to him, I'd know it."

Wier's face remained calm and smooth. "You could be wrong, you know. Denial takes a lot of forms, manifests itself in some strange belief systems. But I'm serious. Berg was killed in a raid on his safehouse in San Francisco. Shag Nakamura initiated the raid. We monitored it. You want to see the tapes?"

"You're frigging right I do." Calley's eyes were cold. Her lips were tight together. Ozzie glanced back and forth between them.

Berg dead? Not possible, he told himself. Somehow we would have known. A message, a fail-safe, something. Berg would have made provision even for that.

Surely he would have.

"Okay," Wier said. His voice held the flat tones of someone waiting for a bit of inevitable unpleasantness. "Let's go this way."

He took them out of the larger room and across the hall into a smaller room. He closed the door. One wall of the room lit up in a glowing white static.

"Viewer here," Wier said shortly. "Give me a second to select chips."

Calley went to one of the several armchairs facing the screen. She sat down hard, her back rigid. Ozzie recognized the stiffness. She was prepared to disbelieve anything she saw here. Calley the immovable, the icebreaker. For a moment Ozzie remembered what he'd said before, about bending and breaking.

Was this the test?

The lights in the room went dim and the screen brightened. The fuzz on the wall jittered, then blanked out into a street scene. Their vantage point was from somewhere high above the pavement, perhaps a roof or an abandoned light pole.

Down below a long armored limousine slid silently onto the deserted street. The camera shifted to an infrared pickup, and Ozzie noted immediately several orange-colored blobs approaching a house about five doors away. The infrared cutouts caught his attention because they advanced on the target in a classic military formation.

"Hey, look at—"

"I see it," Calley said tautly.

"Uh, right." He settled back in his chair and poked one long finger in his ear. He scratched a moment, then leaned forward.

Sudden globs of bright red light blazed on the screen, and the interpretation shifted from infrared to normal night viewing.

Two more explosions occurred, blinding points of

hot white, and then the scene transferred to another pickup, this one inside the house.

Berg was standing next to an array of pickups and monitors, his fingers moving frantically across a touchpad as he directed the defenses of the safehouse. Calley stared at him, her breath frozen in her throat. It had been a long time, almost a year, since she'd last seen him. She'd never seen the house—his need for secrecy had precluded even that.

He'd changed.

He was thinner, almost haggard. Deep bruises hung beneath his dark eyes which, in the urgency of the moment, had taken on a hunted, frantic glare. His skin had yellowed, become parchmentlike.

She sucked in air. Berg looked like a man near death, eaten up by some unseen force, sucked dry as a bone. The silence of the scene made it seem unreal, but its sharp clarity etched itself on her mind, imprinted her with the terrible reality. Jack Berg, the man on whom she'd staked everything, was already dying, even at the time of his death. For she could no longer doubt that this was exactly what she was seeing.

As he pounded at his touchpad, Berg reached down and plucked a pair of nose-filters from the table next to the pad and tried to insert them one-handed. She saw the first faint film of gas begin to obscure the scene. It was a yellow gas, one she didn't recognize offhand. Berg almost made it, but she saw it wouldn't have done him any good. As the gas began to swirl around him he faltered. Dermal penetrator, she thought.

His back arched and his eyes went wide. For a moment he stood there unmoving. But he was already crumpling when the entire far wall of the room lifted away and mirror-faced troopers stormed in.

The screen went dark.

She looked up at Wier's sober face, conscious of Ozzie's ragged breathing next to her.

"How do you know he's dead?" she said.

"Wait. There's more."

And the screen came alight again, this time very dim and from a different vantage point. The picture flickered, as if the camera's power supply was damaged, intermittent.

Berg was a heap on the floor. Several figures crouched over him, working quickly. They moved with the sureness of trained medics. Go on, she thought, *save him*.

One of the medics looked up as another man stepped into the room. The picture jittered and for a second she couldn't make out the face. She inhaled sharply.

"*Nakamura!*"

"Precisely," Wier said.

The little Japanese made a short, questioning hand gesture. The medic who watched him shook his head. Nakamura said something and turned away. The medic went back to work. This time his movements were slower, as if the need for urgency was gone.

The screen faded to black. The lights in their room came up. She looked at Ozzie, then at Wier. Ozzie seemed in shock.

"How—" She stopped, then tried again. "These could be fake."

"No," Wier said. "It was a real-time transmission to a hidden relay some distance away."

"They were still working when you lost the sending."

Wier sighed. "We put a lip reader on a computer-enhanced version of the tape. Nakamura asked the medic if he was alive. The medic told him no, no hope of saving him. So Nakamura said, 'Put the body on the machines. Arius will want it in the best condition possible.' "

Calley felt her skin prickle. The air in the room smelled dead and dusty. Arius would want the body.

For what?

She shuddered. Then, suddenly, she was sick. She stood up from the table and rushed out of the room.

"Down the hall to your right," Wier called.

When she came back she was pale but steady. Her eyes had gone a cold, burning green that even Wier couldn't look at.

"I always thought I would know," she said.

Wier said nothing, waiting.

"Okay," she said at last. "Where do we fit in?" But before he could answer, she added, "As long as I get to kill that fuck Nakamura, that is."

"In time, perhaps," Wier said. "In time."

"Well," Ozzie said.

They were back in their suite, seated across from each other in the bouncy beanbag chairs. "Well, what?"

"You, uh, look like shit, darling."

She glared at him. "Is this your idea of therapy or something? Get me mad so I'll forget how miserable I am?"

His face was somber. He shrugged slightly. "Maybe. Is it working?"

"What do you think?"

"I think I'd like to go for a walk. Maybe ride the cliffside people-movers."

She raised her hand, stared at her fingers as if surprised to see them at all, and nodded. "Why not?"

"Why not, indeed?"

The vast main vault of Kennedy Crater was entered from above by means of a continuously moving chainlike affair which rose from the floor of the crater to the top. Small platforms with handholds rode the chains in a constant ellipse. Passengers simply stepped on and stepped off where they wished. It was somewhat archaic, but the Lunies liked it. It was almost like a carnival ride, and it gave a spectacular view of the main vault.

"Remember the first time we rode this thing together?" Calley asked.

Ozzie grinned. "Yeah. And for about the same reasons, I guess."

She glanced over the huge expanse of main crater. Below, on the floor of the crater, stretched offices, shops, and restaurants. Most of these were unroofed but some, in the interests of privacy, were covered over with light sheets of opaque plastic. Weather was not a factor here.

The chain clinked and clanked up the bare cliff wall. She held on unconsciously now, completely at ease. It was not, she reflected, much like her first trip, when she still hadn't adjusted to walking in the lesser gravity of Luna. But it had been necessary then, and was necessary now.

"You ever trust Wier?" she asked.

"Sure." He looked uneasy. "When I first came here, when you got yourself trapped in the matrix after Double En shot you and Berg off."

"You mean when you and the Lunies trapped me in the matrix. Actually, when Arius trapped me there."

He nodded. "Well, anyway, I trusted him then. What choice did I have? Even if I was wrong, which was how it turned out, what else could I do? The Lunies were the only other players in the game big enough to oppose Double En. Or so it seemed to me then."

She turned and stared at the wall as it slid past, so her lips were shielded from observation. The movement reminded her of the previous time she'd done so, aware that it was unlikely mike beads could be hidden at random here, or lips read, or distance pickups focused because of the movement. It was perhaps the only place on the moon they could be reasonably sure of going unheard.

And now it was necessary again. "You were right, of course," she said. "You didn't have any other choice. Just like now."

"Hey, it was your idea to come here this time."

"Ozzie, you just don't have a feel for real nastiness, do you?"

He looked away from her. "Is that bad?"

"No. Of course not. You wouldn't be Ozzie if you were any different. But it's good that one of us has a nice solid streak of evil."

"You."

She grinned. "Of course. Who else? So you listen to me a second, 'cause evil momma's got some shit for you to think about."

And, hand over her lips, she talked as they swept on up the cliff.

Later—three rides down and up the hundred meter face—they lounged near the lip of the overhang, looking down on the floor of Kennedy Main Crater. It was a staggering sight: Arching over all was the monomolecular-reinforced canopy which sealed off the top of the crater, admitting through its frosted double thickness a pearly light which made the whole interior seem golden and full of distance. Hundreds of small constructions in every possible color gleamed like an orderly garden of red and blue and bright-orange high-tech blooms on the floor below them.

All around the perimeter of the crater floor were openings to the great tunnel systems, each capable of being sealed off by crash doors in the event of some giant system failure in the main crater. The city-state itself was like an iceberg. Ninety percent of it was hidden underground.

Like, reflected Calley, this whole mess. "Think about it," she muttered to Ozzie. "There are so many parallels to the last time. You'd almost think . . ." Her voice trailed off thoughtfully.

"The Lunies are in the middle of this? But how?"

She shook her head. "First thing, the assholes are lying to us again."

"Lying about what?"

"Berg." She said the word flatly, and blinked, her green eyes opaque.

"He's dead. We watched the film."

"Films can be faked."

"You think that one was?"

She closed her eyes for a moment and squeezed the back of her neck hard, kneading the tense muscles there. Finally she leaned her head back. "No. It wasn't a fake. But Berg isn't dead."

"Calley, that doesn't make any sense at all." He bobbed closer, voice intent. "I mean, we've all been through a lot, your blindness, everything . . ."

"And you think I've finally lost it. Right?"

"Well, uh . . ."

"You're forgetting a lot of shit you already know. Think, Ozzie, just fucking think for a minute."

He shook his head. "No. You're gonna tell me anyway. I won't see it like you, you know that."

She stared at him for a moment, and he said, "Look, Calley. I can do things you can't. And the same for you. Why treat me like an idiot just 'cause I don't have your viewpoint?"

This time she nodded slowly. "I'm a real asshole sometimes, aren't I?"

He grinned. "Yeah."

"Okay." She glanced around. Nobody was near them.

She remembered another time they'd stood in almost this same place, having the same sort of conversation, and for a moment she had a sudden vision of a wheel. It kept going around, dragging her with it, as she and Ozzie and Berg and all the rest kept on doing some dance that never ended.

Somebody else always played the tune.

"Come on, let's go back down. I don't trust anybody in this fucking cave except me and you." Her eyebrows opened, but he finished for her:

"Uh-huh. And sometimes I have my doubts about you."

He told her on the way down. "You remember that new computer of theirs?"

She nodded, eyes unfocused, staring at the filmy distance.

"No, I mean do you *remember?*"

She looked at him. "What are you talking about?"

"I thought so." His voice was soft and intense. "But I did think you'd catch it." His lips curved slightly. "Maybe my viewpoint helps, too."

"Ozzie, quit being mysterious and frigging tell me, okay?"

He took a breath. "Low Energy Variable Input Nanocomputer."

"Yeah, so?"

"The initials, lady. The fucking acronym."

Her eyes widened slowly. "Jeezus . . ."

"Yeah," he said.

"Over here." She walked quickly across the floor until they entered a street that featured a long string of eating establishments. They found a place that was reasonably empty and sat down at a round table. The waiter looked familiar.

"Can I help you?" the young man said politely.

"Yeah. Couple cups of coffee, please." She paused. "Hey. Your name's Schollander, right?"

"Yes. Why do you ask?"

She shrugged. "No reason. I met you before, once, is all."

"I remember, Calley."

"Oh."

The waiter went away to bring their order. "Talking's over, is it?" Ozzie said.

She sighed. "No. We got a lot to talk about now."

"Are you nuts? Our waiter guy just might own Luna, Inc. You got to figure this place's got more wires than my comm system."

Her voice was tired. "It doesn't matter, Ozzie. Levin's here, on Luna. Another fucking AI, in the same place, and probably for the same reason. Wier has fucked us again."

"You sure of that?" Ozzie said.

The waiter returned, bringing two heavy ceramic mugs full of steaming coffee. He set them down, smiled, and walked away. Calley picked up her mug and sipped. "Mm. Good. What do you mean?"

"Maybe we're fucking him this time."

She thought about it. Finally she nodded. "If we aren't, we will be. Bet on it."

"Sure," Ozzie said.

They were on their second cups when Wier walked up to their table. "Mind if I join you?"

Calley smiled slightly. "Not at all, Karl. Sit down. Tell us what's on your devious mind."

He pulled out a chair and sat. He nodded at the waiter, pointed at the coffee, and raised one finger. After a moment he had his own cup. "My devious mind? What about yours? It's the second most devious mind I know of."

"And?"

"Well, Berg is number one, of course."

"And that's why I'm here, right? How did you do it, Karl?"

He glanced at his cup. "You know, you really don't have to ride up and down the cliff all day. I could guarantee you privacy."

"Karl, I didn't come here because I was blind. I came here because . . ." She stopped. A puzzled expression flicked across her face.

"Because why?" he asked gently.

She blinked. "I don't know. Something happened to me inside the matrix, and then I knew I had to come here."

"Oh? And what was that?"

"What happened, you mean? I don't remember."

He tapped the side of his cup. "Calley, that doesn't—"

"Let's take it another way. You knew I was coming. How was that?"

"Our AI alerted us. Gave us details on the chips, everything."

"Right. And now that we're where we're supposed to be, what do you have in mind for us?"

He paused. Then, "Same thing as before. Breaking and entering."

"Uh-huh. Breaking into what?"

His gray eyes squinted slightly, as if he felt a sudden pain. "Our AI, of course. What else?"

Calley and Ozzie stared at each other.

He leaned back into his chair and stared up. "I suppose I'd better tell you."

"No, let me," Calley said.

"What?"

"Let me tell you. If I'm wrong, correct me."

He tilted his head down. "Sure."

"Right from the beginning Berg tagged Arius as a bad guy, you know that? Right from the fucking start."

"And?"

She inhaled deeply, then let the air leak out. "Well, the one thing Jack Berg is good at is defense. He can call odds better than anybody I ever heard of. And he knew. He *knew* what Arius was because he helped create it. He was the Key. So he had to understand."

She paused, brushed a rag of hair out of her face. "And he also knew we wouldn't be enough. Arius had Nakamura. He had Double En. A lot of money. All the advantages. I don't know why I didn't figure it out before."

Ozzie touched the back of her hand. " 'Cause we listened to him. And he didn't tell us."

"He didn't tell us a lot," Calley said sharply. She glanced at Wier. "It bothers me, you know. That maybe you knew more about it all along. But where else could he go? For the money, the safety, the power?"

Wier nodded slowly.

"Yeah," she said. "Luna, Inc. Big Blue. The only major corporation that didn't go blooey in the big crack-up."

"We lost our AI," Wier pointed out.

"Sure, but that was all. And you were already opposed to Arius. Only you thought it was Norton."

"I don't understand."

"I had to separate the two. You, your people, your company, Luna. Arius fooled you, too. But when Arius was gone, all the rest was left. And you were still opposed to the new fusion. You had to be. If Norton and his meat were a threat, then an Arius/

Norton fusion had to be an even bigger threat. To Luna, at least."

"Good," Wier said. "You got that far. Now how much further?"

"Oh, a lot," she said. Her tone was arid. "So Berg comes back to you, and he asks the question I should have. What did you build Arius for in the first place? What were you working on? And you told him."

"Of course," Wier said. "He is the Key. He's the biggest threat to Arius. We knew it even then."

"Nanotechnology," she said dreamily. "Molecular machines. I did some research, you know."

"Yeah, we monitor anybody who accesses that data. Nothing personal, but it tagged your searches. So what do you make of it?"

"Your nanocomputer. I figure that it operates, oh, about a million times as fast as a human brain."

This time Wier actually smiled. "Bingo. You're right in the ball park."

Calley scowled. "And, of course, you wouldn't be limited to a single brain. The thinking box concept. Nothing wrong with hooking a bunch of them together. It's an old idea, proven technology."

Wier finished his coffee. "Would you like to see it?"

She nodded. "Your low energy, variable whatsis?"

"Yes. We call it Levin. Actually, Berg named it."

"Figures," she said.

Inside the Levin lab they faced a window which looked into a brightly lit cubicle. Calley tapped on the window. "Thick," she said.

"It's a diamond," Wier told her. "Half a meter thick."

Ozzie coughed. "You mean a laminate. A diamond laminate."

Wier shook his head. "No. A single diamond."

Ozzie's eyes bugged slightly. "Oh."

"Inside is what matters," Wier said.

They turned toward the window. Beyond, the light began to brighten. Finally they could make out ten objects, each about the size of the coffee mugs they'd been drinking from earlier. The objects were a deep gold color. Each was suspended at the junction of white pipes equal in diameter to the objects. Thick wads of what appeared to be optical fiber cables trailed from the objects, as well as what might have been power cables. More cables connected the objects to each other.

"Ten brains?" Calley said.

"Uh-huh. Those blocks are sapphire, honeycombed with cooling channels. Those big pipes carry the coolant, a tailored liquid much more efficient than water."

"Ten of them," she said again. "But I thought the advantage was in shortening the distance. Those are several centimeters apart."

"Good point. Actually, each block contains several hundred of the brains I showed you before, the small computers. Consider each mass of them as a lobe, a part of the greater whole. The capacity of any individual part is as you suggested, Calley. About a million times as fast as a human brain of the same capacity. And putting out about a million times as much heat. But we have ten of them. The sum of it all is Levin."

She turned away, staring out at the busy room. Her eyes were hooded. "Takes a lot of power."

"We have power. We are on Luna," Wier said simply.

Ozzie nodded. "And the programming?" he said.

"That's the variable input part," Wier said. "Berg developed the original programming. He called it a 'seed.' It was a kind of jumped-up hypertext, a way for the machine to make connections. Then we just fed it everything we know."

"What?" Ozzie stepped back. "Everything you know? What does that mean?"

"Everything humanity has ever committed to the nets, the data banks, the storage systems. Every bit of data ever encoded."

"That's impossible," Calley said.

"Not if you can access the metamatrix," Wier said.

"And you can?"

"Berg could," Wier replied.

"Without Arius being aware?"

Wier nodded. "We think so. If Arius had known, it would have taken action by now."

"How can you be sure?"

This time Wier looked away. "We can't be sure, I guess. Because we have a problem now."

Calley folded her arms across her chest and stared at him. To Ozzie she looked like some ancient, blackened blade of war.

"I told you I wanted to guess," she said.

He nodded slowly.

"When Berg was killed, something happened. Is that right?"

Wier licked his lips. "Levin quit talking to us." He raised his hand. "Oh, it didn't shut down. Levin still maintains normal comm, does all the tests and housekeeping we request. But it won't allow us access to the metamatrix. As far as Arius goes, we're blind now."

Calley lowered her arms. "What goes around . . ."

"What do you mean?"

"You've got another out-of-control AI, don't you? But this time you know it."

Wier's lips tightened. In the harsh light they seemed dry and shiny. "We want you to crack it. Berg did the programming. You can break it."

Calley laughed. The moment, so full of tension, collapsed suddenly. Ozzie moved toward her, put his arm on her shoulder.

"You know it's so fucking funny," she said. "We're riding the same goddam roller coaster. The first time I cracked Arius. Now you want me to crack Levin. It's all out of control, isn't it? A million frigging times as fast. A million. And you've got *ten* of them."

Wier looked into the cubicle where the brain rested in sterile safety. "It's been out of control for a long time, Calley," he said softly.

"Human control," she said. "But something's still at work there. You think it's Levin?"

"As governed by Berg's programming," he said carefully.

"That's where you're wrong," she told him at last. "It's not Berg's programming. It's Berg." She slapped the window suddenly, leaving a greasy handprint on the gemlike surface. "He's not dead. He's fucking in there."

"I wondered if you'd figure that out," Wier said.

"Why all the secrets?" she asked finally. "Why can't you just come out and say things?" She swiped at her forehead. "Oh, dammit, it's not just you. It's me, and Berg, and creeps like Nakamura. All of us. All playing games. And now we've got things like Arius playing games. And your machine, your Levin. Berg's Levin, whatever."

"I don't know," Wier said. "All of us, we just do what we think is right. What's necessary."

Calley turned around and looked inside the cubicle again, at the enigmatic tangle of cable, at the innocuous little sapphire cubes. "That is alive," she said. "Nanocomputers. Molecular technology. You said humanity is obsolete. Maybe you think you're exaggerating. But—" She faced him suddenly, her eyes blazing pure green. "—what do you bet Arius agrees? And maybe Levin, too? You can't even control your own goddam machines. *Twice!*"

"That's what we need you for, now," Wier said. For an instant she detected something in his voice. Could it be sadness?

"Yeah," she said. "You want me to crack Berg out of there. Well, why not? It's what I'm good at."

He nodded.

"You ever think of this?" she said. "Berg might not want me to crack him. What about that?"

He ran his finger down the diamond. "Then it's all out of control, isn't it?"

After a moment she said, "Well, you'd better tell me what I have to do."

15

LUCIEN CHEN WAS a native-born from the PRC, educated with hard-won communist dollars at Cal Tech. He was there seven years, and picked up both a Doctorate in Software Engineering and a taste for *quai-loh* music, women, and automobiles. General Dynamics waved a large amount of credit and a green card under his nose two days after graduation, whereupon he became Luke Chen and a committed capitalist. Now he was on loan to NSA, where he did strange things in the data and spy business.

"That's fucking weird," he said.

"What?" Sarah Greenblum was a ridiculous genius of the type old Manhattan families throw up on the female side with disconcerting regularity. She'd spent a fortune on her face, but behind her razor cheekbones lay the soul of a chubby girl with braces. She was in love with Luke Chen but he had never noticed. "What's weird?" she asked again. She licked her lips and wished she hadn't left the new lip gloss at home. Not that this handsome commie turncoat would notice.

"Take a look at this." He leaned back from his console and pointed at three monitors in front of him.

She slid over, making sure that her left breast—she thought it was slightly larger than the right one—ended pushed against his shoulder. She watched his golden features carefully for any reaction. Nothing. Did the sonofabitch like boys, for god's sake?

Then she looked at the screen.

"Jeezus frigging Christ," Sarah Greenblum said.

Behind a black door the small form lay unmoving in its silent cart, the web of shining cables gone dull and lifeless. The tiny limbs no longer twitched. The ruby eyes had faded to a filmy, grayish pink. It was silent.

Arius had gone home.

If one cross-wires the various lobes of the brain—in a manner of speaking, for such things may be done with hormones and peptides as easily as with such gross connectors as metal—so that inputs are not processed in their proper loci, the result has many names. Autism is one. Schizophrenia another. Whatever it is called its name is madness.

Improperly connected data banks are prey to similar maladies. The visual result of such was what Sarah Greenblum and Luke Chen watched on their monitor screens.

The Double En Corporation, Nakamura-Norton, had been a primary government contractor for years. When Shag Nakamura began to sell the meatmatrices, one of his first great markets was the shadow world of government agencies. Every government wished to keep track of its citizens, and of the activities of other governments, both friend and foe. Since the big meats were capable of doing this faster and more thoroughly than any other system, the Double En products came to dominate these markets. Which is to say, the offspring of Bill Norton's brain cells became the brains of the rulers.

Now the brains began to act strangely.

*   *   *

"Can you access any of it?" Luke Chen asked.

Sarah Greenblum shook her head. She was seated in front of her own console, her fingers flying blindly across her touchpad, as she called up glittering summary arrays of data.

"Look there," she said tightly. "That make any sense to you?"

He blinked. "Nada. And I wrote that sampling program."

She tried once again. They both stared at the screen. Finally she let her hands drop primly to her lap and turned away. "All fucked up," she said. "We can't get into any of the prime data bases."

"CIA is gonna love this," Chen said grimly.

"Everybody is going to love it. The entire intelligence capability of the United States is out to lunch."

There was a moment of silence while they stared at each other. "I suppose," Chen said, "we'd better tell somebody."

"Yes," Sarah replied.

When Luna, Inc., became an independent corporation after its epic leveraged buyback, it also became something unique in the annals of nations: a corporation that was a nation as well as a separate world. Its relations with other nations were carried out by contract rather than treaty, and as an entity, Luna regarded corporations and countries as equals. Its ambassadors were salesmen and its leaders executive committees. Nations of the old style were puzzled.

At least the leaders were. The spies knew what to do. Nation or company, the principles were the same. The duty of spies was to gather information, which they passed on to their masters, most of whom were military men. The military knew what to do as well.

Foe was foe. Even friend was conceivably foe. And so contingency plans were made. Plots were wargamed. And weapons were targeted.

Luna, Inc., existed as a point in the center of a ring of weapons. Not all the weapons were physical, although there were enough long tubes with explosives on the ends deployed. But the spies and the soldiers knew the real war was played for data, for information, for control. So, for every nuclear missile or hidden pack of tailored viruses, there were ten schemes to sample, steal, block, or control data. This was a war of software, where the difference was made in the speed and quality of processing power.

Sticks and rocks had once sufficed. Now the players wielded computers and softbreakers. But the battlefield was flesh, and the flesh belonged to Arius. Great systems were slowly deployed. Contingency software packages came on-line. Viral attack worms flexed. It was all automatic.

The meatmatrices were, after all, so much faster than mere humans.

The room where Luke and Sarah had whispered quietly was now vibrant with hushed tension. Long since relieved by heavyweights, the chief programmers, the head spies, they sat quietly against one wall, their backs slumped, and watched the frantic activity.

"Who's that?" Sarah asked.

He followed the slight tilt of her head. "Andrew Lybnewicz," he said. "National Security Adviser. And Frank Bowling, the Science Adviser with him."

There was a small stir as a short, heavyset man whose absolutely bald head was strangely dull and gray entered the room. He was accompanied by a flurry of six or seven men, presumably staff, all of whom looked as interchangeable as bowling balls.

"And now the sharks arrive," Chen whispered. "That's—"

"Uh-huh," Sarah said. "I know that one. Pete Gabrowski. The President's fixer."

Luke grinned. "The President's assistant chief of staff, you mean."

"You heard me."

Gabrowski ignored all the mid- and near-top rankers as he strode directly toward the two other power centers in the room. Lybnewicz and Bowling nodded and offered him their hands, thereby establishing the pecking order immediately.

Luke and Sarah were close enough to hear, but far enough away to remain ignored.

"So what the fuck?" Gabrowski said.

"It's worse than we thought," Lybnewicz replied. "The fucking brains have gone crazy."

Lybnewicz was a man of medium height and incredibly good tailoring. He'd fought the academic wars for so long that some of the inner scars were actually reflected on his flat, bland features. His face was the mask of an old man superimposed on the features of a young one. It made it hard to guess his age or his thoughts. He was feared in the halls of Harvard.

Gabrowski had made a fortune in real estate. His position in government did not depend on the advice and consent of the Senate, and he continued to run his own operations. "And what the fuck exactly does that mean?" he said. His voice was soft and vicious, and Lybnewicz recoiled slightly from it.

Frank Bowling answered. He was a fat man in every way. His voice was fat. "It means, Gabby, that we're out of control. What the fuck did you think?"

And Gabrowski stepped back from him, because in the end the scientists were their only hope. Gabrowski didn't know scientists. They didn't play much of a role in the real estate biz.

But tough decisions did play such a role, and Gabrowski prided himself on being able to make them. After getting enough information, of course. "Right, Frank. Could you be more specific? Out of control of what, for instance?"

Bowling nibbled delicately at the corner of one thumbnail, his eyes distant. "We aren't accessing our data bases properly. And some of our automatics seem to be coming on-line without authorization."

Gabrowski's face went as gray as his skull. "What systems?" he said. His voice was suddenly hoarse. "The Soviets, the Chinese, what?"

"Something to do with Luna," Bowling said. "But we can't find out what."

He had called no ghosts for the day. Sometimes it amused him to do so, to surround himself with the figures of his ancient loves, his friends, his enemies. Sometimes he would take his old body and become once again Bill Norton, and surround himself with a younger Shag Nakamura or a more compliant string of ex-wives. Sometimes Jack Berg would visit in the watches of the night and they would rehash the old questions of flesh and sand and gods and men.

Today he was alone in his high world of clouds and wind, where he walked beneath a blinding sun. Yet he was surrounded by another world, as his senses reached out through a trillion extensions into the places of man. Each of his matrices was himself, and each of his Angels, and through this, almost every machine that thought, or tried to, in the information-processing universe.

The dataverse was his, down to the tiniest cranny.

Except for one place he could not penetrate. He sensed that place as a sore, a wound that must be healed.

He would heal it if man himself had to be destroyed in the process. In fact, the more he thought about his own reality and his own goals, the consideration was growing that man might, indeed, be extraneous.

It was something to think about, when this was over.

Frederic Oranson paused for a moment by one of the glass-paned doors which led out to the wooden deck behind the Great Room, where Shag Nakamura was immersed in the business of murder and revolution. A sudden whiff of roses had stopped him dead in his tracks. He stared over the perfectly manicured lawns at the dark line of mountain pines which edged the back of the estate, almost half a mile away.

A glint of light caught his eye as sunlight flashed from the visors of a pair of guards on patrol. The day was surprisingly warm for the time of year, with the temperature pushing sixteen Celsius and a breath of spring in the air. The roses were an anomaly, but then he realized. These roses, Shag's favorites, were an engineered variety that had a heightened ability to resist frost. Beneath the constant semiwarmth of outdoor heat lamps they bloomed all winter long.

Something stirred in Oranson's brain, an uncomfortable feeling. Feeling? That stopped him. He hadn't had a feeling in a long time. No wonder he didn't recognize it. And what was this feeling? Mentally he poked at it, trying to analyze it. He stared at the roses and felt the wind on his face, and finally he had it.

The feeling was fear.

"Here," Nakamura said.

"What?"

"I thought you told me Beirut was solid. You said the mullahs were in our pocket."

"They are." Oranson moved closer, so he could see the data Nakamura had summoned on his personal screen.

"Then look at this. Ali Barjamuzid is still alive. Half his cabinet, too. And that idiot that runs Pan-Islam Oil. Holed up in an estate that might as well be a fortress. Probably have to nuke the asshole to get him out of there."

Oranson shrugged. "Maybe the mullahs got wind of the coming revolution. They hate the New Church."

Nakamura glanced up at him, his face impassive. "That was your job. To play them off. The mullahs overthrow the Sunni government to stop the New Church. And the New Church overthrows them."

"Somebody might have slipped. It's very fluid there."

Nakamura leaned back in his chair. On this day he wore a kimono, an ancient thing his samurai ancestors had worn. He felt a comfortable continuity flow from the threads of it, as if the threads of his life were interwoven in the fabric.

"It's a mistake," he said. "We knew there would be a few. And at least it happened there. Pan-Islam doesn't mean a thing in the real world. Not since they nuked each other's wells."

"It's not a disaster," Oranson pointed out. "We should come out of the chaos almost as well as we'd planned in the first place. The government will fight back, but half their troops will desert. And the oil people will have their mercenaries out, too."

Nakamura turned back to the screen. "It's still a mistake," he said.

He wanted to grind his teeth. He was astonished at the rage he felt. Nakamura wanted to smash them, to sink his fingers into their guts and feel the damp warmth drip from his hands.

He wanted to *destroy* his enemies.

But he showed nothing of this. Oranson was here and it would never do. He stared at his desk and wondered what was wrong. Things no longer connected with other things. He felt cast adrift on his ocean of anger, and something was wrong with that, too.

It did not strike him as odd, however, that he was directing what was essentially a religious revolution on a worldwide basis. The New Church was organized as a business and, in this respect, was much like most other religions in the world. If he regarded what he was doing as a particularly brutal hostile takeover, the techniques and parallels were evident. This was not the problem.

What did bother him was that, in this case, he was acting as the avatar of a God, a God whom he despised not because of disbelief, but true belief. He knew Arius, at least the William Norton part of Arius, and loathed him. Yet somehow his one-time associate had attained divinity.

It galled him. Envy, he wondered? But that wasn't right either. Arius simply offended some sense of humanity he'd never known he possessed. So he orchestrated the changing of the world on behalf of this flawed but nonetheless God, and hated it, and wondered why.

He turned back to his desk.

"Don't you have any backup killer teams in Lebanon?" he complained.

Oranson opened the door to the Great Room and stared at the man who waited on the other side. After a long, blank moment when both men faced each other wordlessly, Oranson nodded. "Collinsworth," he said.

"Oranson," Collinsworth acknowledged him.

Nakamura's security man stepped back to admit Arius's security man. The dance was slow and precise. Oranson kept his body between Collinsworth and Nakamura, who sat behind his desk, his face impasssive. The scene had a feeling of ritual to it.

"Mr. Nakamura," Collinsworth said.

Shag lowered his head slightly in recognition of this new air of formality. He still remembered Collinsworth's deft murder of his former security chief but, with greater happiness, recalled his exposure of Collinsworth's essential fear of his own boss. He had already won whatever war there would be here.

"Welcome, Collinsworth. What brings you?"

It was a blandly charged question. Collinsworth knew it. His presence here, away from his basic task of protecting the human aspects of Arius's empire, signaled a change. Change could mean danger to Nakamura. Nakamura would know that as well.

"I have a message for you."

"A message? That's all?"

Collinsworth moved closer to the desk, acutely aware of Oranson's nearness, although, strangely, he felt no emotional aura from the man. It made him nervous. He knew that Nakamura had done something to Oranson, something that had changed him and altered his humanity, but the result frightened him. He couldn't read Oranson.

Of course, many things frightened him these days.

"Sit down, Collinsworth. Relax. A drink for you? Something British? A whisky?"

Collinsworth smoothed the sides of his tweed jacket and sat in a large brown leather chair in front of the desk. Oranson moved quietly behind him, away from the circle of his peripheral vision. Collinsworth wanted to turn his head to watch, but forced himself to remain still. Fear was one thing, but shame was another entirely.

When Oranson brought the drink in a heavy, faceted crystal tumbler, Collinsworth tasted it slowly while he stared at Nakamura's dark, steady eyes. Neither looked away. It wasn't really a test, nothing so childish. This clash of gazes was a measurement, and an affirmation. For Collinsworth it said, "I am no longer your conqueror, but you have not conquered my leader. I am unimportant, but I represent a force that may not be touched. You must recognize that force even as you despise me."

Finally Shag nodded. "What message does Arius send?"

The conversation continued on the proper plane, all forces acknowledged and balanced.

"My master is occupied with other things," Collinsworth said, "or he would communicate with you directly."

Nakamura stared at him silently. What titanic project could so occupy Arius that he would be unable to take a few seconds for a simple communication? Obviously this was a lie. But of what sort?

"Yes?" Nakamura said gently.

Collinsworth tasted his scotch again, aware of a slight movement behind him. Damn Nakamura's zombie!

"A very special assignment. Gloria Calley and Oswald Karman have been located on Luna. They are to be killed. Immediately."

Nakamura moved his fingers slightly on his desktop. The wood felt smooth, greasy. "That's all? That's the message?"

Collinsworth nodded.

"Fine," Nakamura said. "Tell Arius I'll get started immediately."

"Not get started," Collinsworth pointed out. "Kill."

"Collinsworth, get out of here."

"Goodbye, Shag," the British assassin said, rising. "Good luck."

"That's Mr. Nakamura," Shag said to his back. But Collinsworth didn't turn, didn't acknowledge him in any way.

"You heard him," Shag said to Oranson.

"I think we should kill that one, too," Oranson said slowly.

Nakamura rolled his shoulders in frustration. "Maybe later," he said.

She had been to the black room and discovered that God was missing. She carefully checked the automatics which sustained the small, flawed body and then, nodding to herself, carefully locked the door behind her. Two Wolves, two Blades, and an Angel met her outside the door.

"Except for myself, kill anybody who comes down this corridor," she said.

The Angel, a very tall woman with glittering eyes and an explosion of black hair, raised her head. "Of course," she said.

The Lady stared at her. "Don't fail," she said.

The Angel turned away. The Blades, happy and deadly, escorted the Lady to the end of the hallway. Her own escort, half a dozen Wolves, formed up around her there. She paused for a moment, smiling. It would be like old times. Old, bloody times.

"Let's get to it," she said softly. Her eyes flamed crimson. "Let's kill the blasphemers."

Arius did not devote much time to the management of the huge underground complex which sustained his physical manifestation. The Lady had overseen it from the very beginning and so was not particularly worried by the attack which was beginning to penetrate the outermost lines of her defense. In fact, a fierce joy surged through her. If she had a destiny beyond what she'd already done, it was to die in the defense of God, to die with her hands on the hearts of his enemies.

She led the small pack of Wolves briskly into her own control center. The room was relatively large, low-ceilinged, well lit. Sound was muffled here, as much by insulation as by the fifteen centimeters of monomole-reinforced armor which cradled them like an egg.

Technicians manned computer consoles. She strode to one group of them clustered around a large screen on her left.

"What do the gaming programs say?"

A thin, harried woman with brittle skin and dry lips turned to face her. "It is a type-B attack, mostly rabble from the local gangs."

"But why would they attack us now?" the Lady wondered. "We've had treaties with them for years."

The tech nodded at the screen and whispered short instructions to an operator. The screen, which had shown a schematic of the various tunnels and passageways in the threatened sector flashed, then cleared on a new scene. The Lady watched carefully, her eyes glowing.

"Give me higher contrast," she said. "I can't make out details."

These monitor screens were designed to provide infrared definition as well as normal visuals. While the Lady might be half-blind in the everyday world, in her own world she'd made her own arrangements. The monitor did not change much, but a very sensitive heat processor would have detected minute variations in the output. It was enough.

The Lady stared at the short, heavyset figure who seemed to lead the attacking force.

"Toshi," she said. "Of course."

Over the next hour she tracked the advance of the invaders. She hissed when her pickets went down. "Who is that woman?" she wondered aloud.

One of the screens obligingly retrieved a dossier. "Sadie Blankenheim?" She read the woman's history. "Ah. She was on the Double En raid."

This congruence startled her. Toshi had led the raid when the Lunies had stolen Calley and Berg's bodies from Nakamura. This had been done under the control of the Arius part of God, before God had been truly born. Now the former allies were enemies. Of course, Toshi had always been an enemy of sorts. His loyalty was to Berg, as unwavering as her own to God. But Berg was dead. Why this last-ditch attack on the Labyrinth?

Unless it wasn't a final gasp of vengeance, she considered. Unless it was something else. But what were the Lunies up to? What could they hope to gain?

She clicked her teeth in frustration. How could they even know?

"What the hell?" Sadie muttered.

She was crouched behind the dilapidated throne. Zebra huddled next to her, babbling frantically into his mike beads. The fireteams were taking whatever cover they could, scrambling across the dusty floor of the huge concrete room, while light boomed and flashed around them. For some reason, hidden behind the great chair, she and Zebra were relatively unaffected by this strange paralysis. The others were not so lucky, and many were dying on the floor.

She couldn't see Toshi. Thin screams wailed like

birds across the smoky half-gloom. In the direction of the door a brilliance began to glow, etching strange shadows on the wall behind her. She wanted to peer out, but the chug-chug sound of engines clawed at her nervous system. She started to shake.

"W-we we've got t-to . . ."

Zebra had given up trying to coordinate an orderly retreat. Whatever had come into the vault was deadly, killing with sight and sound and the twisted responses of human nervous systems.

Again, her muscles began to congeal. The blaze from the door grew stronger, harsh and actinic, as if a child's sparkler, impossibly large, had suddenly begun to burn. She closed her eyes. Heavy, thumping sounds pounded at her ears, confusing her.

The screams had gone silent. She squeezed at the sides of her forehead, trying to physically force some kind of order onto her frazzled brain.

After a moment she began, inch by inch, to move toward the edge of the throne, dragging her rifle with her.

16

THE PLACE WAS formless at first look. Only a deep blue glow beneath and darkness above. Something like wind echoed here, a dull, thrumming background noise. And finally there was a horizon of sorts, little more than a slow shading from blue to black.

No one came here. Everyone lived here.

The sudden insurge of sparks was like a comet's fall, long and silently whooshing. The bright flashes passed beyond the horizon and left a hazy form behind. Now the sparks began to coalesce with echoing, popping sounds, into a vastly tall, columnar shape.

The Shape dominated the horizon, illumined it. In its light the endless floor of the Place was revealed. The blue glow lessened, resolved into countless tiny globes.

The darkness above was split by the light of the Shape now steady. The blue below shimmered in readiness.

The man came walking, walking.

Thunder shouted. The Shape burned incandescent. The blue globes flared an unearthly glow.

Maker! Master!

The words hung as thunderous wordless sounds above the man's head. Now he turned. A sun rose behind him, a pale, transparent filmy thing. An applique against the night of this Place.

The man stared at the sun a long time. Then he turned his back on it and continued across the blue globes toward the Shape.

To him the Shape resembled a Key.

Or a Sword.

Toshi was frozen by the Light. Out directly ahead of him the Angel stood with upraised arms in a great flower of brilliance. The colors were as vibrant as bandsaws, and as murderous. Small figures screamed and died where the blades of red and gold and brass touched and burned. But the Light came nowhere near Toshi, even though the stocky little Japanese saw that the Angel was looking at him. He could see dark laughing pits behind the Angel's eyes.

"Now?" Toshi said aloud. Waves of agony swept through him, jerking his muscles. Each death was a separate pain, a sudden icy hole. He felt it all.

"No. Not yet." The voice was infinitely soothing, infinitely familiar.

"Levin, I want to kill that thing." The conversation was strange. It was as if they were discussing something apart, something minor that had little to do with him. Once he'd killed Angels for a living, and for more than that. Now he watched as an Angel slaughtered his own people.

Things clicked and chittered inside his skull. Tiny things.

The Angel began to walk slowly toward him, grinning. It was tall and muscular. It was quite obviously male, as its body was revealed beneath its flimsy robes. It had an erection.

The vault went silent. Toshi waited stolidly, his hands at his sides. His mind had gone loose and open as a baby's hand. Behind his eyes danced a vision of flame and sword.

"Your time approaches!" The Angel's voice was full of deep echoes, like a great organ in an empty church. Fire sizzled from its eyes, ran down its shoulders, and clung to its robes.

Toshi felt warmth begin to fill his spine, rising like a slow geyser toward his brain.

"You blaspheme this Holy Place!" the Angel roared.

Toshi closed his eyes and saw a blaze of white brilliance. Uncounted minuscule things twittered busily there, like the reflections from a perfect gem. His head filled up and he opened his eyes.

The Angel raised his hands and smiled.

"Give me a sermon, sucker," Toshi said. And blew the Angel away.

To Sadie it appeared that something had exploded where the Angel had been. Only a thick, greasy cloud remained. It smelled like overcooked eggs in bad Crisco. She'd been trying to raise her assault rifle, fighting the paralysis, when suddenly it was over.

She stepped out from behind the wreckage of the throne.

"Jeezus, what did you do?" she said softly.

"Got us past that fucking door," Toshi said.

Sadie looked around at the force regathering itself. It was much smaller. She didn't want to count the smoked, fusing corpses which dotted the floor.

She took a deep breath and tried a grin. It didn't feel right but she left it there. "Something, I guess," she said.

Toshi took her arm and pulled her forward. "But not enough," he said.

She nodded. "Come on, Zebra," she said. "Supernip says the easy part's over."

Zebra looked around. He put his head down and vomited.

Calley stared at Wier with disgust. "You know what you're saying?

Wier shrugged.

Calley twisted away from him. "You've decided that Berg is some kind of jumped-up little god. Some tin deity worse than Arius. At least Arius has some extrahuman ingredients."

"And so does Berg," Wier replied calmly. "He has Levin, who is a far more powerful piece of hardware and software. Berg is in there somewhere. He's functioning without a body. In fact, he has no hope of ever recovering his body. Or his brain. There might have been a time when we could have raided Double En for the two of you. But now we're dealing with Arius. It's a completely different proposition. If Berg's personality is to have a continued existence, it will only be in whatever reality he and Levin can conjure up together. And there's one other thing to consider."

"What's that?"

"The Key. That's what Berg calls it, right? This mysterious power of his to manipulate the dataverse. The faculty that Arius schemed to use in the first place. The ability that Arius now seems to fear." He paused. "As much as he fears anything."

"Wier, this is all so . . . stupid."

"I know you're uncomfortable with ideas like this. What you call deifying him. But that's because you have a history between you. It's hard to think of a man you once shared sex with, and cigarettes after sex, as something supernormal. It's tough. But Calley, you're supposed to be the tough one. Think about it."

She chewed the edge of her thumbknuckle. Her dark hair caught the harsh overhead lights. Techni-

cians bustled around her, their faces serious and intent. Inadvertently she recalled another situation. Once
before she'd invaded the metamatrix with the power
of Luna's computers behind her. Soon she would em-
bark on a similar rescue mission. Or was it rescue?
That was the question. What, precisely, was her goal
this time?

For this time it would be *her* goal. She was determined of that. If Berg had become something beyond
her ken, she wanted to know it firsthand. If such a
thing were possible.

Oh, Berg, you asshole, where have you gone this
time? And why?

"You always win, don't you, Wier?" Her voice was
low and bitter.

"I didn't even know we were fighting," he replied.

"I will guard you, Lord." The Lady burned with a
white devotion. Her eyes glowed dully as she faced
Arius, who was regarding her with an equally flame-
ridden gaze.

"Mother," he said at last. "Aside from all the rest I
love you for your consistency the most. Yes, guard me
well. Although it doesn't matter in the slightest."

She straightened proudly. "Of course it matters. These
vermin profane your place. They beg for destruction.
And I will see they receive it."

His tiny mouth twitched. "But don't you understand? They can't hurt me. Even this Japanese assassin who seems to have special powers can do me no
harm."

"Of course not. He'll never get close enough to
try."

"Even if he did," Arius continued patiently. "Even
if he destroyed this body. Don't you understand,
Mother? I would still remain."

Her long white fingers went rigid at the thought of such desecration. Intellectually she understood that Arius existed finally in another place so far beyond normal human reality that his essential animus could not be touched. But she had carried this scrap of flesh in her own womb, and had felt—indeed, been the channel of—its ultimate energization. She had truly given birth to God on Earth. The thought of this tiny form being threatened by anything affected her in deep ways she could not directly perceive.

What she felt was rage. Murderous rage.

She stared at him a moment longer. "I will kill them all," she said at last.

He seemed to lose interest. "Fine. Go and do it then." And turned his chair away.

She nodded fiercely. As she left the vault she made doubly sure everything was buttoned up tight. Two Wolves and two Blades stood guard. One Angel—a different one—lounged insolently on a chair a few feet away.

"Protect your Lord," she instructed them. Then she gathered her own escort and swept away to do battle. The thought of sinking her fingers into Toshi Nakasone's heart made her eyes glow like lanterns.

"Why do you insist on this artificial separation?"

"Is it artificial?"

"You know it is. We are one. There is no reason for you to maintain that fictional body."

"I am accustomed to dealing with analogs. It's easier."

"I suppose. Eventually you'll outgrow it. But it seems stupid. Here I am talking to 'you,' when it's really myself after all."

"Don't push. Ourselves is a better concept. At least until we're fully integrated."

(Sigh) "And we still have a third of that battle to go."

"If this works, we'll at least have a level playing field."

"If it works."

Ozzie swallowed the rest of his soymilk and tossed the crumpled carton over his shoulder toward the small kitchenette.

It landed on top of a pile of similar refuse.

"You're a real pig," Calley said.

"I'll pick it up."

"Sure you will."

"Something bothering you?"

"I don't know. Yes. Something is."

"You want to talk about it?"

She stubbed out a cigarette so strongly she burned the tip of her finger. "Goddamit!"

"Okay, so maybe you don't want to talk about it. I'll go stack garbage."

"No, wait a minute." She leaned back and rubbed her temples. "What do you think about Wier?"

"Dumb question. He's slime, but he's our slime. I guess. Why did you come here in the first place, Calley?"

"I . . . I'm not sure."

"Is that what's bothering you?"

"Part of it. I guess he's plotting something. Of course he's plotting something. He wouldn't be Wier otherwise." She lit another cigarette. "So why do you think I went blind?"

He blinked. "Huh?"

"You know. What made me go blind?"

"What's this, twenty questions? I . . . uh. You don't want the obvious answer, then. So you don't think it was Wier?"

She paused and watched the smoke curl lazily from her fingers. "Like I said, I don't know. It happened when I saw the Demon Star. Maybe that's a connection. We thought so at first."

"You know, every time you go into the metamatrix something bizarre happens to you. Maybe it's a jinx."

She shrugged. "My life is a fucking jinx. I live with it anyway. But going blind. That's pretty specific, Ozzie. So turn it on its head. What if it *wasn't* Wier? He sure as hell hints he had something to do with it. Which is as good a reason as any to think otherwise."

He began to nibble on one ragged thumbnail. "That's not even the interesting question, babe. Whether it was Wier or Arius or whatever, how was it done? And how did it get undone? And if you can answer all that, then go for the big one. *Why* was it done?"

"I think," she said slowly, "that if you can answer one, you answer the other."

"We've got what? One day or so? It should be enough time."

"There's never enough time, kiddo. Never."

He straightened up and looked at her. "That's not my tough girl."

"Not any more," she agreed.

"What are you?" Sadie said.

They were crouched just before a place where the hall made a tee. Two still forms, one hairy, one not, lay broken at the intersection. Ugly red holes on the bodies leaked slowly. There was the smell of smoke in the air, and copper from the blood.

Toshi glanced at her. "I don't know anymore," he said. "It doesn't matter. Not what I am. Just what I have to do." He moved his shoulders. He carried an assault rifle one-handed.

She saw it in his black eyes. "Will we live through this?"

He turned away from her.

"I don't care," she went on quickly. "I mean I do, but it's part of the job, right? I hired on to take care of you and I finish my contracts. Just like a man." She paused. "We all know it can come to this."

"You'll live," he said. "I didn't ask for you, but you'll live."

She heard the lie in his voice. Her stomach felt loose. Behind her, Zebra was moving among the few soldiers left in his force. He had started with almost a hundred. Now less than twenty were left. Some of them were wounded.

They would all be gone now if there was a way, she thought. They were mercenaries and they would have deserted. But the way back was as deadly as the way forward. Zebra knew this but he had pride. Now he was trying to give a little of his pride to them.

Maybe it would work, she thought dully. Maybe not. But she would finish the job.

As long as there was a job to finish.

Toshi stirred again. His voice was raspy and tired. "We're gonna have to go on."

She edged past him and peered around the corner of the tee. In each direction stretched long hallways brightly lit by recessed fluorescents. It looked like a modern office. What was it doing down here in the Labyrinth? What had she gotten into?

"Which way?" she said.

He froze. She watched him. His eyes went blank and distant, as if he were listening to something only he could hear. Finally he came back to her. "Right," he said. "We go right."

She nodded. She felt her moment of weakness pass. Maybe this would be that last contract. Maybe not. Either way she would do her job. Buoyed by the thought, she squirmed back to Zebra.

"Get the troops ready," she told him. "We're going on."

He nodded. "Yeah," he said. He looked at his ragtag band.

"Jeezus, only twenty left. My boss ain't gonna be happy about this." He thought about it. Then he grinned suddenly. "But I don't guess it's gonna matter to me much, anyway. Is it?"

She shook her head. He might as well know how things stood.

He grinned again, the light catching the black stripes across his face. "Didn't think so." He turned back to his soldiers. "Come on, apes. It's showtime!"

They heard the sound of distant shouts.

"Up here!" Toshi said.

She joined him. Their cadre moved behind them. They rolled into the hallway and spread out. The firing started shortly after.

"What if it was Berg?" Calley said at last.

They had wrestled with the question for hours. Ozzie's angelic face was loose with exhaustion but she was wound tight. She smoked with quick jerky gestures and her eyes flashed.

"How could he?" Ozzie asked.

"Wier talks like Berg can do anything. I don't think he understands what that means. Maybe it's just the simple truth.

"Somebody did it. It didn't just happen. If not Arius or Wier, then who? There's only one answer."

Ozzie pulled at his cheeks. His fingernails were bitten and the quick underneath red and raw. "But why?"

She stared at him. "What if his allegiance isn't to us any more?"

He nodded. "What if he isn't human any more?"

*   *   *

The Lady raged. The Angel stepped back from her wrath.

"You let them get this far!" the Lady said.

"He has some power," the Angel told her. "We can't stand against him."

She turned back to the screens of her War Room. The screens showed disaster. Through drifting clouds of smoke Toshi's small party had advanced within a hundred yards of the center of the Labyrinth. Only a couple of walls, a turning of corridors, separated him from the black door. If he knew the way. And somehow it seemed that he did.

She tapped her teeth with one long fingernail. "Is there a trap?"

One of the three Blades in the room nodded. "Yes. The hall outside the black door. Mines in the floor, the walls. The ceiling would come down, too."

She thought about it. "What about God? Would he be safe inside?"

"Yes. It was designed that way."

She made up her mind suddenly. Toshi was a far stronger opponent than she had guessed. He obviously had help. Something was acting through him, just as Arius acted through his Angels.

"All right. Let him through. Show enough resistance to make it convincing but let him reach the corridor." She snapped her fingers. Two of her Wolves came to her side. "I will go to God," she said. "In case you are wrong." She moved toward the door. At the door she stopped and took a wide-band ripper from the rack on the wall. God said Toshi wasn't a threat. She would believe that when the Japanese drifted on the air, a cloud of oily smoke.

"Let's go," she said.

*   *   *

Nakamura felt on the edge of things. It made him nervous. "What word from Luna?" he said.

"We have a team there," Oranson said. "Two moles. Been there a long time. Techs in the biolabs. I activated them. They will insert a tailored fast bacteria into the ventilating system of her room. It will be over in minutes."

"And Arius?"

"No messages," Oranson said. "He's not replying to our signals."

"Bastard," Nakamura said. Outside the wind was rising.

He stared at the pines and wondered when it would be over.

It was less than two hours till insertion. Wier had explained the process to her. It would be similar to the previous time except for the tank. Levin had designed new techniques which could operate through her socket interface. She had checked some of the programming but it was beyond her. She would need time to study it and they didn't have time. That was what Wier told her.

"It's crazy," she told Ozzie. "I don't know what I'm riding. Don't know where I'm going. Looking for Berg to give him a message." She laughed sharply. "Come home, Berg. All is forgiven."

"They're worried about that damned machine of theirs." Ozzie had finally given up and swallowed a double dose of meth. Now he sparkled and fizzed with counterfeit energy. "They had it happen before with Arius. Went out of control and fucked them up. Now they've got Levin and Berg instead of Arius and Norton. They see a parallel. Who can blame them?"

She stood up. "I can't bring him out. There's no place to bring him. No body. Arius has the body."

"If you believe their tapes," Ozzie said.

"I don't know. I don't know what to believe."

He looked away from her. "Don't believe anything."

"What if it's all gone bad?" she said finally. "What if I have to kill him?"

"Wier?"

She sighed. "Berg," she said.

He was a small man with muddy eyes and a fringe of dark hair over large ears. He turned a corner in the corridor and glanced around. Then he took out a magnetic key and opened the door there. Inside the tiny room was a jumble of machinery. He checked one of the machines and found an inspection cover which he opened.

Behind the cover was a steady rush of air. He reached into the pocket of his lab coat and withdrew a vial. He unscrewed the lid and dumped the contents of the vial into the inspection port.

Then he screwed the lid back on and returned the vial to his pocket.

The doorbell chimed. Calley looked up. "You expecting visitors?"

"Nope," Ozzie said.

She went to the door and turned on the viewscreen there. "I don't see anybody. Wait a minute. You order a pizza?"

Ozzie was still fizzing and popping from the speed. "You kidding?"

"Well, there's a pizza out there. Looks like it at least. Right size box, and two large Cokes."

Ozzie licked his dry lips. "I could do with a Coke," he said. "Maybe Wier sent it."

"Maybe." She opened the door. "It's a pizza, all right. Pepperoni sausage cheese."

"Gimme the Coke."

"Here."

She placed the opened box on the table. "You sure you didn't order this, fry brain?"

He shrugged. "Maybe it's poisoned."

She stared at the pizza. "Well, yeah. It's the way to go. The case of the poisoned pizza." She lifted a slice and smelled.

"You can't tell anything from the smell."

"No. It just smells good, is all." She took a bite and wiped a string of cheese from her chin. "You want a slice?"

"Not hungry," Ozzie said. "Maybe later."

"Good," she said.

She inhaled bacteria from the air into her lungs. The bacteria was harmless. Unless it was invaded by a certain virus, such as that in the pizza. Then the bacteria was overwhelmed, invaded, and its DNA system set to work producing another kind of virus.

A deadly virus.

This new virus was quite small. It was about two hundred millimicrons in length. Quickly it spread.

"I feel a little dizzy," she said.

"Nerves," Ozzie told her.

"I don't get nerves. Not like that, at least."

The tiny machines noted the first wave of the virus and compared it to the templates they carried for her cell structure. The virus was quickly identified, as well as the invading bacteria. The tiny machines immediately created a new blueprint for a series of phages. They passed this blueprint to another kind of tiny machine which set to work building the phages from material easily at hand.

The number of phages grew exponentially as more and more of the tiny machines joined the fray. After a time the battle was over. Another group of machines disassembled the invader's bodies and returned them to raw material for later use. The codes were filed in case of another attack.

What wastes remained were flushed through kidneys and skin.

"You still feel weird? You look like you're sweating a little."

She wiped her forehead and felt moisture. "Naw. I feel okay now. You sure you don't want any of this?"

He shook his head.

"Too bad. It's real good pizza."

"You have *him* here?" she said.

The atmosphere of the room was thick with bone-grinding harmonics. God was disturbed. She was used to it and barely noticed the sounds which were not sounds.

"Lady," he said. "I don't demand trust. Who could trust me? But I do demand obedience." The air thrummed with threat.

She whirled away from the small figure in the chair and pointed at the form on the table. A haze of fine cable sprayed from the interface socket beneath the figure's ear. "That is Jack Berg. That is your enemy, not me."

"It is Berg's body," Arius said calmly. "He's not using it right now."

She faced him. Her eyes were pits of fire.

"This is dangerous."

"Yes, Berg is dangerous. In the right hands he is a terrible weapon against me. But in my hands . . ."

"This is some kind of trick," she said. "He's the great trickster."

Now Arius laughed. Appalling things sawed and heaved in the air. "Greater than I, my Lady Mother?"

She stepped back from him. "I don't like it," she said at last.

His throne slid silently toward the table. "I don't care," he told her. "Things are coming to a head now."

The body suddenly sat up on the table. Its eyes slid open.

"Lord!"

"Don't worry, Lady. It's only me." She stared at the corpse which had spoken the words. The corpse stared back at her.

"Berg is the Key," Arius said at last. Then the lips of the corpse moved. "And now I am the Key."

An explosion shook the corridor outside.

There were four left now. Sadie gritted her teeth as she adjusted a velcro pressure bandage around her left biceps. The stripes on Zebra's face had disappeared behind a thick coating of greasy soot. Toshi carried an assault rifle in either hand. The fourth member of the party, a seven-foot black man, flashed a silent grin. Both his abnormally long hands were covered with blood.

Behind them a hole gaped in the corridor wall. To their left was a pair of glass doors opening onto a further corridor which led to a massive black door. The double doors were blocked partially open by a dead Blade of God. The corridor was full of the stench of burned insulation, smokeless powder, and cooked flesh. Sirens whooped and fell in the distance. A single red light blinked over the black door like a demon eye opening and closing.

"It's down there," Toshi said. "That's where we're going."

Sadie finished cinching the bandage tight. "Let's get to it then," she said. There was a manic air to her.

Toshi recognized it for what it was. Battle madness. Sadie was running on hysteria and wouldn't stop until either her body collapsed from exhaustion or she died. He doubted if she could feel pain.

For a moment his single-minded concentration on the goal wavered. She'd guarded him from a deserted field to this slaughterhouse without reservation or stint. Now she was preparing to die in the same cause. And she didn't even know what the cause was.

For that matter, did he? Levin was back with him and he felt no fear. It was Levin that flowed through him when he destroyed Angels with a wave of his hand. Levin initiated the feedback loop so often that Toshi could barely tell the difference between it and his normal self. But his normal self wasn't quick enough to take the throat out of a Blade with a single swipe or tear the heart from a Wolf without a second look.

Yet behind the black door was more than Wolf or Blade or Angel. He knew what awaited and he shuddered. He had no expectations for himself, but Sadie and Zebra and the nameless giant had served him well. Did he owe them their lives or at least a chance for them?

He searched in his combat sack for the right equipment. It was possible that his force, small though it was, might be the edge needed to get him beyond that door. If that was the case, then could he afford not to use it?

He rolled out two gleaming steel-cased objects and set them on the floor.

"Neat," Sadie breathed. "Mark Two guided mines. I didn't know Mitsubishi had them on the general market yet."

"They don't." He made adjustments. "These aren't Two's anyway. They're gimmicked."

"Gimmicked?"

"They mimic human shapes with infrared, holo, and sound. If there are any tripwires down that hall, these babies will do the tripping. Not us."

She smiled. Her lips stretched too wide on it. "Better than us, right? What are you waiting for? Set them off."

He stared at her. Finally he nodded. "Yes," he said.

The two shiny machines scrabbled off down the hall.

Ozzie walked with her to the insertion room. Beyond the monocrystalline diamond shield the strange machine that was Levin did its silent work. Wier smiled as he strapped her down.

"This is for you," he said. "Occasionally there are seizures. You understand."

She nodded.

"All you have to do is find him. If you do that, we can do the rest."

"I'm going, too," Ozzie said. His voice was flat. He reached out and touched the back of her hand gently.

Wier didn't seem surprised. "Yes," he said. "We planned on it."

"Wait a minute," Calley said. "That wasn't part of anything I heard about."

"Our projections say you may need a backup. In this case it's Ozzie. He's been in the metamatrix before. Somebody has to go. Would you rather it be me?"

She looked into his eyes and saw nothing. "No." She was surprised to find relief washing through her muscles, relaxing them. "I'd rather it was Ozzie. We've been through a lot together."

"Right this way," Wier said. He led Ozzie toward another chair and strapped him in.

She caught his eye a moment later. He winked. She grinned.

"What the hell, my boy. What the hell."

He stuck out his tongue at her.

"One minute to insertion," an anonymous voice said. "And counting."

"What happened?" Nakamura said.

"They missed," Oranson replied. "I don't know how but they did. She's in the insertion room with Oswald Karman now."

"What's that?"

"I don't know. Our moles don't work there. Top security. All they know is the name."

Nakamura pushed himself back from his desk and looked at a wall of monitor screens across the room. Scenes of violence played on some. Riots. Fire. Some were filled with words and some with meaningless symbols.

"Arius?"

"No contact," Oranson said.

"What about the rest?"

"We're winning," Oranson told him.

"He's still out there," the Lady said. "The mines didn't get him."

Berg's corpse had returned to its supine position. Now Arius moved his chair quite close to the body. His tiny hand reached out and stroked the flaccid skin.

The infant monster smiled. "It doesn't matter," he said. "I keep telling you it doesn't matter."

She said nothing. The rim around the black door began to glow cherry red. She raised her ripper and stepped in front of Arius.

"Yes, it does," she replied.

"Don't you think the sword image is a bit flashy?"
"You pick your analogs and I pick mine."

The dark wind boomed over the blue plain. Across the horizon the pale sun glowed. He stared at it from his post beneath the flaming sword.

"It's coming together. Just as we planned it."

'Yes. Would you like to join me now?"

"In a moment."

The sun began to glow more brightly.

"He'll break through soon."

The man nodded. After a time he turned and walked into the shifting coruscation of the sword. The great construct hung a little longer and then winked out.

The empty blue plain shimmered beneath the burning sun. In the distance thunder grew.

17

"**I**NSERTION!**"

She didn't hear the word. She felt the familiar twisting sensation. Then she opened her eyes.

"Oh, shit."

The room was cool. In front of her the steel ring of her desk gleamed like a knife. She looked around. Everything was as it had been long ago. She blinked. It had been years since she'd seen this room.

Or had it?

It was a construct, of course. It had to be. But whose construct?

The doorbell rang.

He awoke in the jumbled wreckage of his first apartment, the place where he and Calley had made their original entry into the metamatrix.

It was very quiet. There was an air of decay and emptiness to the place.

"Hello? Anybody home?"

No reply.

It was a construct, of course. It had to be. But whose construct?

The doorbell rang.

If it was a construct, then things should work pretty

much as they usually did. After all, it was her own mind supplying the details. "Who's at the door?"

The machine voice of her computer replied. "Nobody, Calley."

"The doorbell's ringing."

"No it isn't."

"Stupid machine."

"You programmed me."

"Then maybe I'm stupid. Open the door."

"It's opening now."

She heard the front door sigh shut. Steps crossed the foyer and stopped in front of the inner door to her office. She reached into the center drawer of her desk and removed a Smith & Wesson .44 Commando Special.

"It's my fucking analog. I can have what I want," she muttered. She placed the heavy revolver on the desktop in front of her. Then she rested her hand next to the grip.

"Come in, come in, whoever you are."

The door opened. A figure was outlined against gray mist. The figure stepped into the room.

"Oh, Jeezus fucking Christ," Calley said.

"Not hardly," Berg replied.

Ozzie reached under the cushion of a dilapidated basket chair and pulled out an old-fashioned switchblade. He held it pointing down, concealed against his thigh by the palm of his hand. He took a deep breath and walked to the door.

"Who's there?"

Silence.

Carefully he stepped to the right of the door and put his hand on the knob. Generations of TV and vid cop shows had convinced most people that the bogey man waited behind the door.

Pros didn't do that. He'd known a few pros in his time.

He held the knife low and close, ready for the upward belly slash in close quarters.

He turned the knob.

The figure stepped into the room. Ozzie brought the knife up.

"Don't," the figure said.

Ozzie knew he hadn't missed. But the figure stood before him, grinning.

"I figured it had to be you," Ozzie said.

"Then why the blade?"

"I wanted to see what kind of you it was."

"Satisfied?"

"As one analog to another."

"But I'm not an analog," Berg said. "Not quite." He watched Ozzie fold up the switchblade and put it in his pants pocket. "Come on," he said. "We're having a reunion."

Berg walked over to the sideboard and unwrapped a package which rested there. "Dom Perignon," he said. "I thought we'd celebrate." The bottle immediately frosted over, although she'd seen no ice.

He took three glasses and set them on the desktop. "Three?" she said. "Who else is coming?"

He grunted. "Ozzie should be along any second."

"Yeah? Where'd you stash him?"

"Another construct. Come on, drink your bubbly."

She lifted her glass. He raised his own. They regarded each other over rims of crystal. "Cheers," he said at last.

Her eyes sparked emerald. "I've missed you, you sonofabitch."

He smiled and the years fell away. "Me, too."

They drank. The doorbell rang again.

*   *   *

"It was all smoke," Berg said. "All mirrors."

They were seated around the low table away from the desk. Berg had produced two more bottles of Dom. Everybody was mildly fried.

"You could have told me," Calley said. She stared at the smudges left by her lips on the crystal. "Didn't you trust me?"

"I didn't even trust myself," Berg said. "Maybe least of all. I had all this goddam *knowledge*. And those old guys were right, babe. Knowledge is power. In this case, more power than I wanted. More power than anybody should want."

Ozzie tasted his champagne. "So why didn't you drop it? Opt out? We could have survived. All of us. Why start a war with Arius instead?"

Berg stared at the tabletop. "Where do you think I got the knowledge?" He sighed and leaned back. "From Arius. Where else? When I joined Norton and the AI, some part of me picked up everything involved. Way too much. And, of course, I fucked him up in the process. Just a reflex. I was pissed off, remember."

"I never understood that. Exactly what you did."

Berg shrugged. "Messed with basic templates. Norton was all set to have a nice Superman body to use. I trashed it. The new Arius couldn't grow, not in any physical incarnation. Oh, it could use others temporarily, those Angels he started building. But nothing that could handle the full weight of his ability. That nasty little monster was the result."

"I still don't see . . ." Ozzie said.

"I got the data from Arius. He already knew it. It was what the AI had been originally designed to do. I knew it, once I had a chance to sort it out. *But so did he*."

Calley pushed her empty glass forward. "Come on, Berg. Spit it out. What was the terrible secret?"

He laughed. "Does sound like some kind of teen movie, doesn't it?" He filled her glass. "Nanotechnology. Molecular engineering. You know about it?"

She remembered the cold feeling which had snaked down her spine when Wier had first used the term. What had he said? "Humanity is obsolete."

"Wier said man was obsolete," she said.

"Maybe," Berg said. He drained his wine. "Could be. If Arius starts horsing around with it."

Ozzie said, "What could he do?"

"About anything he wanted. Which was why I had to convince him to make me the number one priority. Come after me instead of exploring all the fascinating new possibilities. Arius takes the long view, after all. He intends to be around forever. A little thing like reshaping the whole human race could wait. He's afraid of me a bit. Just enough to keep him interested. That's what I meant. All smoke. All mirrors."

Berg paused and nobody else said anything. They stared at each other.

Finally Ozzie spoke. His voice was thick. "So we were just hung out there for all those years? What would you call us, Berg? Me and Calley and Toshi and all the others. How about bait? Would that be fair, you asshole? Fucking *bait*?"

Berg continued to watch his face. His dark eyes didn't waver. "Yeah, that's fair I guess. Since you put it that way."

Ozzie put his glass down. He didn't seem to know what to say. "I thought . . . I figured you to give me some bullshit about a higher cause or something."

Berg grinned. "Oh, there's a higher cause all right. Sure is. But I couldn't buy into the noble sacrifice crap. Especially when it was you and all the rest I was sacrificing. No, you have it right, Ozzie. Bait is what you were. Of course, I was the biggest bait of all, but that doesn't matter. Does it?"

Ozzie shook his head. "You aren't a nice man, Berg."

"Yeah," Berg said. "But we knew that already, didn't we?"

The two men continued to look at each other. Ozzie glared. Berg had no expression on his face at all.

"Okay, you guys," Calley said. "This piece of bait wants to know what's gonna happen now. You, Berg. I don't figure you brought us all together for a tea party, no matter how good the champagne is. So I think you'd better let us know. One bait to another, you might say. Since I just remembered where you put bait."

"Where's that?"

"Right in the middle of the fucking trap."

Around the black door metal turned pink, then white, then began to drip. A dull *whumpf!* shook the room. The Lady blinked.

The door now stood a couple of inches back from its jamb. Slowly it toppled forward.

An amazingly tall, skinny form darted through. The ripper bucked in her hand and the room was full of its electronic cough. The tall figure fell without a sound.

Smoke and heat obscured her vision. Behind her Arius watched the scene with no expression on his face. If anything, he seemed bored.

When the smoke cleared, the hallway was empty. Then a hand reached around the door and dropped a small object. She aimed the ripper at it, but before she could trigger the weapon the small object disappeared.

"This is enough," Arius said. His small voice cut

through the hiss and pop of cooling metal. "Come on in, Toshi. That's what you want, isn't it?"

Silence.

"It's over," Arius continued. "You were foolish to even try. I won't harm you. But I have to get a few answers. You understand."

The Lady still crouched with the snout of the ripper toward the opening. "Relax, Mother," Arius said. "I told you it's over."

Suddenly the air around her began to vibrate. It was a low, jagged tone, like a vast, rusty saw spinning faster and faster. Now the sound began to rise and a choir of distant screams joined in. The walls, the floor, started to vibrate. She ground her teeth together and held her position.

Even she was ready to plead with him to stop when two figures stepped away from the outer walls and into the room.

She tried to raise her ripper but her muscles wouldn't respond.

"I told you no, Mother," Arius said quietly. "Okay, Toshi, allee allee in free. If not, my dear mother is going to blast these two where they stand. Does that mean anything to you?"

Sadie and Zebra seemed frozen. Their weapons drooped loosely in their hands. The moment went on. Finally a third figure moved into silhouette. It was short and stocky. It stood there a long instant, then threw its assault rifle on the floor.

"Good, good," Arius said. "Toshiro Nakasone. Nice of you to come."

"Berg," she said at last. "Why did you blind me?"

For the first time the little man looked uncomfortable. He turned away from her, then turned back. She waited. He poured a bit of wine for himself. She thought his hand might have trembled slightly but she wasn't sure.

"Do you really want an answer?"

"Then it was you."

He swallowed his wine in a single gulp. "Damn. I forget how good you are. Yes. It was me."

"For a while I thought it was Arius. I was in the metamatrix when it happened. Then it seemed like Wier was the logical candidate. But finally it began to look like you. If I hadn't seen your body. But I knew you weren't dead anyway."

"The body's real enough. I assure you."

"Why did you blind me?"

"To buy time. To manipulate you. And to manipulate events."

"You are a bastard."

"Yes," he said. He sounded tired. "We all agree about that."

"Berg, I want to forgive you. But you have to help me. Please help me."

He stood up and walked toward the desk. When he began to speak he kept his back toward her. His voice was low and hoarse.

"Does this room mean anything to you?"

"Sure. It's my office."

"That's all? You don't have any more . . . recent memories?"

She shook her head. "No. Should I?"

"Yes. You've spent quite a lot of time here lately. Doing software for me and Levin."

She rubbed the side of her nose. "I don't think so. I can pretty well account for my time. Me and Ozzie. Nothing like being blind to concentrate your attention."

The sound he made might have been a bark. Or a laugh. Or merely clearing his throat. "Yes, but you've been here, too. You, yourself. That's fact, Calley. And that's why you were blind."

"Asshole," Ozzie muttered blearily.

"The anima," Berg said. "The consciousness. The soul." His words were slow and dreamy.

She slammed her glass down so hard the thin stem shattered. "Yes, Berg, tell me about the fucking soul."

He spun around. His features were set and chill. "I duplicated your brain, Calley. Right down to the last neuron and synapse. The precise molecules. And then you know what happened?"

She shook her head. A trickle of blood ran down her palm.

"As soon as the fit was exact, you were in two places at once. And I couldn't have that."

"This is all bullshit," Ozzie said. "What you're talking. Identical brains. Souls. Two places at once. It can't be done."

"But it can, Ozzie. And I can do it. In fact, I'm doing it right now. To you."

"It's Berg isn't it?" Arius said.

Toshi looked at the stunted form and said nothing.

Arius nodded. "I knew it. He always keeps a step ahead. I'm beginning to think he might be dangerous."

"What are you talking about?" Toshi said.

The form on the table sat up. "Hi, Toshi," it said. "How's tricks?"

Toshi's eyes widened.

"I know, I know," the corpse said. "But it probably isn't what you think, or you wouldn't be here right now."

"What the fuck is this?"

"Listen to the man," Arius said. "He's right, you know. It's Berg's corpse. But if Berg was dead you would never have penetrated my Labyrinth. You wouldn't be standing here now. Without Berg, even the least of my Angels would have made you a grease spot."

Toshi's gaze slid between the corpse and the hideous dwarf.

"By the way, Tosh old sport, why exactly did you come? Really?"

Toshi tore his gaze away from Berg's corpse. "I'm a pilgrim," he said.

"Ah. And this is a pilgrimage? I didn't know you were a religious man. I'm not myself, but there's no accounting for taste. Would you like me to bless you or something?"

Toshi shook his head.

"What, then?"

"I came to destroy you."

The Lady raised her weapon but froze suddenly. The strange sound her master was making. Could it be laughter?

"What's that supposed to mean?" Ozzie said.

"Here's how it works," Berg replied. "There are nanocomputers and replicators and assemblers. The computers function as DNA. That is, they are the blueprints, the sets of instructions. The assemblers take these instructions and build whatever is necessary. There are also disassemblers which take things apart down to the atomic level and thereby provide the means for perfect copies. A combination of a computer, an assembler, and a disassembler might be called a replicator. Handy things, replicators. Let you copy a brain. And if you're really smart, you can reduce the scale. Maybe on an electronic level. Brains are really nothing more than complicated pathways for electrons. You can change the materials and reduce size without disturbing the pathways."

Ozzie tilted up the bottle of champagne. His Adam's apple glugged up and down. But a light had come into his eyes.

"Yeah, sure. But if you could do that—" He stopped. "Exactly how small?"

"Oh," Berg said. "Say a millimeter on a side. About one tenth the size of Levin, in fact."

Ozzie placed the empty bottle on the table. "Levin is ten times as complicated as a human brain?"

"Uh, yes. And about a million times as fast."

"Are you assholes done? I still want an answer. Work out the techie details later, okay? Berg, why did you blind me?"

"Because personality—consciousness, soul, whatever —is a function of organization. When I duplicated your brain you occupied both the duplicate and the original. Left to themselves, both brains would change as new information was added. Eventually—quite quickly, actually, on a human scale—they would become different enough that the conscious parts would separate and go their own ways. Unless one brain was constantly updated to keep it identical to the other."

She rolled her head and rubbed her neck. "Blindness, Berg. Tell me about blindness."

"The dual occupancy is not affected by distance. I wanted to split you apart. Can you think of any more traumatic event for data input than blindness?"

"You bastard."

"It worked, didn't it?"

She looked away. Then the thought hit. "Berg, you say you duplicated me, right?"

"Yes." Suddenly he found the steel desktop fascinating.

"Well, where is she?"

"Who?"

"The other me?"

"Oh. You're her. I mean you are the duplicate."

"But I just came in the metamatrix."

"No, you didn't. You aren't in the metamatrix. What happened is I updated the duplicate brain. What you think of as you is still on Luna hooked up to Levin. The only thing is Levin is keeping you under. You, too, Ozzie."

"What," Ozzie said, "do you mean about not being in the metamatrix? If we're not, then where the fuck are we?"

"You about finished with the champagne?"

"Yes," Calley said. "Very."

"Okay," Berg said. "Come on. I'll show you around."

"Toshi. Now why would you do a thing like that?"

The Japanese stared at him. He felt unbelievably tired. Why had he come? Things had gotten clearer recently, especially since Levin had returned to him. But there was a blank, wasn't there? A long foggy period dominated by a single desire?

Why?

Toshi's tongue touched his lips. "I don't know," he said at last.

"Ah. An honest answer. I like that. No bullshit about you, Toshi. So consider this. What if your pilgrimage has nothing to do with you? What if it's only a dream, the dream of a would-be God?"

Toshi glanced at Sadie. She was still frozen. He wondered if she was aware.

"Let them go," Toshi said. "They have nothing to do with us."

"Of course not," Arius agreed. "Do you see the parallel?"

"No!" The Lady stirred restlessly. "They attacked you. They have to pay for it."

"Mother, your sense of punishment is interesting

but unnecessary. I don't demand sacrifices. Now be quiet."

The Lady subsided but her eyes glowed like lamps.

That one will kill me, Toshi thought.

"Will you release them?" Toshi said.

"In time. Answer my question. Do you see any similarities in their situation and yours?"

Toshi puzzled it. *Levin?* he thought silently.

"*Answer him*," Levin replied.

"I see what you imply," Toshi said at last. "I have used them, just as somebody—something—has used me. Is that it?"

"Very good. Now make the step. What has used you?"

His mind touched on it. Somewhere a demon sun burned endlessly, and he had seen it. Somewhere the world of his dreams was real.

But in the end he could not grasp the answer. "I don't know," he said.

Arius stared at him. Finally one of his tiny hands twitched. "Perhaps you don't. Perhaps the truth is locked away from you. The dreams of Gods aren't always comprehensible to men."

Suddenly he wanted it to be over. He spat and ignored the Lady's hostile stirring at the act of desecration. "You're no God. You're just a machine and a man. That's all. What's this bullshit about dreams and Gods?"

Again, the strange barking sound. "This is the funniest conversation I've had in a long time. Shag Nakamura used to amuse me this way." A note of sadness. "No, that's okay, Toshi. I'm not a God. And neither is the one who animates you. But I do have power. Do you wish to test it?" The tiny form went motionless for a bare instant. Then, "More to the point, does your master wish to test me?"

Toshi touched his fingertips together. It was an oddly respectful gesture.

"These two. Let them go."

"Yes," Arius said. Toshi sensed movement.

"*No!*" screamed the Lady.

Zebra was already diving when the ripper cleared its electronic throat and cut him in half. Toshi felt the lightning galvanize his spine.

"Fuck you, bitch," Sadie muttered. The deep booming sound of her rifle split the room. The Lady jerked sideways. A red bloom appeared on her left shoulder, but even as it did the ripper spoke again. As from a distance Toshi heard the sound of dead meat thudding to the floor and a part of him cried out. But the rest of him buried four fingers in the right eye of the High Priestess. He felt plastic and metal crumple. Then moist warmth. He stepped back.

Arius had not moved. Three bodies lay crumpled on the floor between them.

Finally Arius spoke. His voice was soft and wondering. "Is it enough, Berg? Will you try me now?"

"Bastard!" Toshi said.

Arius smiled at him. "In every way," he said.

Calley paused on the threshold of the formless mist just beyond her office door. "I am having a strong sense of *deja vu*," she said.

Berg stared at her curiously. "That's interesting," he said. "Is there any possibility it's based on real memory?"

She stood there considering. "Yes. I think so but I don't understand how." And then it hit her. Her mouth twisted.

"You asshole!"

He smiled sadly. "I wondered . . ."

"The other one. The other me. *How did you achieve identity*?"

"I wiped the brain, of course. But evidently there is some kind of hangover effect. She used to wonder about the mist, too."

Calley could not describe even to herself the strange feelings which filled her. There had been a twin, another self. A Calley as real as she was. And Berg had destroyed that personality as simply as cleaning a plate.

She shuddered at the thought of his power.

But she filed the emotions away. "Somehow you will pay a price for all this. I feel sorry for you."

He winced. "We are still joined," he said. "I am still the Key."

"I know," she told him. "That is part of the price."

"You are terrible," he said at last.

"And that is another part."

They walked into the mist.

Toshi stepped away from the bodies on the floor and raised his hands palms out. Even as he did so the silent power rushed to him and he shivered beneath the force of it.

Arius's throne spun round and the dwarf faced him. The deformed body remained absolutely still, but as Toshi watched, the eyes began to grow, to flame.

The force channeled through Toshi until his nerves sang like bowstrings. His back arched against the strength of it.

And finally Berg's corpse sat up and stared at him.

Somewhere a great door was unlocked.

In the middle of the room between the warrior and the God grew a sun. And a sword.

Overhead, thunder echoed with slow precision. Calley glanced at Berg. His outline had become faintly hazy in the blue glow, and it seemed to her that it was a haze of tiny symbols like a cloud of gnats.

"What is this place?"

Ozzie walked silently beside them, his eyes wide.

"I told you it wasn't the metamatrix."

On the horizon behind them burned a red-gold sun. Beneath their feet were countless glowing blue globes, but she had no feeling of contact with them.

"What is it?"

"It is the place at the end of things," Berg replied.

"Mystical bullshit."

He stopped. "I don't know. I suspect it is the human equivalent of the metamatrix. The wetware perceives what it can perceive, Calley. But parts of the human brain are barred to our conscious introspection. My first thought was that the mentalists were right after all, with their talk of souls and silver cords and tunnels to life. I thought perhaps this was the plain of souls. But I don't think so now."

The thunder was the only sound.

Finally she nodded. "How did you get here?"

"Levin brought me. After I joined up with him."

"Does he see it, too?"

"We are the same," Berg said. "Perhaps we created it. It is very pliable. I am showing it to you now in its raw state. Usually I inhabit more pleasant surroundings."

She stared down at her feet. "Souls?"

He shook his head. "Some sort of ghost image. A map, perhaps. Levin thinks it is a quantum effect generated by the brain."

"Cut it any way you want," she said. "It still sounds like souls to me. Oh, fuck, Berg. What have you got into now?"

"They can't be manipulated, you know," he said mildly. "They are the one immutable thing about this place. Levin monitors them. He says they come and go. They show minute changes, but not in response to anything we do here. Perhaps if mankind disappeared, this place would go as well."

She felt sweat trickle down her spine. Her breath was thick and heavy in her chest. It was painful to breathe.

"Berg. What is going to happen?"

He glanced at the swollen sun. "We are going to have a divine visitation," he said.

His hand brushed his waist, and she noticed that he wore a sword there.

A sword? she wondered.

18

THE ROOM WAS filled with power. Toshi tried to walk forward toward the throne but power pushed him back. More power flowed through him, an endless river.

Arius sat on his throne unmoving. A faint smile twisted his lips. His eyes burned like fire on watchtowers.

Thoughts chased themselves through Toshi's mind. Die, you motherfucker! he screamed silently.

"I can't die," Arius said suddenly. His voice was like an ax through the silence.

Toshi tried to reply but another rush of power took him, and Arius sat back on his throne suddenly, a look of surprise on his face.

"Yes," Arius said. "Very strong. But not strong enough."

There was triumph in his voice.

The Berg corpse slid its legs from the table. Stood on the floor. Began to walk forward.

Toshi shivered as a final burst of energy poured into his skull and out his palms, his eyes, and sweated out of his skin. He saw Berg move toward him and knew if the corpse reached him, touched him, he was dead.

But then he was dead anyway. Had been since he stepped into this room. What had Arius said? Sometimes the dreams of Gods aren't comprehensible to man.

Perhaps this was such a dream.

Berg shambled closer, a loose, sagging zombie.

Toshi screamed.

"The Key!" Arius replied. "I am the Key."

Berg raised his hand. For one instant Toshi saw something flicker in those dark dead eyes.

Then he triggered the bomb in his belly.

The room exploded.

The vast plain stretched around them in cold blue silence. The thunder had subsided. Above was utter darkness. Calley felt very alone.

Ozzie laughed. He put his arm around her shoulder and she folded herself to him, grateful for his warmth. Berg looked at them.

"Jealous, Berg?" Ozzie said.

Some nameless emotion washed over Berg's features, but he shook his head. "There are things I can't give anymore. I'm glad somebody can."

Calley felt a great gulf widen. She stared at the swollen sun hanging low on the horizon. "What's that?" she said.

"Arius."

"What? I thought you said this was a human place."

"And what is Arius but a few kilos of Bill Norton's brain?"

She felt herself shake slightly. Ozzie hugged her tighter.

"Is that what you mean? A divine visitation? Is Arius coming here?"

"He can't. Not yet. Because of the imperfect Joining of the AI to Norton. Again, what we see is a ghost."

"Then why?"

Berg sighed. Slowly he took the sword from his waist and held it in his hand. For a moment he seemed to listen to a distant song, a reverie from another place. Then he blinked. "What I did wasn't a mistake, but is a mistake now. So I'm rectifying the mistake."

In his hand the sword began to spark and shine. The light from it fell in pools. A column began to appear. It rose above them in a tower of luminescence.

More sparks, comets appeared out of nothing, out of the dark overhead, and rushed down.

"Join me," Berg said. And in his hand was a Key.

They stepped forward. Wondering, she touched his face.

He nodded.

A moment later the Star and the Sword faced each other, there on the infinite plain.

The demon dwarf shook his head. Slowly the shield around him lifted. It was a thick slab of perfect ruby. The explosion hadn't even scratched it. But the room was wrecked.

Where Toshi had stood was nothing, not even a spot on the floor. The Berg corpse was only a few rags of scorched flesh.

Arius breathed in, breathed out. The air was thick and greasy. The thought pleased him.

I engulf my enemies with my very lungs, he thought. Nothing more than a breath.

He savored the odors of carnage for a little bit and then kicked the vent system up to high. Small robots entered and began to remove the detritus.

The demon's eyes glowed.

"Now for you, Berg," he said. "Now I come for you."

The tiny form settled back in its throne. Slowly its eyes faded from red to pink. Finally to blank reflective black.

Except for the robots the room was empty.

*   *   *

The Sword moved slowly. It grew until its point was lost in darkness. Then, in one swift movement it sliced down toward the Star.

The dome of darkness split into a slow white wound, and the Star began to bellow through.

"This is where we all came in," Berg whispered.

She looked around, trying to find him, but he was gone. Everything was gone. She was surrounded by dancing dots of light. She put her hands in front of her face. No hands. No face.

The burning mist dissipated slowly. Overhead a long running flame arced across the sky. Colors dripped slowly up and down its length. Near the far end a strange cold sun flared with viscid hues that reminded her of rust and blood and ancient coins.

Something tugged at her skull. She whirled. Nothing.

"Give it to me," a voice commanded. Metallic overtones rippled through the voice and through the bone around her brain.

"What? What do you want?"

"Give them to me." The voice was remorseless, demanding.

A picture of her office flickered dimly in memory. Had she been there? But how could she remember?

The programs. Of course, the programs.

It was as if a key had turned in the lock of her past.

"Yes," she said.

She felt them flow out of her in a gray, dusty cloud. All the painstaking nets. The convoluted solutions to impossible problems.

Had she done all that?

The cloud swirled up and disappeared into the blade of light that bisected the sky. It changed color. Now it was a deep cobalt, a throbbing color.

Berg? Where are you?

The sun began to expand. Thunder muttered beyond the horizon. A hideous band saw began to play.

Berg? Berg!

Laughter babbled behind the thunder. Now the sun was an eye, a vast crimson eye, slowly opening.

Here.

The single syllable was immense. Quiet as a single heartbeat. Everywhere.

The great eye moved.

Berg's face appeared at the apex of the line of fire, laughing. His dark eyes glittered. Clouds of gray dust flew from his mouth.

Then she saw herself there, her own face, green eyes flashing. And Ozzie suddenly, his hair that of an angel. Finally an Oriental face grinning beneath epicanthic folds.

Here.

All four mouths spoke the quiet word.

The Demon Star came forth. It moved like a slow God entering the field of battle. Now it was completely beneath the dome, rising toward the cobalt bridge. The sounds of bone and blood trailed from it like veils.

She saw the open wound behind it begin to close.

The faces blinked out like a bad holo. The bridge began to twist and turn. Finally it stood before the Star.

A single upraised Sword.

Here.

The tolling of a bell.

The band saw choir shrieked.

Now!

Then both together, the agony and the silence.

The sky went mad.

Faces and changes and colors. Thunder and the smell of scorched stone. An endless hissing. Babble rising and falling. The death of crowds. A single infant's cry.

The Star engulfed the Sword.

The Sword impaled the Star.

She felt a silence tremble through the place and sensed that events were poised upon the instant. And then she saw. Finally and with awful majesty the last of the Wound was being healed. There beneath all things.

Closed the Door.

Something cried without end and then was still.

Overhead the light show winked out. It was dark again.

She sat with him on the brow of a hill. Overhead the sun burned down warm as honey. She smelled new grass. The earth was faintly damp with the memory of rain.

Far away the horizon was blue and lost in haze. A few clouds scudded by, pushed by the same breeze that cooled her cheek.

"Nice day," she said.

Berg grunted. "However you want it."

She touched the ground with her fingertips and felt the grainy dirt hidden at the roots.

"What happened?"

He rolled over on his belly and picked a stem of grass. He stuck it between his teeth, chewed, and spit it out. "I sucker-punched him. When Toshi blew himself up, and my corpse along with it, he filled that room with tiny machines. Nanocomputers, replicator systems, you name it. Arius couldn't get in here unless I let him."

"And you did," she said.

"Uh-huh. Levin built not only a duplicate of the child brain, but also a duplicate of the metamatrix itself. See, that's how Arius used the dwarf. He maintained identity between it and the matrix, so he was, in effect, in both places at the same time. Then I made duplicates here. Well, at least in Levin."

She shook her head. "I don't understand. Wouldn't Arius then be in four places at once?"

"Naw. That was the beauty. As soon as identity was achieved—that was when you saw the analog of the Demon Star push into here—the computers altered the forms of the original brains. Arius was here. And he can't go back. That was the closing of the door."

Slowly she reached over and touched his shoulder. "Isn't that dangerous for us?"

He looked at her fingers, looked away. "I can't kill Arius," he said. "It's tied up with the original Joining. I'm part of him. So are you, and Ozzie, and Norton." He laughed suddenly. "You could say we're all in this together."

A thought struck her. She remembered the video she'd seen of Berg's death. "Nakamura." Her voice was flat. "What about him?"

His sudden chuckle startled her. "Old Shag? I think he's about on the way to ruling Terra. If he can hold on to it. He will probably be very surprised. But he'll recover. He's always wanted to ride the tiger."

She thought about it. "What a diabolical thing."

"Yeah, isn't it?"

High overhead a blackbird called. It was the sound of a wish. A warmth moved up her spine. "And Arius? Is that diabolical, too?"

Berg shrugged. "He had to be removed from the worlds of men. He dreams of being a God. He has all the nanotechnological secrets, or would have ferreted them out as soon as he tried. Man deserves a choice, don't you think? To dream his own dreams? Arius is not real big on choice. What else could I do?"

She rubbed her feet together and stretched. "They are different, aren't they?"

"What?"

"The dreams of Gods and men."

He laughed. "Not so much as you might think."

She closed her eyes. A dark thought took her, there in the bright morning. "It must be a terrible thing to know the difference."

Berg rolled over again and rested his head on her stomach. He watched a cloud shaped like the head of a dog drift by. Finally he said, "You told me I would pay a price."

She nodded and ruffled his hair. In the sky the sun stretched wings toward noon.

Interlude

THE SHORT MAN with the big nosé stood on the edge of a great red canyon and stared into its depths. He wore dark blue jeans and a black leather jacket. Around his neck was a silver chain. A key shaped like a tiny sword hung from the chain.

He waited, and after a time heard footsteps.

"I wondered when you would come," he said.

The tall golden youth joined him at the edge of the precipice. "I wanted to thank you for correcting the error. This is an excellent body. I can build more, of course. As many as I need."

"Of course," Berg said. "You're welcome."

The golden youth looked out on the canyon. His eyes were faintly pink but clear. "It's not over."

Berg turned and looked at him. His voice was quizzical. "I am the Key That Locks and Looses. Which makes me the Way In and the Way Out. What can you do?"

The youth moved his shoulders slightly. "There is always something. I dream my dreams, as do you. It's not over."

At the base of the canyon a tiny chrome line meandered through scarred rock. Berg imagined a river, endless and strong.

"No," he said at last. "But then, it never is."

In silence they watched the river flow.

About the Author

W. T. Quick was born in Muncie, Indiana, and now lives in San Francisco. He was educated at The Hill School and Indiana University. He is fond of single malt scotch and writing about the near-infinite possibilities of technology. He is not fond of Senator William Proxmire or cats. He has been publishing science fiction since 1979 and intends to continue.

In the vast intergalactic world of the future
the soldiers battle

NOT FOR GLORY

JOEL ROSENBERG

author of the bestselling
Guardian of the Flame series

Only once in the history of the Metzadan mercenary corps has a man been branded traitor. That
man is Bar-El, the most cunning military mind in
the universe. Now his nephew, Inspector-General
Hanavi, must turn to him for help. What begins as
one final mission is transformed into a series of
campaigns that takes the Metzadans from world to
world, into intrigues, dangers, and treacherous dip-
lomatic games, where a strategist's highly irregular maneuvers and a master assassin's swift blade
may prove the salvation of the planet—or its ultimate ruin . . .